The Summer Land

The SUMMER

by BURKE DAVIS

LAND

 Random House · New York

FOR
Evangeline, Angela and Burke

AND FOR
Jane Carson, Bill Gravitt, Cecil Houck, Jake Keyser, Bob Loomis, Betsy Rouse, Virginia Sneed and John M. Virden

Contents

x   *Contents*

The Summer Land

1

Papa's Enriched
Watermelons

We whispered in the hay. The barn loft was deep in fresh
bluestem hay and I hid up there with Jimroe, keeping a
drowsy watch. Swallows dipped in and out over our heads
and a buck quail kept whistling *Bob White* in the cornfield. Voices called from the tobacco patch, where we were
supposed to be, but we weren't fools enough to answer.
Cousin Tree Poindexter finally yelled and he was as sore as a
scalded cat. He could evermore yell:

"Jim-ROOOOE. You Jiiiiiim-rooooooo!"

Jimroe was my brother just older than me—James Mon-

roe Starling was his real name, but it had been bobbed off
when he was a baby and we never thought of him except as
Jimroe, any more than we stopped to think that Cousin
Tree's name was Trevilian. Nobody had time for all that.
Most of our names had been worn down. Papa's given name
was Henderson but everybody called him Hence, and my
name is Fairfax but all I ever got was Fax.

Our folks were suckering in the family tobacco patch,
pulling off stringy shoots that would sap the strength and
ruin the leaf if they were left to grow all summer. They
pulled off the big horned tobacco worms too, squshing the
green bodies with a snap of the fingers. It was galling work.
In five minutes your hands were black with gum, and prick-
les from the leaves ate you up, so that you had to wear
everything you could stand in that heat. It was hotter than a
depot stove in the field, because in North Carolina the sun
knows how.

We watched them at work through heat waves that made
them seem small and far away, shimmying like dolls in bib
overalls and yellow straw hats and faded blue shirts. Far
behind them was the timbered shoulder of . Wildkitten
Mountain where the road hung like a scar above the river
gorge, and northward over the river we could see into
Crown County, in the State of Virginia. The river was the
boundary between us and Virginia in our county.

Cousin Tree was our straw boss when we worked tobacco, and he had licked us that morning for horseplay in
the field, so we were trying to lie low. Raising tobacco was
no joke. It broke our backs all year long, and at the end put
into Papa's jeans the only hard cash he had coming. You
could tell the way it was when Papa talked about money. He
would say, "Well, a hundred pennies make a dollar—but
they just barely do, dammitall." So tobacco meant bread and
meat to all of us, and it was easy for a young one to get a
licking in the growing season. It made everybody serious.

If we could just hide out until they quit work, we might
sneak to the creek for the rest of the afternoon. We lazed.

Until that minute I had forgotten there was such a day in the world as the Fourth of July—much less a year of 1916. Jimroe jabbed me with his elbow and I saw Papa down in the barn with two men, who came in quick and quiet. One was Jess Sixkiller, the biggest Indian halfbreed in our county, and the other was his trifling cousin, Pembroke. They had a jug of white corn whiskey. We knew what was up. Papa was loading watermelon for the Picnic. Jess wrenched out a corncob stopper and gave Papa a whiff. "Prime, ain't it? Old Pem ran it off last winter, just for his own folks."

"I hadn't thought to sell none," Pembroke said.

Papa had ordered Pem off our place the summer before, but now he looked like he bore no grudge even if they had fallen out over Pem's sorry ways. Papa held the jug to the light. "Looks like you used mountain water, all right."

The little Indian was a dried-up foxsquirrel of a man, with a head of hair like a bearskin. He stuttered, "H-h-hell I reckon. I l-l-live so far back in there that the hoot owls lay eggs with my ch-ch-chickens."

Papa took a deep breath from the jug and closed his eyes. "It's as easy on the nose as a man could ask. It'll do the job."

I knew Papa despised Pembroke because he was such a no-account worker, and Mama sniffed about him because he was always moving his family around. She said, "That Pem could walk out in his back yard and every hen he's got would flop right over on her back with her feet held up ready to be tied."

They funneled the liquor into pint bottles and Papa paid Jess some money. Pembroke Sixkiller watched the money pass, then shifted from one foot to the other while Jess talked to Papa about what a choice tobacco crop we had. That touched Papa on his pride and he made light of it, but grinned so that he showed his wide front teeth. "Why, I reckon we'll meager it out this year, somehow."

The little Indian said he'd like to see the day he could

make such a crop for himself. They were quiet for a bit, looking at the field where a light breeze from the river was stirring the leaf.

"I expect you'll take in mighty big money this fall, Mister Hence," Jess said.

"Well, it couldn't happen to a needier cause," Papa said.

The Indians grinned and raised their hands, and as they went Pembroke mumbled "Cap'm" to Papa in a way colored people had, so that nobody could say whether it was more of a bark or a question—or whether he thought anything of it at all. Pem had a big whiskey bottle in a hip pocket.

Papa began cutting cotton-string wicks for his bottles and we looked down as still as could be, holding our breath. We didn't fool Papa. Without glancing up he said, "Come on down here, now."

He let us help with the bottles. We cut grooves in the corks for the wicks and then drove home the corks, and followed Papa into the melon patch to the lower end, where the Georgia Blackseeds were coming in ripe. He cut slits in the vines close to the biggest melons and stuck a wick in each vine, wrapped the joints good and tight with old cloth strips and shoved a bottle deep in the sand beside each melon he had fixed.

Papa thumped a melon. "Um. Ummm. By dark these old fat gals will be moaning with content. Inside a week they'll have sucked up every drop of that liquor, and the vines will thrash around so happy that I'll have to pull melons before they get worn out."

"When's the Fourth, Papa?"

He fingered his watch from the breastbone pocket of his overalls the way he did when he was puzzling out which day was which. "Tuesday week."

His silver watch was as big around as a biscuit and almost as thick. Papa had it tied to a gallus with a greasy black rawhide thong. He dropped the watch back and made a quick move with his hand, slapping away a fly at his ear, and

Jimroe jumped like he had been shot. Papa laughed. "Duck, dammit. You know you need a lick." He wasn't stingy with lickings for us but he was fair, and we hardly ever got whipped unless we had it coming.

Jimroe commenced talking fast, about nothing, to keep Papa's mind off sending us back to work, but Papa flipped open the cover of his watch again and this time looked close. "I'm giving you forty seconds to get back where you belong before I sic your Cousin Tree on you two."

We made it.

"I'm going to get me some of that melon this year," Jimroe said. "I'm a suck-egg mule if I don't."

"It'd be your last mouthful if Papa caught you at it."

"Ah, poot. What do you know about likker, Fax Starling? You ain't hardly old enough to button your own britches."

He ran his gummy fingers inside my collar so that the tobacco stickers would aggravate me for the rest of the day. I couldn't take that off him, even if he was too strong for me. I lunged at him, but he held me off the way he always did when he provoked me to fight, with his hands on my forehead, laughing while I flailed the air with my fists. Papa broke it up.

Papa was built for comfort more than speed, squatty and short-coupled, but he could come and go like a cat. He sneaked up and took us by the collar and shook us. He wasn't sore with Jimroe. "If you feel so frisky, you could pick on somebody your own size. We ain't got but one book scholar, anyway."

He grinned and Jimroe laughed and that made me so mad my eyes blurred, and if Papa hadn't held me I would have jumped Jimroe again. Papa always called me the odd whelp of the litter because I never minded going to school and would sometimes read books if they didn't watch me. He never ragged me about it the way Jimroe did, but I knew that Papa couldn't make me out.

Papa flung us together and made me and Jimroe hug each

other until we quit our scowling. It was bitter for me to hug
that hateful thing, but after a little I simmered down. Papa
got after Jimroe. "I wouldn't want a misreckoning about my
loaded melon, now."

Jimroe had a mind like a mink. He could think up anything in the line of meanness, but Papa read him like he was
using a looking glass.

"Now, chaps, those melons are meant for grown folks.
And if some little booger cuts a plug in one to get at that
whiskey-soaked meat, then I'll have to fix his little red
wagon."

"What would you do?" Jimroe said.

"It'd have to be something he'd remember, wouldn't it, so
it would improve his character?"

"I reckon." Jimroe didn't want to talk about it.

"Well, it'd not be much of a lesson if he forgot, would
it?"

"Naw, sir. What do you aim to do to him, Papa?"

"I might take the skin off his butt in little strips to make
shoelaces or guitar strings, something like that."

You could almost see Jimroe's brain twist and turn.

"Papa, suppose somebody else robs your melons."

"Yeah?"

"I mean, somebody who don't know you've loaded them,
and helps himself. You'll not blame *that* on me."

"That's your lookout, Jaybird."

"How you mean?"

"I mean you might have to stay up of a night to guard the
patch if you want to save the seat of your britches."

"Hell, Papa, that ain't fair. I'll not stand for that."

Papa laughed. "You'll learn no younger. You stick your
nose in somebody else's business and you're liable to pick up
burdens you never counted on."

Jimroe poked out his mouth. "It won't our fault we saw
you loading melon."

"Wasn't, hey?"

"Naw, sir. We was just up in the loft . . ."

"Holding Sunday School, or hiding from your duty?"

Papa hugged us both around the shoulders, but it was Jimroe that he talked to. "Boy, you won't do. You just won't *do*."

Papa went away.

We had never tasted Papa's loaded watermelon, but I knew that it made the old folks red in the face at the Picnic every year and put them to singing. The oily liquor in those bottles had a sour, sickening smell, and I couldn't imagine the melons tasting sweet after a dose of Papa's medicine.

Pretty soon Cousin Tree called for fresh water for the tobacco crew. It was Jimroe's turn to carry it. "I tell you, Fax. I'd trade you somethin' great if you'd go this time."

I knew from his voice that he was about to fleece me, because he had a buttery way of talking that he used only when he wanted to skin you out of something. Nobody could resist Jimroe when he really worked on them; Papa said Jimroe was like no Starling he ever knew—and that his ways made him suspicious about those old snake-oil peddlers who used to come through our county and hang around the house, talking to Mama. So Jimroe hooked me.

"What'll you trade?" I said.

"How about the cool spot by the window when we go to bed tonight?"

"Ain't yours to trade."

"I mean, if I get there first."

"Yeah, and suppose you don't?"

"It's kind of like insurance," Jimroe said. He went on about how smart people bought insurance for everything, and in the middle of that, Papa himself bellowed for water —the last time before trouble set in. So between Jimroe's nattering and Papa's hollering I gave up, and shouldered the old yoke and the two buckets and went.

. . .

I walked up the hill toward our house, where the well was, but Papa yelled for me to go the the spring instead— away down in another direction. Papa would wash his hands and face with water from the well, but when it came to drinking he wanted spring water. He claimed that he could tell the difference blindfolded if you put one drop on his tongue. Papa said spring water was what had put the spizzerinktum into the manhood of John M. Virden County, North Carolina.

I let my legs loose and they carried me down the hill where the steep path wormed back and forth under the mountain laurel brush, that we called ivy. I went so fast that I had to stop by snagging onto the smooth gray limbs over the tunnel of that path. It got cool near the bottom.

I sat in the springhouse and looked through the slat walls to make sure nobody came down and caught me loafing. Mama's crocks sat in the spring branch, gray stoneware jars about three feet tall, full of milk and buttermilk and clabber cheese, with white cloths draped over their mouths and old plates on top holding them down. The sides of the jars were beaded in cold sweat. I peeped into a crock and saw butter flakes swimming in the milk and wanted a drink so bad that I could taste it, but didn't dare chance one. Mama would have a fit and fall in it if she thought one of us would drink from a family jar, and I didn't want her on my trail.

The spring flowed through the springhouse and then downhill into Dirty Butter Creek. I lay flat and drank from the spring with my face in the water and saw the salamander, that we called the spring lizard; we all believed that you couldn't have a sweet spring without a lizard to keep it. The water was so cold it made my teeth hurt.

I felt all alone down there, because our farm was cut in two by a razorback ridge, and the house was on the north side, out of my sight. From the house slope you could look down on the river and see into Virginia. Our big barn and the outbuildings and about a dozen tobacco barns were clumped together south of the ridge, with lots of trees around them, so that you'd never know there was a farmhouse anywhere around.

A minty smell drifted in, and I raised up on my arms and saw Jess Sixkiller and old Pembroke not twenty feet away, squatting in the horsemint beside our spring branch, drinking whiskey and slapping up water in their hands. I held still inside the springhouse and hoped they couldn't see me. They wiped their mouths and looked downhill to our tobacco patch.

Jess gave Pembroke the money for his whiskey. Pem had just four teeth in the front of his mouth, and he took a half dollar and bit it with his eyeteeth. "Hod amighty. It tickles me good to git a piece of that damn Starling money."

"If you was worth a plugged dime you could have all you'd earn."

"Who the hell said anything about earn?" They drank again.

"I hate a damn Starling," Pem said. "They've got the notion they own the whole blooming valley."

Jess wagged his head. "They've mortally got money leaf, you've got to give 'em that."

"Is that how come you to say 'Mister' so pretty to that son of a bitching Hence?"

Jess gave him a sour look. Pem cut homemade chewing tobacco with a hawkbill knife and stuffed his cheek. "Wouldn't it be too damn bad, now, if they n-n-never get their fine leaf to market?"

"Hell."

"Don't talk like it'd be the f-f-first time. They did a lot of sh-shooting and burning down south last season over the bad m-m-markets—but in the end the big dogs ate up the little folks like always. I heard it'd be worse this year."

"I ain't heard it."

"Well, I sure G-g-god did." Pem waited for a second and said, "I reckon Wash Strawn ought to know."

"I might have known it. The biggest looselip in the county, and you listen to him."

"Well, he's the deputy, ain't he?"

"The nearest no deputy there ever was."

Pembroke whittled a toothbrush twig and switched it about in his mouth, then spat in the branch and snapped shut his knife. "If anything sets my teeth on edge it's a damn white man that's got rich and too big for his br-br-britches," he said.

"I can't say no Starling ever done me harm," Jess said.

"All you've got to do is wait. I found that out. They'll get around to you." Pembroke took out a kitchen match and rolled it between his palms like he enjoyed it. "But I've got the cure f-f-for 'em, if anybody was to ask y-y-you."

"Like what?"

"Like this here."

Pem lifted a leg and struck the match on his overalls seat and held it up, grinning, until the match burned and curled into a hook, then snapped it into the branch. It hit the water with a blue hiss. I knew what he meant—I could see our tobacco barns burning as plain as if he'd really touched them off before my eyes.

"I knew there wasn't but just so much sense in your gourd," Jess said, "but damned if I knew it was plumb empty. Come on."

Jess jerked his head toward the hill behind our spring and climbed into the farkleberry thickets. Pem followed him and they went out of sight.

I came to myself with my arms trembling under me, still reared up over the spring. I had almost forgotten where I was, and what I was doing.

They trumpeted for water again from the tobacco patch, and I dipped my buckets deep in the spring and ran. I had the feeling that the eyes of the halfbreeds were on my back as I went, almost like they were touching me with sharp fingers between the shoulder blades.

2

Mama

I tore up the path under the ivy branches, with the buckets
sloshing cold water down my legs. There was a clearing
halfway up the hill and from there I saw Mama against the
sky, leaning to look down from the ridge. She had her
mouth open, staring at me. I was panting when I got to her.
Mama caught me. "Boy, as soon as you set down your
water, tell your papa I need you worse than he does, now,
and I don't mean tomorrow morning."

She was really my stepmother, but I never stopped to
think of that, because we got on together better than most
anybody else in the household. Mama had a big fire under an
iron pot in the yard and was making soap. The only thing

worse than suckering tobacco in late June was helping
Mama boil lye soap. We made the soap from scratch. All
year long, every time we passed the lye barrels in the yard
we had to pour water over the fireplace ashes that Mama
kept there between layers of straw, to leach out her lye. We
saved every drop of grease from the kitchen for her soap,
too.

Mama stood over me while I punched up the fire and
poured in two buckets of rancid grease. The smell was
enough to keep buzzards at bay, but it didn't faze Mama.

"Ut, ut," she said. "Not quiiiiiiite enough. Just a skimp-
tion more. Just a think-you-do."

I stirred the bubbling pot, but kept looking over the valley to see if Pem and Jess Sixkiller were still hanging around,
and forgot what I was doing. Mama snatched the boiling
stick from me, an oak paddle that she'd cooked for years
until it was as white as an old bone. She began to stir. Making soap was so tricky that we sometimes had to boil five or
six times for a good batch. When neighbor women left our
house they might call, "Luck with your soap, Linden," instead of saying goodbye. Linden was Mama's name.

Mama handed me the paddle, and I waggled it in the pot
to keep things barely moving while she put in salt to harden
the soap. Her face was sweating and she mopped hair from
her forehead and patted the bun behind her neck. Even at
making soap, Mama was as neat as a bird. She wore her gray-
and-black striped dress and an apron, and her sleeves were
rolled, showing her freckled arms with long ginger-colored
hair. She counted the stirs while the soap thickened. All the
time I was looking over to the next hill, afraid of what I
would see among the ivy, but I saw nothing. The Sixkillers
were gone.

Mama was red-headed and lean and full of going. Papa
said, "She's all whet leather and gristle, and feeds on buttermilk and gunpowder. The most even-tempered woman in the
world—mad all the time." He was joking, for Mama was as

changeable as an April morning. She wouldn't have weighed a hundred pounds with a rock in each apron pocket and her hair combed down wet. She had an even hand for her own young ones and for us older ones, and we got on together and never thought of one another as half brothers or half sisters. It was hard to remember that Mama wasn't my real mother, because she'd been there since I was a baby.

The soap made fast. At first it was a jelly the ugly color of a fresh bruise, but when I paddled it into Mama's molds it was a cloudy gray paste. The molds were flat wooden boxes as black as soot from years of soapmaking. I filled them all. Now Mama could make do until cold weather.

Nobody in our family ever came out to say "Thank you" for anything, but Mama came closest. When the soap was done she said, "Well, you didn't ruin it after all. I guess you've earned your victuals for one more go-round." She popped me on the tail to show that we were friends, but hard enough to sting.

I started for the creek but she called me back. "What was all that down at the springhouse?"

"Why, nothing."

"Who was with you?"

"Nobody."

"Faaaax."

"I never spoke to a soul."

"Don't let me catch you in a lie, sir. You know I can hear things from that hollow like they were right under my nose."

I gave her my sheepy grin. "I reckon it was me you heard."

"A-Lord have mercy."

"Yes'm, it was. I was only practicing up for school."

"I just imagine you were, boy."

"Yes'm. I said my arithmetic up to the nine-times table, and all kinds of things—oh, I said 'The Boy Stood on the Burning Deck.'"

"Well, I never knew you to lie out of a thing—but I know it wasn't your voice down there, young man."

"I was trying to talk bigger, Mama, like Jimroe or Damon."

"I vow. Well, what scared you so that you lost your mind and flew up here, spilling your water all over creation?"

"They flustrated me, yelling for water of a sudden."

I couldn't say why I fought to keep her from learning about Pem Sixkiller and his match; something just told me she mustn't know. I knew it would mean trouble because a barn burning was a thing we had been brought up to fear above anything; it could mean a lifetime of hard work gone up in smoke. It would be better to have your house afire than your barns. It was the first time I had ever thought, too, that somebody might hate our family and wish us harm, and I didn't know what Mama might do if I told her. She looked me in the eye like she saw clean through my head, then gave a deep breath and let me go. She didn't half believe me, but couldn't find me out. I broke for the swimming hole.

I got back to the house as Cousin Tree was going home for the evening, slouched sideways on his little mule with his feet almost dragging. He looked at the sky. "You'd better sleep one-eyed, Tadpole. It's nightwalking weather if ever I saw it."

He meant that we might go hunting. I told him I'd be ready. Mama came to the kitchen door, with flour on her arms to the elbows, and flung a hand to Tree.

"Heigho, Cuz. What's the good word tonight?"

Everybody played a game with Tree, trying to see if they could worm some kind of a story out of him. He was never known to be caught without a joke, or to tell the same one twice. He didn't care how old they were, because he said the old stories were so true that people ought to be reminded. You never knew what he would tell. He slowed his mule.

"Why, I'm thinking of joining the She Say Baptists."

"What in Jee-rusalem—"

"It's right out of your Holy Writ, honey. You know when old Miriam found that baby and said his name was Moses and the Pharaoh's daughter asked her where she got him and she said in the bulrushes?"

"Sure thing."

"Well, that's what *she say*. We've done taken that for our text and way of living. That's the way I want to carry on."

He left Mama sniggering, and poked off down the hill.

After supper Mama and Papa came to the porch swing to watch the sun go down behind Wildkitten while the girls beat the dishes around in the kitchen. Damon tromped up and down in Mama's new shoes to break them in for her, Cornelia played the parlor organ and Frank watered the horses and mules and threw fodder down to them. Some of the girls drew fresh water and slipped pails of milk and cream into the well bucket and let them down to cool for morning.

Mama gave Papa his daily message. They talked every evening about each little thing that happened all day, like they wanted to be sure they didn't forget. If Mama had something on her mind she would ease Papa into talking about it before he knew what was going on, and then pop it to him out of the blue. Now I thought she had caught Papa.

"I expect that if they could test out the blood of every man in this county, you'd run about half black-eyed peas and half corn liquor."

"What else do you think made this country great, Little Bit?"

"I'd as soon they'd grow great while they were drawing a few sober breaths around me, in particular at picnics and Sunday meetings."

She heard me tip down the steps behind her into the yard, and snatched two little boys at her feet. "Trout, you and Gonville help Fax, now. He's going to fetch down the apples for me—aren't you, Fax?" It was against her law to complain about your chores.

It was easy enough to get in the apples, but a nuisance. Mama and the girls had cut up bushels of June apples and put them to dry on the roof, between old sheets and a cheesecloth cover, where bees crawled them all day, the slices shrinking browner and sweeter all the time. When the sun went down they had to come in out of the dew. I scaled the ladder and handed them down to the boys. We borrowed a handful apiece on the sly.

"I don't see why you don't put 'em on the barn roof and have done with it," Papa said. "It'd be so much quicker."

"And have them parboil on that old sheet iron? I reckon not. They'd taste like the insides of a threshing machine. When I bite into dried apples about Christmastime, I want to taste that old oak and shingle moss and rain and sunshine."

"Whooey," Papa said. He went for the barn lot, but Mama wasn't about to let him get away.

"Henderson, do you aim to expose your women and baby girls to that drunken crew at the Picnic every year that comes?"

Papa turned. "Lin, if a man wants a sminch of tanglefoot on his holiday, there's no way on God's green earth we can stop him—I thought you enjoyed the Picnic."

"I do. We all do. But one of these days, you mark my word, one of these days we'll see a brawl."

"Goddlemighty, Little Bit. You'd worry the teats off a boar hog. Let somebody else do some of the fretting. If it'll make you feel better, I'll promise you—we'll have peace and quiet up there this year. I'll stomp out them sinners till hell won't have it."

He went off whistling and Mama started swinging again with her mouth shut like a trap, but she couldn't hold it. She melted to a grin.

"I ought to wash that ugly talk out of your ears," she told

us. "But take a good look, for you'll never see another like
him. When the Lord made Henderson Starling he broke
the mold and threw it away where he'd be sure not to find it
again."

We took the apples into the hall for the night and eased
upstairs before Mama thought to make us wash our feet on
the porch with the others. The apples smelled like we had
perished and gone Above. It made my mouth drip to think
of the fried apple pies Mama would put in my dinner pail for
school in winter. They would taste of spice and summer all
over again. It made me feel better just to think of school, and
of the new teacher who was coming. Folks said there was
something wrong with me the way I loved school, when
Jimroe and Damon and even the girls hated it like poison—
but so long as I got to go, I didn't care what they said.

Papa claimed he had gone to school just one day in his life.
"The first time I went was on a Friday," he would say.
"Then I went back on Saturday and nobody was in the
schoolhouse, so I came home and told Pap that school was
out—and I never went back again."

It gave Mama the whiffets to hear him tell me things like
that.

The little boys were excited that night because we had put
one over on Mama by getting abed with dirty feet, and they
didn't mind even when I made them say their prayers. When
he was asking the Lord to pass around blessings to everybody, Trout told Him to keep some for Himself for having
helped us out of the foot washing. They giggled and rooted
around and gave me no peace until they dozed off.

Pretty soon Jimroe snaked in bed beside me and started
whispering. I was glad of it, because Jimroe could think up
more good things to talk about than the next dozen boys,
and when he wanted to, he could be the best friend you'd
want. But Jimroe would rather argue than eat when he was
hungry, and from the time we were little nippers disputed

with me over everything that came along, just to keep in
practice. That night he whispered me into a corner, arguing
over which one of us had the earliest memories.

"What's the first thing you remember, Fax? The very
first thing of all?"

I said it was when the big boys fed lightning bugs to
hoppy toads one evening and I saw them light up inside—
toad frogs jumping in the grass with lights going off and on
in their bellies, making little bottle-green flashes. Jimroe
snorted. He talked so crazy with lies of what he remembered
that I finally said I remembered the day I was born. But
there was no such thing as catching Jimroe Starling.

"That ain't a nothing," he said. "I can remember back
before I was born."

I hooted.

"Oh, yes, I can. I remember hearing the keys in Mama's
apron pocket. They were in her lap, and I heard 'em jangle
when I would kick. I remember plain as day wondering
what the devil them keys were to. I had sense enough to
know one was to the smokehouse and one to the icehouse
and one to the dairy—but all them others!"

I laughed but Jimroe wouldn't give ground, and for a
minute or two I thought he was accidentally telling the
truth, but of course I got over it. Jimroe began to yawn and
gave out.

The katydids raised a racket that night until I could
hardly hear myself think, like a million rusty little hinges
swinging back and forth all night, just outside the window.
Field mice caroused in the loft over our heads, the screech
owl in the box elder by the barn gave a half-hearted whoop,
and there was a stud whippoorwill in the creek bottom
woods who couldn't sleep. I got drowsy, and then, as clear
as a picture in a stereopticon, so plain that I felt I could reach
out and touch things, I remembered the first time I ever saw
my new mama, to notice. It was a thing I didn't even know I
knew until Jimroe stirred up my memory. I had the habit of

not thinking too much about Mama, because I was a little ashamed that I loved her better than what I could remember of my real mama.

This time in my memory that came so clear, I was no more than four years old, squatting on the back porch on a rusty plow point, using it for a play saddle, rocking red scars in the planks. Mama came out in the yard and her hair blazed like fire in the sun, so I watched her, thinking that I didn't know that red-headed woman.

Mama ran like she had been taken by a seizure, and hemmed an old Dominecker hen in a fence corner and snatched her by one leg, whirling her around flapping and squawking and feathers flying. She got pecked on one arm, but she held on and took the hen to the chopping block. She tried over and over to lay the hen's neck across the block, but couldn't do it until the hen was worn out at last and laid her head flat, looking up without a blink of her orange eyes. Mama took the hatchet.

She raised the hatchet and held it until it trembled in her hand and the sun ran silver on the edge where Papa had honed it. Mama let the hatchet down slow with a sound like she was crying but without making tears. She crouched down over the block and looked back with her face upside down under her arm, to see if there was anybody who could help, then turned and stared at the hen like she had never seen a chicken before.

"I can't do it," she said.

She raised the hatchet a dozen times or more and waited at the block with that hen, trying to get up her nerve. The hatchet barely rose the last few times, until she went off carrying it in one hand and the hen in the other, bawling as hard as she could. I got up off the plow point and paddled after her. She walked to where Papa was working, at least a mile away over the hills.

She was still crying when she got to Papa but she never said a word and neither did he. She held out the hen and the hatchet and Papa looked her over quick, took the hen and wrung off her head with one whip of his arm, and when the chicken quit flopping handed the body to Mama. She went back to the house with her face wet and working. Papa looked after her with a little bit of a smile I never saw him smile again.

It never came to me till all those years later that Mama was trying to kill the first chicken of her housekeeping, and that Papa had the sense to help her over the hard time. Since then she had killed one million and one and never bothered to think about it—and in all the time since, I never saw a tear on her face.

I went to sleep thinking that the owl at the barn was like the squawking of the old hen from away back on the first day I had learned something about Mama.

Later I had a nightmare. I dreamed that our tobacco barns were burning and that I kept trying to yell for Papa, but that all I could do was stutter like Pem Sixkiller. I could hear the snapping of logs burning all through the dream, like gunfire from far away.

3

A Three-Ring Coon Hunt

Something woke me going *pip, pip* at the window. Cousin Tree was down in the yard on his mule Lize with his hounds about him, and all of them looked up as he thumped bird shot against my window. It was his signal. I looked first to see that Jimroe was still asleep, then threshed into my clothes and swung down our rope without a sound, toeing barefoot against the house. We had worn a stripe down the weather-boards, scuffing off crackled paint with our feet. I went easy so that I wouldn't rouse Jimroe.

I was glad to have Tree to myself. I had a feeling that

Jimroe wouldn't follow us because if there was anything he feared it was the creek bottom at night, where he thought snakes were as thick as fiddlers in hell. I went everywhere with Jimroe, but half the time wanted to kill him. He didn't boss me around so bad when we were alone, even if he was seventeen and more than two years older—but when other people were around he changed, and picked at me just to show off. So it was Jimroe that I sneaked away from that night. Tree knew how it was. He sometimes said, "You shouldn't be so all-fired uprighteous. He's a cross you've got to bear—but if it was mine, damned if I wouldn't drop it now and then."

Tree started his jokes on me right away. "Who's that coming here with that two-by-twice throwing arm on him? It's a wonder to me you can stand up straight."

He liked to tease me about the way I was forever throwing rocks, and claimed that I was the only boy in the known world who could carry five rocks on a coon hunt and come back with five coons every time. He said my right arm was a foot longer than the left, just from heaving rocks.

I crawled up on the mule behind Tree and we rode. The moon was full and had a gauzy ring around it and Tree said that was good luck. It was about three o'clock, and warm mist washed around us as we neared the creek. Away up-river, maybe four miles, some hounds were running, and their music came thrumming down the Redwine.

"Can't afford sleep tonight," Tree said. "Coon's going to waste. How many rocks you got?"

"Three."

"I'm glad to know we'll have a mess of coon to say grace over. My mouth's all fixed for it."

Tree was my tombstone buddy, especially for hunting. He hunted any game that moved the year around and paid no mind to the season. "I eat anything that don't eat me first, is my motto," he would say.

He wasn't really our cousin, but by his daddy was some

kin to Mama. On his other side Tree was a good part Indian, or a crossbreed called Redshank. The Redshanks were a branch of the Hockaway tribe in our county, but the Hockaways didn't brag about it.

In the town of Randolph the courthouse had four backhouses in the yard: white, Negro, Indian and Redshank. The Indian-blood business was something men fought over, and a man could be killed for calling an Indian a quarter-blood when he was really only a sixteenth.

Of all the mixed-blood people we knew, Tree was the only one who came and went in the house of a white family. He sometimes ate with us. He never came to the back door the way colored people did, or stood with his hat off when he was talking with Papa. That was because Tree and Papa had run together so much as boys, and because he and Mama were kin. Tree and Mama never said boo about their being cousins of some kind, and I wouldn't have thought about it except that Tree never let it get dark when he was in our house. He would always grab his hat and go home. It was like there was a law that he wasn't to stay the night under our roof.

Little old Lize waded the creek about hock-deep because she wasn't much bigger than a toy. I hung on to Tree's middle when she skittered up the hill into the woods. He hummed one of his funny songs, and held the lantern away out front so that Lize could see where she was going. The light made him look like the Giant in *Jack and the Beanstalk*. Tree had a head about the size of a peck basket, bulging in the forehead, with salt-and-pepper gray hair poking out every which way from under his blackened Panama hat. And his jaws were always working, either gnawing East Tennessee Crosstie Chewing Tobacco or raw peanuts. I thought that if a coon could see him, he'd be scared to death.

Tree was the most famous man in our township. It wasn't humanly possible to spend an hour in a store or the tobacco warehouse without hearing a story on him. He lived in a river cabin, deviled by a wife and a nest of children, so that he was always finding things to do somewhere else. Tree could do anything. He and his boys ran the chain ferry over to the Virginia side of the river, and he was a jackleg carpenter too. He had forgotten more about guns than Winchester ever knew. Our people thought there was nobody like Tree.

I held Tree tight around the middle when we went up that hill on the mule. You could tell it was a man you had hold of. He was as hard as an oak stump, and had a fine smell.

His black-and-tan hounds ambled ahead of us in and out of the light, going stiff-legged like they might be on their last hunt, but they covered ground and Lize was beginning to blow, just keeping their pace, by the time we climbed the bluff over Dirty Butter Creek. Tree didn't waste breath on the dogs.

"*Haaaaaak!*" was all he said.

The hounds loped out of the lantern light and began casting through the woods.

Tree wouldn't baby a hunting dog. His hounds were so broke that they wouldn't turn off a coon track after a rabbit even if they came close enough to lick one in the face. Tree said their noses wouldn't smell a thing but coon. He trained dogs by starting with a couple of dozen and weeding them down to four or five coon hounds he could bet on. He never had to pepper dogs with shotguns to break them of bad habits, like other hunters did, but he was hard. He said it was too bad that you couldn't bring up children along with your dog pack.

Tree had tied Lize to a bush because it was against our principles to ride after a coon, and we waited on the hillside while the dogs worked. Every minute or so Tree yelled to let them know he was in behind them and that they had better do right. He was sitting ten feet away, but I was close enough to smell him out when he changed from tobacco to peanuts to a sweet potato, and then to whiskey. He passed me a yam from a pocket of his old blue Army overcoat, the one he had brought home from the War with Spain. It was as thick as a blanket, with brass buttons the size of half dollars drooping from wire staples.

We sat in the woods listening to hound music from the hollow. I tried to talk to Tree about Pem Sixkiller, without his making a joke out of every word I said. It was hard to have a straight talk with Tree. He despised to say a serious word as bad as anybody I knew.

"I'm getting up a list of all the people who hate Papa."

"Why, sure, Sport," Tree said. "You can put me down."

"I mean it, now, Tree."

"Son, I could come out flat-footed and say your daddy's the biggest stem-winding son of a bitch in the Redwine Valley, but it ain't so that I can. I'm done committed to Wash Strawn when it comes to honors like that."

"Aw, Tree."

He squeezed my knee with his big hand until I yelled.

"Fax, you've got the wrong bee in your bonnet. You couldn't find an enemy of Hence Starling in a day's ride."

"How about the Sixkillers?"

"Whatever gave you such a notion? The worst you can say is that they were born lazy and all had relapses."

As much as I wanted to tell Tree all about it I couldn't get the words out of my mouth, the way he was teasing me. So I said, "Old Jess is a good man."

"Not a mean bone in his head unless he's likkered up beyond reason. But you've got to take him like he is, with the bark on. Deep inside, them Sixkillers run quick and wild."

"Well, how about Pembroke?"

"He don't amount to a poot in a whirlwind. And atop everything else he's such a liar. He's just so big a liar he'd have to hire somebody else to call up his own dog for him."

Tree tried to find out why the Sixkillers were on my mind until he saw that I wouldn't tell, and then he said that I must have been eating after supper and got the mulligrubs. I told myself that I was a goose to worry so over Pembroke when he had done no more than strike a match and talk ugly about our family, and I tried to forget him.

I shut up and got another yam, but before I could choke it down a hound belled out like the track was red-hot. Tree sat still.

"That's the youngun, Miss Annie. She gets all worked up like a June bride in a feather bed. It ain't really so till Carlyle says so."

The pack soon bugled and Tree grabbed the lantern. When the old daddy hound joined the others, we moved. We knew they had treed a coon. It was all I could do to keep up with Tree, gobbling my sweet potato and quartering down the slope with briars and limbs whipping at me in the dark, and trying to stay close to that rocking ring of light that flew through the woods. I was damned if anything would stop me, because I knew I would get the coonhide for my share, and if I was lucky and the weather hadn't made the fur too ratty, it would bring a quarter from the dealer in Richmond.

We found the dogs standing against a shagbark hickory, one of the tallest trees in our bottom woods. The ground was swampy and they hopped in the water, the young one scrambling about five feet up the trunk at each jump, like she would climb it. Tree tried to shine the lantern up and catch the coon's eyes so that I could knock him out with one of my smooth river rocks, but the branches were too thick to find him and I had to give up. Tree took off his shoes.

"I'll shake that dude out of there, old Fax. You stand here with the light and we'll soon make him sorry he ever left Mama this night."

He took another pull at the whiskey bottle. "Now, you needn't tell your papa that I had my constitutional. I promised him I'd not fall off the wagon—even to pick up a whip —till tobacco season was over."

He shinnied up to the first limb and his feet went out of sight. The hounds cut off the baying at that instant except for a few nervous barks from the young one; they looked up into the hickory and trembled on their haunches and whined, but they held.

"Lookit them fine dogs," Tree said. "There's no known way to make 'em leave, once they've treed—they know durn well that if they did leave, I'd kick 'em so far and so high that the bluebirds would build in 'em before they ever hit ground."

He bulled up through the hickory, growling. It was the whiskey talking. "I'm a good mind to arrest your papa, letting his dratted trees grow so big and bushy they ain't fit for coon hunting."

Then he cussed the coon because he couldn't find him, and said he'd better, by God, be a nice big one if he knew what was good for him, after all our trouble. Then he got quiet and I knew he was high enough to study the limbs against the moon, trying to spot the coon.

I couldn't see much with that little old lantern, and the dark seemed to be closing in. A ground fog humping along over the swamp gave things a creepy look, and foxfire glowed on rotten logs like animal eyes. I wasn't scared exactly, but when I moved the light and shadows spun around I remembered Papa's tales about wildcats in our woods when he was a boy, so I took the lantern bail in my teeth and went up the hickory to the first big limb. It was a good ten or twelve feet off the ground and I sat there with the lantern, feeling better about things.

Tree gave a coon squall with his mouth, so real that it made my hair stand up, spitting and snarling and yowling like forty tomcats tied in a sack. Then he yelled, "Ho, cooooooooon! Yo, you coooooony cooooon coon."

He shook a limb so hard that it teetered me on my seat away below him, and I hung on tight. The coon squeaked and started down, slipping and slapping against branches over my head, trying to hang on but tumbling faster and faster, with Tree right on his tail. They made a fuss together. Cousin Tree had a way of falling through the limbs that would scare you to death—just turning loose and dropping, catching onto anything that came in his way to break the fall, so that he could reach the ground before the dogs tore the coon to pieces.

The coon hit in the swamp under me *kersplash!* and the dogs were all over him in a jiffy. There was a thundering fight. He was a good-sized boar coon full of the Old Nick, and he ripped and cut and drove dogs in all directions. They screamed murder but kept coming back for more.

And then, here came Cousin Tree.

He whisked down to where I was and caught himself on a limb overhead and winked at me. Then he stepped out in thin air and fell like a rock. When he passed me in the light of the lantern I could see surprise on his face. He went reared back at full length, with hands and legs pawing for a hold, and even his toes arched out stiff, ready to grab.

"*WooooooooOOP!*" he said.

He lit on his back in the middle of the coon fight. Everything blew up—dogs and Tree and the broken whiskey bottle and mashed yams and peanuts aflying. It looked like the dogs were in a hurry to eat one half of Tree and the coon the other half, before he could sink into the swamp mud. I never expect to hear such yowling and snarling and grunting again, and some of Tree's cussing was an education to me.

Before I knew what was happening, Tree flew up the trunk and snatched me down and frailed the fire out of me, cussing between grunts.

"Hod! Uh. Damn! Uh. Youngun! Next time I tell you to

stay on the ground, you'd just by a damn sight better."

He stopped as suddenly as he had begun, like he had for-gotten himself. "Aw, Fax, what the devil possessed you to pull a trick like that?"

It didn't come over me till then that Tree had thought he was down to solid ground when he reached me and the lantern, and it hit me so hard that I didn't give another thought to the licking, but righted the lantern and scrambled among the dogs with Tree to save what was left of the coon and look for broken ribs and legs on the hounds. Tree pulled down his britches and I tried to pick slivers of glass out of his rump by the light of the lantern. I didn't find them all but he got up laughing and sent the dogs limping home. We skinned the coon about daylight and went back.

"Now weren't that a regular dog's breakfast of a coon hunt?" Tree said. "I hope I don't have to learn that lesson another time."

"I'll bet you wish you'd brought Jimroe instead."

He wrinkled his big mouth in a grin and said he could no more do without me than he could his dogs or Lize or even his bottle.

"Of course, now, Jimroe's got eleven times your sense, but he uses it all looking out for Number One. He wouldn't know a good coon-hunting trick if it was to come up and bite its initials in the seat of his drawers."

"Tree, I hate it that I hurt you."

"Hell, boy, I pretty near enjoyed it. I'll put up with most anything if a boy wants to learn how to hunt. And then—there's something curious about you that reminds me of your daddy when we were chaps together. You make me feel like old times all over again."

There was something wishful in Tree's voice. After a minute he said, "Boy, one way and another, it's got so that your daddy and me ain't so close as we used to be. He's got things to worry him these days."

I wondered what Tree was talking about.

"It's not the least bit my business," he said, "but I fret about your daddy. He'd never let you know it, but he's way yonder in debt to Biscoe Allen for seed and fertilizer and all, and no place to find the money except in the tobacco patch. I expect he won't sleep much till his crop is laid by and sold."

"Don't Biscoe know Papa would pay him back if it took his last breath?"

"You ain't old enough to know how ugly a debt can be. It's got a habit of turning into a mortgage—and a mortgage has turned many a planter into a tenant. But don't let it vex you, boy. Life ain't nearly as serious as it's made out to be. And all you Starlings seem to scrape by, one way and another."

Tree's hands and face looked as if he'd been run through a cotton gin at least once. Lize snuffled at him like she wondered who in the goodness he was, and was at first shy about letting him mount her. I got up behind him and we started off on the mule. Then Tree straightened to listen.

"Speaking of Brer Jimroe," he said, "here he comes despite snakes, gallinipper mosquitoes and all. And he's burning wind."

Then I could hear Jimroe. He was yelling "*Eeeeeeeeeeee-oooooo!*" at the top of his voice. He was afraid on the path through the bottom woods and was yelling to keep up his courage in the dark places, hoping to scare things out of his way.

"He couldn't stand it," Tree said. "We woke him up when the dogs treed that coon, baying so loud—but he didn't dare come till it got light enough to show him where to step."

Pretty soon Jimroe was there with us, making a fuss over the coon and Tree's banged-up face, and trying to catch his breath without letting us know how fast he'd come through the bottom. He begged Tree to let him ride Lize home with us, but Tree said nothing doing.

"You're too big," he said. "She can't carry an ounce more than me and old Fax, to save her soul from mulehell."

Jimroe hated it, but he walked along just behind Lize, up on his toes, as if he expected a snake under every leaf. We were halfway home, in the worst of the bottom, when Jimroe toppled over, yowling.

"*Iiiiiiii!* I'm a goner. Take me home quick—before I die."

We got over to him, and he slipped up a britches leg and showed us a red mark. "Right there. A durn snake popped me, like I told you he would. I know he was a cotton-mouth."

We loaded him on Lize and he rode until we came to the ridge near home. Then Jimroe slid off the mule and leaned against me. "Tote me up the hill, Fax. I ain't got time to go clean around. The poison's ataking hold." His hands quivered.

Lize couldn't have made it up that steep place, so I grabbed Jimroe and went up, holding him around the seat with one hand and pulling us up by bushes, until somehow I got him to the top. Tree led Lize over the path.

I was half dead when we got to our big barn because Jimroe was a good twenty pounds heavier than I was.

I staggered around with him, blowing hard, hoping that Tree would hurry and help me—but just then Jimroe fought loose from me and slid down and ran, like nothing was wrong with him. He laughed over his shoulder, and was so quick that he was almost out of range before I could get a rock from my pocket. I sailed one after him so hard that it whistled, but too late. I wanted to kill him, and would have if I'd had another try. I wanted to lie on the ground and cry, in the way I had done when I was little and he had deviled me with tricks like that, but Tree came up, so I laughed.

"I knew he had a sore on that leg," I said. "I ought to know better by now. He never came within half a mile of a snake."

Tree watched Jimroe run over the ridge and out of sight

on his way to the house. "Well, don't forget that brothers are harder to live with than anybody else. If you can live through it with him, everything else will be rosy."

We got home in time for breakfast and Tree wheedled Mama into frying the coon. She groused about it stinking up her kitchen but she couldn't help doing what Tree wanted.

4

Good Men Don't Cheat —Much

It was a holiday to have Tree in the kitchen with us. Mama waited on him hand and foot until he was ready to explode —like he was company from far away instead of having been there the day before.

He made the little ones laugh by singing some of his homemade songs. Trout and Gonville and Sheba and Quail crawled all over him, or beat their spoons on the table and sang one of Tree's songs:

> "Mama pass the corn bread
> Papa pass the coon.

Baby's little belly growls
About a empty spoon."

The kids didn't drag it out for fear of missing a mouthful of the coon. It was scandalously good, and even Tree, who was an expert, said it was just about fit to eat.

"Linden," he said, "it tastes like cooked music from a brass band."

Tree made a story out of his fall from the coon tree, and said it was my fault and that I was just scared of his dogs. He went on until it was almost solid lie, and I knew that I'd never hear the last of it. I liked it, though, because Tree joshed me and didn't even look at Jimroe. He wouldn't give Jimroe the satisfaction of telling folks about the trick he'd pulled on me that morning. They all enjoyed his tale, and somehow Papa got wound up and started telling yarns about how they had carried on when they were boys. We sat there listening like it wasn't a Saturday morning at all and we hadn't a lick of work to do in the fields.

Tree and Papa had worked together on the railroad over on the Virginia side of the river when they were young, and Papa had funny tales that were still good to us even after years of telling. This time Papa thought of one we hadn't heard before.

"Well, sir, one night T. finally got a bellyful of that railroad. You know that high trestle over Gravitt's Creek? In the middle, it's a drop of about fifty feet to the bottom."

Tree began to shake, laughing, as soon as Papa said that, keeping his eyes on Papa like he wanted to make sure he told it straight and was half afraid that he would.

"Old Tree was just prancing, so full of corn juice that his back teeth were afloat, when 'The Creeper' came chugging up behind him. He could see her headlight in the gorge and hear the engine bell, and he went up on his tippytoes, flying over the crossties as fast as he could go.

" 'The Creeper' got so close that old Tree had to give up, she was gaining so fast. He dropped down between two crossties and hung on for dear life."

Tree beat himself on the thighs like he couldn't stand to hear another word, and tears rolled down his cheeks. We couldn't see that it was all that funny but we laughed at Tree's antics, except for Jimroe, who looked from Tree to Papa as if he saw something nobody else could see. It was one of his ways. He understood funny things, all right, but he was anxious to look behind the laughing and see what else was there.

"Poor old Tree hung there till his fingers like to have popped off," Papa said. "When that freight train got past he tried to pull up, but he couldn't make it. He was stuck between ties and had to hang there or give up the ghost. His arms most came out of his sockets, but he hung and he hung and managed to last till daylight.

"And then, when it was light enough to see"—Papa grinned at us—"why, then old Tree looked down, and after all his suffering saw his toes hanging just about eight inches off the ground. He'd come that close to making the bank."

We laughed over that, and when he got a little pause Papa said, "*Ah-whoo!* And that ain't all. It made Tree so mad that he hung there till dinnertime that day, just out of spite."

Tree and Papa went weak from their whooping, and to us their laughing about it was funnier than the story. They beat each other on the back, and I thought that I had never seen Tree and Papa touch each other that way before. It made me wonder why they weren't like they'd been when they were boys. I knew it couldn't be just that they'd grown up, for Tree was always playing around with other men just as if he was a boy himself.

"Great June," Papa said. "The times we used to have, nobody knows. They don't make boys like they used to."

It took us a while to quiet down because one of the little

ones would suddenly see what was funny about Tree hanging on the trestle that night, and erupt and start everybody
laughing again.

Then Mama made a prim mouth and her humor changed
in the snap of a finger. She didn't have to say a word. All of
us were used to her fussing about Tree and his ways. Now
she was thinking less of how good it was to have him
around, laughing and making all of us feel better, and more
of how he was always flat-broke and would sometimes have
liquor, and neglect his family and his own crops to go off
with other folks. That set her off, and she spoke to Tree
sharper even than you'd expect between blood kin. That
abrupt manner was something we had learned to live with in
Mama. She couldn't help it. She was one way one minute
and another the next, now giving her howdy-do smile and
then blessing you out. Now she had taken the notion that
Tree was the enemy of householding and churchgoing and
the motherhood of the Redwine Valley, and she wanted him
out of there. I'd heard Tree mock her so many times in those
selfsame words.

Tree got the change in climate right now. "Hence, I expect we ought to be at it if you aim to work tobacco today."

Papa came to himself and we hustled to the field. The
sun was high and we were sweating from the start. We had
to go easy that morning, since wet weather had choked the
field with crab grass, and Tree worked the rows with Lize,
using a scoop plow to kill the grass. Even Lize had trouble,
as tiny as she was, and now and then she popped off a tobacco leaf. Papa tried to pretend that he didn't care, but
sometimes he turned his head from Tree so that he wouldn't
see the damage.

Tree would sooner have died than admit it, but he loved
Lize better than anything in the world. You'd never catch
him saying a kind word to her, but when he cussed her he
didn't have his heart in it. He gave her a good try that

morning. He picked up a rock, and held the lines and plow handle in one hand with his right arm cocked, ready to pop Lize. "Damn your good-for-nothing hide. I'd sell you for a song and sing half of it myself. You snap just one more leaf and you're as good as in the glue factory."

Lize couldn't help herself; she broke another leaf, and as soon as she came to end of that row, Tree hit her with the rock, good and hard. She jumped, but she went on working and didn't come close to breaking another piece of tobacco. Tree was mighty proud of her, but we could tell it only from the way he walked. Except for when he stopped for a dipperful of water, he cussed her that livelong morning.

Papa let us knock off at noon. The field looked good. We had never grown finer, darker tobacco, or more of it. If the hail didn't catch us we would get rich in the fall. Papa and Tree walked up and down feeling the leaves like they were made of gold, not saying much, but nodding and looking. Papa knew he owed a lot of the good crop to Tree.

Mama and Tree kept picking at each other while we were at dinner in the kitchen, pretending to be joking. They smiled, but didn't mean it. They were a sight together, the spitting image of each other, even though he was twice her size and lots older. They had faces to remind you of foxes— long and handsome, with wide jaws and neat little eyes set sideways in the head, with the same kind of sly grin. Their end of the Poindexter family had what was called a hook-and-eye complexion, with red hair and freckles, and Tree had it too, atop his halfbreed flush of skin. Papa called them the Red Muzzle Poindexters and said they were devoutly to be avoided.

After dinner Tree said he ought to go to town. "Hence, if you'd make me the loan of your buggy . . ."

Papa said it was all right, but Jimroe and I begged Tree to let us go, and Mama said that it was high time somebody took her goose feathers to the store.

"Take the wagon, then," Papa said. "Take the whole caboodle and maybe I can get some work done around here."

Mama's feathers were bundled in sheets, and when we got them in the wagon it looked like we were hauling a cloud to town. It made Lize skittish.

Jimroe said he thought he would go trading, too, and came from the hog lot with a little shoat he had raised, and went in the house for his other plunder. He had a dollar watch that he had earned by clearing new ground for old man Billy Lufler on the next farm, and a brass knife he had traded for at school. Trading in town was something new for Jimroe.

Papa said, "If you think you're going to trade that outfit for a horse, you've got another think coming."

Jimroe said he'd have a horse or bust trying.

"You're a captain," Papa said, "but you'll learn. You'll learn."

Tree got a gallon stoneware jug and a sack full of dusty medicine bottles from the barn, and washed them up.

Mama came onto the porch and watched while he sloshed water around at the well house. She took a walleyed look at the medicine bottles and yelled, "Bring me a paper of needles, and have the rest of my feather money put to my credit on Biscoe Allen's books."

After a minute she yelled louder, "And don't you come about me with liquor, T.T. Poindexter. I'd just better not catch you trading my feathers for a drink."

We went off looking like a set of gypsies, with Jimroe perched on the tailboard of the wagon, holding the little white shoat in his lap, the shoat squealing and both of them coughing and sneezing in our dust.

Tree drove for half a mile before he said a word. "Boys, I'm a hog about your mammy, but I ain't above giving you one piece of advice. Don't never—and I mean, by God, never—get mixed up with a woman who goes by the name of Poindexter."

Tree taught us a couple of dirty verses to the song "In the Southern Part of France Where the Women Wear No Pants." I couldn't tell quite what he meant but Jimroe begged for more, so I knew something was wrong.

Just then my sister Cornelia reared up from under the feather bags. She had two eggs in her hands that she had stolen from under Mama's bed, out of the pin-money basket. She was going to swap them for candy at the store. She sat up whistling and pretending that she hadn't heard Tree's dirty song or didn't understand it. Even Jimroe didn't tease her, though, because she might tell Mama all she knew. Tree himself couldn't think of much to say to her.

"Well," he said, "the whole buzzard flock together. It looks bad for old Biscoe. When we get through with him he'll feel like he's been drove hard and put up muddy."

At the edge of Corona Crossroads we passed the Boneyard, where people from our end of the county went to trade livestock. The lot was about half full and a little dickering was going on. Deputy Wash Strawn stumped toward the road on his wooden leg and yelled to Jimroe, "Hey, boy, here's your chance to get shut of that there pig." Everybody knew that Wash was a hard trader.

"They ain't made enough money yet to buy her."

"That so? It ain't every day I get to see a solid-silver shoat. You'd better let her and me get acquainted, son."

"I might, some of these times."

"Oh, I'll cheat you right, boy." Men in the Boneyard laughed.

We rode on. Tree hawked his throat. "You want to watch how you trade with that devil."

"What's wrong with Uncle Wash?" Cornelia said.

"I'd trust him about as far as I could throw the Redwine River. That's all that's wrong with him."

"I'd be ashamed to talk so about the poor old thing," Cornelia said.

"Yeah," Tree said. "You'd feel different if he'd plucked your feathers once. Nobody ever knows whether he's playing deputy, or mail carrier, or horse trader, or just working for Biscoe Allen on the sly—mostly, I expect, it's all at once."

"Well, I like him, I don't care what. I learned to talk on his knee."

"I guess you think he got that red mark across his nose from wearing tight spectacles while he was reading the Bible."

"Well, how *did* he get it?"

"Drinking whiskey out of a fruit jar."

"Well, pot call the kettle black," Cornelia said. Tree said there was no doubt she was her mama's daughter. He talked about how Wash had been making a shady living since the Civil War. Jimroe wouldn't listen to him either.

"I aim to try him out," Jimroe said. "He'd better have on his trading britches when I get ahold of him."

"Well," Tree said, "if you're fool enough to try that, you'd sure better have a solid-silver shoat, is all I can say."

Tree drove to Biscoe Allen's store and hitched Lize, and swung out his heavy jug.

"Let's see if old Tree ain't got a little trick up his sleeve to entertain the good merchant," he said.

A one-lung gasoline engine chugged behind the store and we knew that Biscoe was out grinding corn for somebody. Tree took his jug on the porch, where a line of men sat propped against the wall with their heels hooked in chair rungs. One of them yelled, "Evening, Pinedexter. Whatcha know good?"

"Well, we just saw Wash Strawn have a mighty close call."

The men turned their heads all at once, grinning, to see what lie Tree had thought up.

"Why, how's that, T.?"

"You know he's always said he'd hang himself if he had just one more youngun, and this new baby at his house has mighty near drove him crazy."

"Yeah."

"Well, we passed his place just now and Wash was poling up from the barn with a rope, shaking his head and saying he couldn't bear to take his own life. When Fax asked him how come him to change his mind, you know what that scannel said?"

"No telling."

"Why, he said, 'Boys, it come over me in a flash. I got to thinking, hi God—what if I was about to hang the wrong man?' "

They cackled while we went inside to trade, and told the tale to one another several times and said Tree was a curiosity in this world.

I took a deep breath when we went in: tea and coffee and molasses, bananas, cheese, sugar, beef in brine barrels, cured hides and harness, old onions and kraut kegs and dogs and raw tobacco, kerosene, pickled fish, lap robes, yard goods, mildew left from the wet weather, fertilizer and dried herbs from the country.

It was so dark in there that women who came to pick over bolts of cloth had to take them to the porch to finger them. And dangling down from the rafters, to the height of a good-sized man, was a world of cobwebs Biscoe and the spiders had been making for forty years. He had everything that would hang up there: plows and chain and chicken wire, saddles, animal traps, broomcorn, plowline, grindstones, women's dress forms and grimy sacks of things that only Biscoe could remember. The cobwebs were dusty and woolly and thick as ropes, and shuddered when people walked on the floor. The counters were stacked out of sight into all that truck with piles of straw hats and chamber pots and overalls and hunting boots and salt-lick blocks for cattle.

In front near the door two old men had made an island in the mess and were playing checkers on a greasy board, using corncob rounds for the men.

Jimroe and I took the feather bags to Biscoe's platform scales. It was all we could do to squeeze through the aisles, and we walked barefoot through the wet spot under the kerosene barrel and in rice and coffeebeans that had spilled from bags.

The only sounds were the buzzing of flies over the molasses barrel, about a hundred dirtdauber wasps butting their heads against the dim windowpanes, and the feather duster slapping back and forth while Biscoe's clerk, Red Dowd, tried to look busy. Red's eyes were sleepy, like he had been rousted from under the counter where he took naps.

While we weighed the feathers, Cornelia ran her nose over the glass candy counter. Red Dowd took her eggs and put them in a bucket of water to make sure they were fresh, and when they sank to the bottom and he was satisfied he said, "Whatcher want?"

Cornelia was smart enough to count everything in the store, but she knew better than to ask how many candies she could have for the eggs; she just poked her finger at things until he got tired and stopped her: "Gimme three black babies and a green jawbreaker and a red one and a licorice whip and two of the wax bottles and a banana marshmallow and a chewy piece and a lemon suck and a strawberry rose . . ."

Tree came in and went to work on Red Dowd. "Red on the head, draw me half a gallon of that good government likker, won't you?"

Red put Tree's jug under the spigot of his barrel and ran the whiskey and knocked the cob back and slung the jug on the counter with a grunt. Then Tree ordered Mama's paper of needles and told Red to be sure and give her credit for the feathers. Red checked the weight behind us and scratched figures in his big ledger.

"All right, then," Red said. "She gets seven dollars and forty cents for the feathers. That's less ten cents for the needles, leaves seven-thirty. You tell her that."

He put his hands flat on the counter and leaned toward Tree until his fingernails turned white, like a man who couldn't be budged. "Now. That'll be one seventy-five for the likker, Tree."

"Yeah. Just charge it to my account, Red." Tree hefted the jug and turned it upside down.

"Naw, I can't do it, Tree."

"How the hell come you can't?"

"You know as well as you know you're standing there that Biscoe said I wasn't to charge nothing more to you till you paid up. I can't help it."

Tree rubbed his hands together like he wanted to reach over and coldcock Red Dowd. Red straightened and said, "He's out back there if you want him."

Tree gave Red a half-hearted cussing, not so bad that Red would want to fight over it, and said, "All right, sir. I know it's no fault of yours. That son of a bitch Biscoe is as tight as one bark on two trees."

Biscoe walked in the back of the store at that instant. He was a bony man, so thin that you'd think he was walking around to save funeral expenses. His face looked like it had worn out two bodies. Biscoe had a clenched smile.

"It would take something like a Poindexter to be so free with other folks' money, and their name too. What's ailing you now, good friend?"

"Why, *there* he stands in the flesh," Tree said. "Speak of the devil. I was just saying how pleasant you're looking, Biscoe—like you'd been born in crab-apple season and put up in vinegar."

Red Dowd told Biscoe about the whiskey that Tree wanted to get on a credit, and Biscoe got fuller and redder in the neck.

"Well, by God. I told you twice, goddammit—no! What

makes you think you can wipe your feet on me till dooms-day, Trevilian?"

Tree had such a mild voice that I was ashamed. "I didn't have no idea you felt that way about it, Biscoe. Redhead, just pour the damn stuff back, then."

"You're damn whistling pour it back," Biscoe said. "You sure God ain't going out my door with one drop that ain't paid for, and I mean cash on the barrelhead."

Dowd sighed and poured from the jug into the top bung of the big barrel. Tree barked at him, "Make good and sure you don't pour back one ounce more than half a gallon, now—that's all I ordered."

"Don't get your bowels in such an uproar," Dowd said.

Tree nodded to us and we all went out in front of him: Cornelia first, with her cheek full of jawbreaker, and beads of licorice at the corners of her mouth; then Jimroe and me; and Tree last, scuffing his feet like he was as sore as a boil. But outside he hopped into the wagon and we went off fast.

"How come you to take all that off Red and Biscoe?" Jimroe said. "They treated you right common."

"Oh, don't go on so about it. Me and Red and Biscoe have been friends from way back."

"I'd like to know what kind of friends you call that, the way you let Biscoe wolf at you."

"Jamesroe, when you are a grown man, and have developed in your calliwhacker a taste for the finer things of life and are without funds and have experienced no likker lately to amount to anything—why, then you'll endure most anything for a drink. Not most anything. Anything."

As he rounded a bend, Tree took up his jug. "Excuse me, little folks. I'm obliged to wet my poor old dried-up whistle."

"Ah, hell," Jimroe said. "You ain't got a drink. We saw him pour out that liquor."

Tree gave us his foxy Red Muzzle Poindexter grin. "Cousins, I'll tell you a little secret just in the family—what Red and Biscoe never knew is that when I went in that den of thieves, I already had this jug pretty near half full of water."

Cornelia laughed.

"Of course," Tree said, "you couldn't say what I've got left is pure drinking likker by any means—but a little Adam's ale never hurt a good honest jug of whiskey."

He took a long drink of the watered liquor, and drank it down so that it didn't touch his lips but just glugged in the back of his throat. He smacked his mouth.

"It'll be a long time before that sip ever catches up with the first one I ever took. Ahhhh. Who was it said that one swallow never made a summer?"

He clucked Lize into a trot.

5

The Unexpected Mare

The nearer we came to the Boneyard on the way home, the
whiter Jimroe got in the face. He wiped his sweaty hands on
his sleeves and talked about the slick trick Tree had pulled
on Biscoe Allen, but Jimroe's mind was on horse swapping.
He couldn't hold still.

He jumped off the wagon before it stopped rolling and
went toward Wash Strawn, leading his shoat. Wash was
busy trading, so we settled to watch.

The old man was something to see. His overalls were tight
as a drum around his droopy belly, though the rest of him
was skin and bone. His string of white beard was tucked into
a breast pocket. One leg of the overalls was ripped off above

his wooden leg, showing a big round leather cap for a knee.

Wash had hooked a stranger, a town man who had come to Corona to begin farming and who wanted to buy sheep. Wash had a couple of dozen moth-eaten sheep under a tin-roofed shed out of the sun, looking like they were half dead. Wash pumped up and down between the sheep and the man, barking.

Wash's peg leg had been burned off through the years against hot stoves in winter, and was too short, but he kept wearing it, since it was made of oak from Cold Harbor, where he'd been shot in the Civil War. He looked like he was climbing out of a hole at each step.

Washington Strawn had been in my grandpa's company in that war, and had been stumping around Corona on his one leg ever since, waiting for the next heavy thing to fall on him. Nobody took him seriously, but he could trade livestock to a fare-thee-well. He hustled that town man so fast that he trapped him with those sheep before he knew what had hit him.

Pem Sixkiller's boy Jiggs was helping Wash at the trading. Wash yelled to him, "All right, son. Fetch me out another one. I want this gentleman to look in every single solitary mouth in that flock."

The town man tried to get into the sheep pen to look at the flock himself, but Wash said it was too hot in there under the tin roof, and made him wait for Jiggs to haul out the sheep one by one. Everybody except the town man could see what those two were doing.

Wash had just two young sheep in the flock, the only ones there with teeth in their heads. The others were so old that their teeth were gone and they were fit only for mutton, and hardly even for that. Jiggs had marked the young ones so he could find them, and dragged them out over and over, one after the other, opening their mouths for the town man to see. He put them back in the flock to get lost, then dragged one out again. Wash and Jiggs kept that up until the town man had looked in the same two mouths about twenty times, and said that was enough for him.

The town man paid Wash and went off to get help to herd them. The men laughed and the old man said, "The durn fool will be back in a day or so, raising hell because somebody's teased him about the toothless old things, and I'll have to give him another dose."

"What'll you do then, Shurf?"

"Why . . . hell, boys. I'll give him the Gospel according to St. Wash. I'll say, 'Friend, them things is just babies and ain't cut their teeth yet. You wait a season or two.' "

The men laughed so hard that the town man turned to look from the road, and then drove on.

Jimroe stepped up, but Wash wasn't ready for him. He had an Indian farmer waiting to buy a horse. The Indian looked at an old bay gelding, and when Wash saw his eyes light on that nag he hobbled over and put his hand on the horse's backbone and leaned there while the Indian went over the animal.

He covered the horse from tip to tail, looking at the worn cups in the teeth to see how old he was, poking him in the ribs and listening to be sure Wash wasn't trying to hide a case of windbreak. The Indian squatted to peep at the legs for signs of ringbone or spavins—but he paid no attention to Wash's hand on the horse.

Wash said not a word through the whole thing. His head was as bald as a china darning egg and he wiped it a time or two with his bandanna—but he kept that one hand on the horse's spine.

The Indian was finally satisfied and took out some money and handed it to Wash and said, "All right, Shurf. It's a swap."

Wash took his hand off the gelding's back. Tree punched me. An awful blue-green saddle sore was puckered on the horse's back. The Indian shook his head, but he knew that a

trade was a trade and he took the gelding off without another word. He walked hard and fast on his heels. We knew
that it would take him months to cure that sore.

"It was worth money to him," Tree said, "little as he
knows it now. That Indian thought he was a horse-trading
fool until he had the luck to run into old Wash."

Jimroe faced Tree with his eyes dark and shining, the way
he got when he was trying hard to convince somebody of
something. His face was like a mercury thermometer; you
couldn't see a thing in it until he got all wrought up, and
then his eyes changed.

"Now, you all go away, Tree," Jimroe said. "I can't trade
with you holding my hand. Go on home, now."

He wouldn't listen to Tree's warnings, and so we drove
out of the Boneyard. When we were a little ways down the
road, Tree stopped to see what would happen.

Jimroe led the shoat up to Wash Strawn and kept his
other hand in his pocket, holding on to his knife and his
watch. Wash slapped him on the back and poked the shoat
with his walking cane.

Jimroe talked thirteen to the dozen, throwing his head
back in the way he did when he was nervous. We could hear
them but not make out anything they were saying. Jimroe
led Wash along the line of plug horses, shaking his head at
each one and trying to joke Sheriff Strawn—all the time
studying the legs of the horses. Then he pointed to a horse
that he hadn't seemed to notice before, and Wash unhitched
it and pulled it back and forth by the bridle, running a few
steps as he pumped along on his peg leg. Jimroe shook his
head and started out of the lot with his shoat, like it was no
trade. Wash let him get almost to the road, and then called
him back.

"I swear," Tree said. "I think he's going to pull it off. I'd
give a pretty to hear what they're saying."

"You ought to have stayed with him," Cornelia said. She
managed to sound like Mama.

"No, siree. He could skin me trading the day he was

weaned. He took it in with his Mama's milk. By God, he did make it. Look at that son of a buck coming here with that nag."

It was true. Wash had the shoat, and Jimroe was coming out of the Boneyard with a horse, a plump claybank mare. We couldn't believe it. Cornelia and I yelled.

"Shut up," Tree said. "This'll never happen to him again. His first swap. Let him have his say-so."

Jimroe was swaggering so that I thought he might fall down. He got up on the tail of the wagon to hold the horse's rein.

"Let 'er go," he told Tree. He was trying not to talk biggity, but without much luck.

Tree drove away from the Boneyard and in a few minutes stopped and went back to Jimroe's horse. He handled her knee tendons and her hocks, and looked at her teeth, which weren't bad, and told Jimroe he had got a bargain.

I heard myself say, "I bet there's damn sure something wrong with her."

Jimroe gave a brassy laugh, he was so proud and scornful. Tree leaned close to look at me. "Funny," he said. "I never noticed before that your eyes were green."

It made me hot in the face.

"That nag moves like a three- or four-year-old," Tree said. "I don't see how you got her with that flea-bit shoat."

Jimroe grinned and showed Tree a new half dollar Wash had given him. "I got me a little to boot, too."

"Boy, boy." Tree slapped the horse on the withers and touched Jimroe like they were men equal, and we rode on. In less than a mile Tree stopped of a sudden, like he had just thought of something.

"Uh, oh," he said. "I should have known it." He went back to the mare and waved a hand before her eyes. The big cloudy eyes didn't blink and the horse looked straight ahead into the wagon.

"Well, boy, she's blind."

Jimroe was so quick that I couldn't tell whether or not he was surprised and trying to hide it.

"Heck, yeah. She sure is. How do you think I'd ever have got her, if she wasn't? But I'm aiming to double my money on her. I'll guarandamntee you that."

"I for one ain't betting you won't," Tree said.

We headed home with Jimroe trailing the horse, and I guessed from the set of his shoulders that he had been fooled high, wide and handsome and wished he had back that shoat and that watch and knife. I came close to feeling sorry for him.

I fought myself all the way home, trying not to feel glad that Jimroe had been tricked, but I couldn't forget the sight of Tree being so friendly with him when Jimroe came out of the Boneyard with his mare. I had never been so mixed up about Jimroe.

Tree stopped and put his liquor into the old medicine bottles when we were nearing home. "I know I'll be needing my tonic, the rest of the hot weather, and I expect this Miracle Prescription to do me a world of good." He took a drink and pulled up a sassafras root at the roadside and chewed on that, to hide his whiskey breath from Mama.

Tree told Jimroe that he ought to ride his mare to the house, and Jimroe jumped on her and made her trot. Our family stared from the porch like Jimroe and the mare had fallen out of the sky, and the first one who found her voice was Mama.

"What's her name, Jimroe?"

"Lydia Pinkham."

"Lydia Pinkham, my foot," Papa said.

It was such a fool name for a horse that it woke them up, and they crowded around to pinch and poke the mare, and asked Jimroe to tell everything that had been said in the trade, and none of them found out that the mare was blind until Jimroe took her to the barn lot and Tree told them. That made them solemn until Tree said it was only the start of Jimroe's fortune and that they shouldn't worry.

The family treated Jimroe like he was different at supper and passed him things to eat like he was one of the grown folks. Cousin Tree went home on Lize and we waved him off, and Mama and Papa sat in the swing.

"I guess I know my Scriptures as well as the next one," Papa said, "but I'll be swiggered if I remember a miracle to beat the way Jimroe turned that shoat into a mare, even if she is blind."

Mama appeared not to hear him. She stared after Tree. "Hence, you don't reckon I hurt Trevilian's feelings, talking like that this morning?"

Papa put an arm around her. "Little Bit, you couldn't hurt his feelings with a loaded shotgun. He loves you the same as all the rest of us do, maybe worse."

"Well, I don't know, Hence. The poor thing's been sipping some old medicine all evening. There, look—he's taking a dose right now."

Papa looked like he wanted to laugh. "Whatever it is, it'll never cure the Tree Poindexter Disease."

We knew by heart how Tree had gone to a doctor and told his symptoms: "Doc, I eat hearty and sleep hearty—I just don't feel worth a damn when I work."

I was afraid Papa might tell the story again and say it was the catchingest disease in John M. Virden County and that the whole family was coming down with it, but he didn't.

Mama said she believed she would pray for Tree, and she got a little huffy when Papa said, "You can bear down all you like, but you've got about a snowball's chance in hell to change Tree Poindexter, and I don't care how heavy a hand the Lord puts into it."

When Mama left the porch Papa sighed and shook his head, looking down toward Tree's house. "Ah, Fax, be careful you don't grow up and get old. The world has a way of running out from under you." Something in his voice reminded me of Tree.

6

The Way Grandpa Was

Then, before we knew it, we woke up one morning and it was the third of July and we had to start for the Picnic. It began like any other summer day. The first sound was the birds—purple martins twittering in and out of their nesting gourds. They hung in gourds on tall poles outside our windows and never missed getting out before daylight to scout for bugs. They beat even our early roosters.

Papa's feet hit the floor at four-thirty and everybody knew it was time to get up. Upstairs in our big bed we didn't stir. A door slammed below and somebody went toward the barn. The well windlass squealed and a bucket banged.

Things rattled in the kitchen, and we smelled woodsmoke from the chimney and then coffee beans parching in the oven. Cornelia stuck her head in the stairwell and called.

She yelled the same thing she did every morning of her life, just like it was the first time, "You gonna lay up in the bed till the sun blisters you? . . . All right, then—starve!"

We had fourteen children in the family, in both sets, but because the old ones were always marrying and moving to town, we had only eight or nine about most of the time. Except for a few girls, most of us slept in one bed. We slept crosswise in the biggest white iron bed in the world, an old one rigged with rope springs. Our summer mattress was a straw tick, two feet thick when it was fresh-made, so that it smelled fine and you could hear crickets deep inside. By winter we had slept holes in it and beaten it to a wafer and were just about on the ropes. We slipped and slid on the straw tick and it crackled every time one of us took a breath. When it was just about worn out, in winter, we got our feather tick again.

Every night when it was especially cold or hot we raced for the bed to get a warm spot in the middle or a cool one on the edge, so we had fights enough. You never knew there were so many cold feet and bony knees and gimlet elbows until you crawled in with those smelly little boys. We had chamber pots under the bed. One thing we learned about sleeping in that bed: when the fellow in the middle yelled to let him out at night, you'd sure better clear out of his way.

On this morning I got up early and ate with the first shift at breakfast, and squatted on the porch to watch Papa shave. He started in the first light of the sun when it struck through the orchard on the river side of the house and laid twiggy shadows on his red face.

When he shaved in warm weather, Papa wore nothing but a pair of funny drawers that Mama had made for him from feed bags, puckered up around his waist like a tobacco sack so that lather could run into his chest hair without making such a mess. A black mat of hair grew right up to his neck, and his legs were furry except the back of his calves where overalls had worn away his hair. He was mighty bowlegged. Mama liked to tease him about that.

"If you ain't a picture," she said. "I vow, Beau, you couldn't stop a pig in a ditch."

"I do my best," Papa said. "I don't get so many chances."

"Well, it looks like to me you don't half try to stand up straight."

"We've all got some little defects of character. I can't help it if mine settled in my legs. God knows they ain't pleasure-bent, anyway."

Mama hissed like she was scandalized. "Henderson Starling!" She ducked away from the kitchen window.

Papa fixed his nose. He poured a spoonful of salt into one hand, doused it with water to make a paste and breathed it up each side of his nose. He went "Snork! Snork!" and spat over the porch. "Just the thing for catarrh of the head," he said. He'd never had catarrh or much of a cold either, but he kept the inside of his head cured like smokehouse bacon. I tried his salt once and almost popped my head.

Papa got his Wade & Butcher razor off the shelf and slapped it a few times on the horsehide strop on the wall, and to finish honing worked the edge back and forth on the heel of his hand, where the steel made as much noise as it had on the strop. He yanked a hair from his head and sliced it in two and then shaved.

He used a cake of Peel's Soap in a chipped cup and slopped lather over his face. He mumbled to Mama through the window while he shaved. "Whatever 'came of the new schoolteacher?"

"Why, she'll come over in the fall, I guess." Mama said she couldn't come for summer, when we had a break in farm work for a few weeks.

Papa splashed and blew spray. "Great God in a haw bush. Not another marm? I thought you had all the skirts you

could stand in school last year, with Jimroe and his goings-
on."

Jimroe had squatted beside me and pretended that he
wasn't the one Papa was talking about. The year before,
Jimroe had half accidentally popped our schoolteacher on
the head with a bat in a baseball argument, and she'd gone
away.

"Suppose this'n won't take old Jamesroe back," Frank
said.

"It'd be nothing lost," Papa said. "What he needs to know
they'll sure not teach in the schoolhouse. If tobacco goes
bad, he'll have to save us with his horse swapping."

Mama gave Papa a look, and he hushed and went on cleaning up. After a little he stopped and surprised us all. He was
serious. "I know one thing. We've got to stick together this
year. There's never been a dime's mortgage on this place,
and I hope to die before I see one. We can't stand another
crop of debt tobacco— Boys, you've got to help me pull
through. Looks good now, but then . . ."

"You know Biscoe Allen wouldn't hurt us," Mama said.
"And him a deacon."

"Hell. He's like too many other churchfolks. Honest as
the Holy Ghost on a Sunday morning, but when it comes
to a deal he wouldn't give you the time of day."

He threw his shaving water in the yard in a flat sudsy
sheet that made chickens flap and run, and stared over at the
tobacco patch. "A hell of a come-off," Papa said, "when a
man has to worry over a crop that looks as rich as all that."

I thought to myself that he had more to worry over than
he knew, with Pem nursing a grudge. I wished that I'd told
Papa at first, but now I couldn't, with him so wrought up
over things. I had a curious feeling that I'd swallowed something hard and that it was growing in my gullet.

All of us except Frank and Creed went to Grandpa's. Somebody had to care for the stock, and they said they'd been to an even hundred Picnics and that was enough to do them. We loaded the wagon with tools to help clean the cemetery, two coops of Dominecker chickens for the Picnic, and a couple of dozen of Papa's watermelons packed in straw. The boys piled in the wagon and the girls rode with Mama in our hack, a two-seater Hawkeye with a black oil-cloth folding top. Jimroe rode Lydia behind the wagon and we all went off to Grandpa's.

John M. Virden County was a perfect square except on top, where the Redwine River separated us from Virginia. There wasn't a foot of railroad track in the county, and roads were scarce. From the north the only way into Corona Township was to cross the river at Osmond, Virginia, on Cousin Tree's ferry. We lived on that road, the second place back from the river, where the canebrakes and tag-alder thickets gave way to hardwoods, and little hills shouldered up toward the mountain. It was country that strangers didn't give a second look, but we loved it. Tree's saying about it was: "I know the Redwine Valley was created on Wednesday afternoon, after the Lord had made his mistakes and learned how on all the other places—but before he got tired and careless, and took to making places like Texas."

We left our house, going west, jolted down a clay hill and began to climb Wildkitten. It was mean and rocky threading the mountain road, and scary with the river away beneath us.

"If we happened to fall off right here," Papa said, "a body would have time to read the Richmond Sunday newspaper, cover to cover, truss ads and all, before he hit bottom."

We stopped on top of the mountain and Papa pointed up and down the river with a faraway look on his face. "There was a time when your grandpa owned every bit of it on this side the Redwine, almost as far as you can see.

"Pap never wanted to go to the Civil War. He was exempted because he had more than twenty slaves, but he said that a man couldn't stand to be kicked around, even if he didn't believe in Secession. So he called his slaves to the house and showed 'em their manumission papers and told 'em they were as free as any white men, and made a little speech. He said, 'I don't favor this war, but I'm bound to go to it. If you'll stay here and take care of my folks, and I live to come back, we'll divide this place, share and share alike. Now, I could run you to Richmond and sell you all for a thousand dollars a head. But you're part of this family. I never sold a person nor bought one, and I never will. Just stay while I'm gone, is all I ask of you.'

"And when old Pap walked back from Appomattox he found the house and barns burnt by the Yankees, and Grandma and all us younguns living in the cellar—but those slaves still here. And so he divided it the way it is now, and left himself just a hundred and twenty acres, and we've been poor ever since."

We looked at the cabins up and down the river, where the only Negro families in our township still lived, most of them bearing the name of Starling.

"And don't you take old man Grantham Starling for having been a fool all his life," Papa said, "just because he's failing in the mind now. He was a man when it hurt to be one." He slapped the reins and we started down the far side of the mountain. Nobody spoke until the ride was over.

Grandpa lived on the far side of Wildkitten in a house for all the world like ours: two tall lean stories with peeling white clapboards and fading green trim—the kind of house that made people say of our folks, "Too poor to paint and too proud to whitewash." It had the same lightning rods on the roof with bright-blue insulating balls shining in the sun, and stone chimneys daubed with mud. The house perched off the ground on stone pillars, like a woman holding up her skirts, and underneath, the chocolate-colored dust was deep and cool, and boys and chickens and dogs and pigs hid there from the heat. The yard was swept so clean with twig brooms that there wasn't a blade of grass.

Grandpa's yard was full of buggies and wagons because most of my aunts and uncles and cousins had come. The women chased Grandma from her kitchen and the place looked like they might have been cooking for the U.S. Army. They fried chickens till the yard was blue with smoke, and late in the night were still fixing vegetables and pies and nobody knew what all.

I hunted up Grandpa. He was on the back porch with my boy cousins about him, telling his yarns. His eyes were as blue as china marbles, and a long red scar ran from one ear into his lemon-colored beard. Papa said that was a bayonet scar and that soldiers never got cut like that unless they were up front, where they played mean and dirty. Grandpa pointed a finger at me. "Ho, Buddy. Come see Grandpa."

Grandpa was in his eighties and couldn't hear thunder unless it was something special he wanted to hear. He didn't know the names of half his grandchildren, and to be on the safe side called all the girls Sissy and all the boys Buddy.

When he was younger nobody could get him to open his mouth about the Civil War, but since he had grown childish there was no way to shut it. It was hard for him to find people to listen now. When he could think of no other way to worry the subject around to his battles, he rapped the floor with his hawthorn walking stick and held his hand to an ear and broke in on the conversation. "What in hell's that? Cannon fire? Sounds like the third day at Gettysburg. Did I ever tell you how I fought and died in that war?" And he would go on and tell who shot who.

Sometimes on a foggy morning he would scrooch up his shoulders and blow through his mustaches. "By God, boys, my wounds hurt me today." Then he would tell about war times and might start singing dirty songs he had learned in the Army.

I sat near the old man to see if he was telling things the same way he usually did. That day was his big chance and he told some of his best ones. One of the boys had asked him a question. Grandpa took a thoughtful spit at a rooster out in the yard.

"No, Buddy, I couldn't say General Forrest was a *good* man, not God-fearing. But by God, he was a diddler and a fighter and a wild horse rider. I can hear him to this minute hollering the way he did in battle, 'Shoot low, boys! Keep on acrawlin' and hold your fire, then shoot low. Shoot for the belly. Make 'em die hard!'

"But one day we got in a fight in middle Tennessee with Forrest, and the Yanks shot me through the body, down about here." He punched himself in the groin. "I laid there in the rain all night long, scared that I was bleeding to death, but I knew the Ginral would not go and forget me, because he cared for his own. And sure enough, boys, a wagon came for me at sunup and a doctor pulled his silk handkerchief clean through me, and my wound healed in jigtime. I was like a pine knot in those days, and you had to be to ride somewhere with Bed Forrest."

One of my cousins broke in, "Grandpa, how come you to shoot them Yankee spies at sunrise?"

"Why, to keep from giving the sons of bitches their breakfast, that's why!" He looked at the boy like he must have been wrong in the head. The old man told a new story:

"Didn't you boys know Ginral Lee hisownself come up to me at the battle of Sharpsburg in Maryland, where Yank bodies were piled hip-deep around me? He rode up on that dapple-gray horse of his and said, 'Hold on there, Sergeant Starling, they ain't nothing but Yankees. After all's said and done they're human beings. Think of the widders and orphans you've made this day. Stop it, I say. You've spilled blood enough.' "

He made the eyes of the little boys pop and we all loved him, but something made us guess he was spoofing and that it was mostly for our entertainment. The only thing that stopped Grandpa that day was Judge Bucktarrel, who came up about that time.

He was Judge Furnifold M. Bucktarrel, an old man who wasn't much over middle-size but walked like he might have stood nine feet tall. His hair was as white as a boll of cotton and so thick that he could hardly keep his black sugarloaf hat on his head. He wore a shoebrush mustache and had hair long over his collar. His year-round uniform was a black suit with a long-tailed coat, congress gaiters, a pleated shirt and celluloid collar with a white string tie, and a ribbon in his lapel for the Grand Army of the Republic. He was the only live Republican most of us had seen, and had fought for the North in the Civil War.

He came up and yelled to Grandpa, talking way down in his dewlaps like he was playing on a brass horn, "Brother Grant, you must've fought in some war all by yourself. Damned if I ever heard of such things as you tell."

Grandpa squinched at him and made the walking stick hiss in the air over his head. "Damn your bluebelly time, Furn Bucktarrel, it's a wonder you lived through it. I was just telling these boys about the time I chased a Yank lieutenant in a hollow log and shot the no-good devil from both ends, just to make sure. A fellow just about the size of you, Furn. He had the prettiest pair of boots ever I saw, soft as glove leather. I wore them boots the whole winter of sixty-three."

Judge Bucktarrel squeezed in beside Grandpa. "I expect that if the War had gone on another week or two, you'd have won it single-handed, Grant. Now, when I was at Fredericksburg . . ."

"What! You wasn't at no Fredericksburg, sir! We killed off every damn Yank present on the field that day. If we ever have another war I'll kill you yet. Right now I'm a good mind to mash your mouth flatter than a flitter, just for getting away and living."

They jawed like nobody else was in hearing, until you'd

have thought they'd splashed through gore to their horses' bits at Fredericksburg. The little boys stared, but I knew the old men hadn't been near that battle, because Papa had told us all about it. We stayed on the porch to listen, slapping flies off our legs while they talked on.

Judge Bucktarrel had brought our Aunt Ly Sue Poindexter to the Picnic. He had been courting her night and day for more than twenty years and she kept putting him off, yet wouldn't have another man. She was a good-natured old soul with a face like the map of West Virginia, as Papa said, but she wasn't as poor as Job's Turkey, like the rest of us. One of Judge Bucktarrel's sayings about Aunt Ly Sue was: "Money! Now that's what I admire in a woman." He was some judge.

John M. Virden County was the newest one in North Carolina and had been cut from the counties around it, and our people had to make a county seat and a courthouse from scratch. Even worse, they were caught without a lawyer to their name and couldn't make a proper judge. They had sent into Monell County, the next one west, and got Judge Bucktarrel, who was then a half-starved lawyer strayed in from Ohio. He owed everybody in his county and was glad to come and be our judge for a hundred dollars a month. He came with nothing but a saddlebag of old law books, a few spare clothes and two bottles of mountain liquor.

By now nobody stopped to think that Judge Bucktarrel was different from the rest of us, and he was re-elected every time. Grandpa loved the Judge like a brother.

Judge Bucktarrel ragged Grandpa that day until he cut off his war tales. Then Papa came out and joked about Grandpa's Confederate lies, but he was really proud. "He'd burn the last shirt off his back to make a light to cuss Yankees by," Papa said.

Grandma had the Judge ask the blessing at supper. The kids had to wait on the porch while the grown folks ate first in the kitchen, but when the Judge blessed, we were made to crowd around the door and drop our heads and squeeze shut our eyes and listen. The Judge was as bad as a preacher.

He had cornered all the voters and big talkers of the Starling tribe where they couldn't get away, and he carried on about how the Lord had given our county good government and a passable court, and he even said the North Carolina State Toast, that we had to recite so often in school:

"Here's to the land of the longleaf pine,
The summer land where the sun doth shine.
Where the weak grow strong and the strong grow great—
Here's to Down Home, the Old North State!"

The fried chicken got cold and the beat potatoes went gray, and we stood it as best we could. The Judge blessed for about half an hour and then they started eating. We waited on the porch while the first shift ate. Grandma apologized for the biscuits, saying they were burnt.

Jimroe whispered, "Now ain't that too bad?" And like a fool I answered aloud before I thought of what Jimroe was up to, "Heck, I wish I had even one of them old burnt ones."

Papa scampered out of the kitchen and had hold of me before his knife and fork quit clattering on the plate. He slapped me so hard that my head rang like a church bell.

"I'll learn you to act like you're starving to death," he said. When he went back in the kitchen the Judge mumbled at Papa about dinging so hard at his younguns, but Papa wouldn't back down. He said I had to learn something some time—but I knew what he meant was that I had to do right in front of company, no matter what, and that I would have got by with it any other time.

We went to bed before dark. Children slept on pallets all over the floors, even in the halls. I slept with Grandpa, because they said I was the least likely to keep him awake. He fell to snoring as soon as his head touched the bolster and I

couldn't have roused him with a stick. We slept in the parlor, that Grandma kept shut against drafts, and there was a
close smell in there. Grandpa woke up about three o'clock in
the morning and fumbled until he struck a match and lit a
lamp. It was spooky in the parlor but there was plenty to
see.

A white-painted spinning wheel was threaded through the
spokes with a red ribbon. A pillow on the wicker sofa had a
picture of a girl beside a waterfall and said something about
the Columbian Exposition, St. Louis, Mo. On the walls were
tintypes of old people in our family, and pictures of "The
Last Supper," "The Crucifixion" and "The Resurrection"
that had come from the Cloverine Salve Company and were
under glass in gold frames, and not tacked up like the
Poindexters had theirs.

Best of all was a picture of Papa and my real mama, taken
on their honeymoon when they were sixteen years old and
had run away from home to get married. They looked like
they had been caught stealing something.

Grandpa had a new pair of mail-order shoes, the same
hook-and-eye kind he had always worn. He cussed about
them. "Damn Yankee swindlers. It used to be they gave a
man a year's guarantee, and now they've downed it to six
months. Something crooked going on. Look how thin these
things are—why, it could thunder in Georgia, and I mean
South Georgia, and my feet'd get wet."

He was a goose about his hat, a high-crowned black felt
with a wide brim that hung on a bedpost over his head for
the night. It was the first thing he put on when he got up. I
hadn't seen him mother-naked before, and he was a sight,
with skin loose where muscle had melted away and a spiky
little bottom showing bones at the hips. His legs were
stringy but he was still wide at the shoulders, and on his

back was a blue lump the size of a sand plum that waggled when he moved his arms: a Yankee minnie ball that he wouldn't let a doctor cut out. Something about him made my eyes fill. He looked helpless, like a picked chicken, with only his hat on, but he came back strong when he put on his clothes. He wore long winter underwear the year round because, he said, "what'll turn the cold will turn the heat."

After his underwear he put on rough gray socks with white toes and tops, which he usually wore until they could stand alone. He dusted his shoes and socks with powdered alum, and put on a fresh hickory shirt with no collar and fastened the band with a gold collar button riding under his Adam's apple. The shirt was so loose at the neck that he could have reached inside to scratch himself. He put on a pair of dark wool britches, and scuttled into the kitchen and snorted around until the tired women were up and about breakfast.

We didn't eat as much as usual for breakfast, since there were so many of us and we had a good ways to go, but we couldn't get by on nothing. We were used to hearty eating. Everything you pick up on a farm is heavy and makes big eaters of everybody. We had biscuits and slabs of ham and brown-eye gravy—Mama's special kind of red-eye gravy made with a little slosh of coffee in the hot ham skillet—and small hominy and plenty of honey and butter and preserves. The big folks had half a setting of eggs apiece and drank gallons of coffee.

Grandpa had his pie. He wouldn't sit down to breakfast unless he could see two kinds of pie on the table. Today he had apple and sliced sweet potato. He had almost got down in his chair when he remembered his nip of morning whiskey. He leaned into the pie safe and hid behind the pierced tin door and came out clearing his throat. "Ah, Lord. Got to have a little something to start the blood of a morning."

Grandpa wouldn't speak a word so long as he was eating.

He was so stubborn that he never asked for anything to be passed to him, but would just give Grandma a look and expect her to know his mind. She always knew what he wanted and passed it without a word. Grandpa was still at the table when the last shift finished breakfast, ready to talk with the children.

He peered at a plate of biscuits that had been left over and glared around like somebody had done him a foul deed, then sighed and gave one of his old sayings: "All right, feed 'em to the hogs and we'll get 'em back with gravy in the fall."

Jimroe was there and was the only one who laughed, just to please Grandpa. The old man clucked at him and said, "You're a right bright boy. I bet your hand never did fit a hoe handle. I heard you were a great hand to swap a horse. That's the kind of spunk I like—you're worth a dozen of these good old mealy-mouthed Starlings. I'll remember you in my will with my horse and buggy."

He and Jimroe yarned about trading horses until the women had cleaned up and it was time to go to the Picnic. "By God, you've got the sleight to make a horse trader," the old man said. "That's the ticket. Just like your great-grandaddy Sylvester. He just about cleaned out this country with his trading, boy. I know it's in your blood."

I had never seen Jimroe so roiled up.

Grandma's name was Columbia and we called her Aunt Lumbie. She was a lot younger than Grandpa, and was gentle with him. She swung him up from his chair when they were ready to go. "Come on, Grant, honey. They can't start a thing till you get there."

Grandpa pretended to scowl at her. "I swear and be-hold, Lumbie. You want 'em to think I'm a cripple? Any man that's lived through what I've seen ain't to be led about by women."

Grandpa held to his hawthorn stick and did a buck and wing around it in a circle, tapping and singing an old song:

"Chicken in the bread tray,
Pecking out the dough.
Granny, will your dog bite?
No, chile, no!"

Grandpa was puffing and Aunt Lumbie made him stop. "Do you want to pop a gusset and ruin the Picnic for every-body?"

She smoothed his hair with her hand and grinned at us. "This old boy is so timid of the traffic in the big road—even the wagons and buggies—that he hates to leave home. And the automobiles! Why, I've been working on him for a week, getting him used to 'em. I tied him to a persimmon bush and rolled a wheelbarrow round and round him just so he'd get accustomed to all the hurrah."

Grandpa was so put out when we laughed that he went into the pie safe and took another drink.

7

Papa Calls Upon the Lord

Grandpa was so nervous about automobiles that he made me ride backward in the buggy and peep out the tiny square of glass to watch for them. He called them Steamers.

"All right, Buddy. If you see one of the damn things, just job me."

So I sat on a pile of folded towsacks and watched out the back as we rattled along. His sensible little red mare was named Ladylove, and she had seen automobiles for several years; she wouldn't have shied if one had run over her but Grandpa thought she was as scared as he was, and whenever we met a Steamer he would turn her out of the road and stop, no matter where.

When a Ford tore up behind us I bumped the old man with my elbow and yelled "Steamer!" and he pulled the mare to one side into somebody's fine grain field. Ladylove stood there, patient and knowing, and when the dust died down he turned her back into the road.

We went on toward the church.

It was eight miles to White Oak Limb Meeting House, in the direction of Randolph, the county seat. The road was better than most and full of people going to the Picnic. The township was turning out in spring wagons and carts and buggies and a few automobiles. There was one chain-drive Franklin, brand-new, and four or five brass-head Fords went by.

I tried to get Grandpa talking about the war again, but he wouldn't say much. "Ah, Buddy, dammitall, I've lied so much about the War that I've clean forgot what really happened."

He finally cleared his throat and rumbled a little and said, "I can tell you one thing I ain't lied about—when I was in that Army, way back yonder, they put some kind of stuff in our eats to keep us from hankering so after women. Saltpeter, I think it was. Oh, Lordy. That's been fifty years ago and more. Long time. You know, Buddy—I think that damn stuff is beginning to take effect on me." He cackled.

After a while he said, "Ah, me. Youth. By God, if I had teeth I'd run out and bite me a damn woman this evening."

We were really in the crowd by now. It was a Corona Township Picnic and all the Corona people came. From the lower end of the county, along Lost Boy Swamp, were the Indians who called themselves purebloods—the Hockaways. They were really mixes of white, Indian and Negro blood, but were more Indian than the Redshanks were. They had a name for violence. There was a tale that they had come down from a wrecked colony of Englishmen on the North

Carolina coast and had lived for a long time in our county
before the first white men came. Their young women were
sometimes pretty, with blue eyes, and complexions running
from pale cream to the shade of an old saddle.

The Indians were there, anyway—the Gowers and Kinnamons and Oxendines and Locklears and Yubas—and then
I spotted the Sixkillers. Jess's head was sticking up over the
crowd. Pembroke was with him, and I was so startled that I
jobbed Grandpa in the side without thinking, and came close
to yelling "Steamer" again.

The old man still had women on his mind. He looked over
the crowd and said, "Where, Buddy? I don't see no prime
women. I've seen better at a dog fight." The old man pulled
Ladylove aside and stopped.

The crowd filled the churchyard. White Oak Limb was a
homemade white church, used as straight Baptist one Sunday, Methodist the next, then Presbyterian and then Foot-
washing Baptist, all in turn. They used the same preacher,
Charlie Raper Billings, and pretty much the same people
were in every congregation, so that one church was all we
needed.

Since it was the Fourth, they cut short the preaching and
the women worked over the picnic tables in the grove.
Preacher Billings could preach a blister on you, and he
yelled about all of us being bound for hellfire. There was no
place to hide from him. He preached the selfsame old hard-
shell Gospel sermon as ever: "Ah, brethren. What's to be
will be—whether it ever happens or not. The Lord God's
done made up his mind. He's got his finger on the last one of
you, and never mind trying to sneak away."

Late in the morning Cousin Tree got on the church steps
and yelled, "Come on, boys. Fall in on the burying ground."

They marched to the cemetery lot with spades and shovels
and grubbing hoes and bush hooks. The brush hadn't been
cleaned for a year, and briars and saplings were moving in.
That was something our people did every Fourth of July. In

the old days it happened on Decoration Day, mostly for old soldiers buried there, but later it had spread to the whole cemetery, and since everybody turned out on the Fourth for our Picnic, the affair was moved into July. And so everything was combined, and horse trading had got to be a big thing on that day.

The men loafed in the cemetery, telling dirty stories and keeping an eye on the women down at the tables. A few sneaked drinks of liquor, and as it got hotter they swung their hooks and sickles faster. The Indians felt the liquor before anybody else.

Jess Sixkiller was the loudest. Jess got away with being an awful bully when he drank, because of the look of him. He was almost seven feet when he straightened from his slouch, and was all man and not so rounded in the body as most of our Indians. He was as thin in the waist as a girl, but across the shoulders measured at least an ax handle. Cousin Tree was Jess's friend, and said that Jess was as good as they come when he was sober but something else when he'd been patting the jug. There was a neighborhood joke about Jess: "He can't remember his own strength when he sobers up—and thank God for that."

Jess had been in the state pen twice, but for nothing we thought was serious. He had shot up Biscoe Allen's store one Saturday night for the hell of it, and pulled a year and a day. Then he lost patience with A.D. Strong's cows that were always ruining the Sixkiller sweet-corn patch. Jess doused a couple of them with kerosene and set them afire and got another year's time for that, and some people began to think of him as a hard man.

Jess Sixkiller worked beside Tree and Papa and some of my brothers in the grove. Pembroke was close by too, but I shied away from him. It gave me the willies to look at him, knowing how he felt toward us. I could stand Jess, but was afraid that Papa would read my thoughts about Pembroke.

Jess talked and the men mounded graves and reset leaning

stones and cut back brush. Our cemetery was a knuckle of high ground, hard clay between flint rocks that had been hacked out inch by inch to make graves. The men talked about the comfort of having a good dry grave to put their people in, and paid close attention to the work, but they listened to Jess, too.

Jess stopped and hung on his shovel handle and looked down in the grove, where the horses and mules were tied. He was eying that blind mare of Jimroe's, and he went tense, like he wanted that mare. Jimroe was down with the others who were trying to trade. Most of the animals were old plugs and swaybacks, and Jimroe's blind Lydia stood out from the bunch. Jess had her spotted. I knew he was turning it over in his mind, trying to remember every horse he had seen around there, and wondering where that mare had come from. Jess Sixkiller was known as a sharp horse trader.

The tools scraped and snicked and threw sparks off the rocks while Jess told about his time in the pen until he began to drag with his yarns. He finally stopped short in the middle of one and went down to see Lydia Pinkham. With liquor in him, Jess didn't act like much of a horse trader. He didn't seem to care if Jimroe noticed that he was in a hurry. He walked once around Lydia with a quick look in her mouth, showing off for the men who had followed him, grinning, to see what would happen.

All of them saw at a glance that the mare wasn't rump-sprung or spavined, and when they got close to her, saw that she had no heaves or anything like that. She looked like something, with her mane combed out and her hide shining in the sun, and Jimroe was so slick at whipping her around to keep her head away from the crowd that it was always the best part of her that Jess Sixkiller saw. Jimroe was trying to stay clear of Jess because he was afraid of him while he was drinking; he would rather sell the horse to anybody in the grove than to fool with Jess.

Jess was impatient. "I want that mare, hi God."

Jimroe circled her again, showing her springy gait. "You don't want her atall," he said. "They say she's hard to work, Jess."

"I won't born yesterday. I know a horse when I see one."

"Don't crowd me, now."

"How'll you trade, boy?"

"Naw, I won't do it, Jess. She's ornery, and you'd just come back on me and kick about her."

"I never saw one I couldn't handle," Jess said. He hung around trying to decide what kind of game Jimroe was playing, and when Jimroe kept talking about how mean the mare was, Jess and Pembroke Sixkiller went off in the crowd.

Jimroe sweated at it, trying to get somebody else to buy Lydia, but hadn't had a nibble when Jess came back. He had been drinking more and talked louder now. Pembroke was leading a mule colt, a big-boned young one that everybody recognized from the Sixkillers' good stock.

"Here you go," Jess said. "Here's my bait. I've done made up my mind to have that mare, I don't give a damn how high she goes."

Jimroe let out a deep breath. "All right, then. I've told you time and again she's not going to suit you, but if you're bound to trade, I'll talk."

Jess yelped a little when Jimroe said he wanted five dollars to boot, but Jimroe said, "My great-grandaddy told me on his death's bed, the last thing he said to me, 'Boy, don't never trade for a thing unless you get a little to boot.' I know you'd not want me to go back on his dying words."

Men in the crowd laughed to hear a youngster talk that way to a grown man, and Pembroke tried to pull Jess away. But Jess reached for his pocketbook like he wasn't going to let the crowd think he was a piker, and gave Jimroe five dollars and the mule. He went off with Lydia.

Everybody swarmed for the picnic tables. The women stood on one side of the tables, each one in front of the stuff she had brought. They were supposed to have just enough for their own households, but everyone had brought enough to feed three families, and they hung around to overhear what people said about their prize dishes. Some women whispered to their kids as they passed down the tables, "Be sure you get some of that pie. She's one woman who keeps a clean kitchen." They made sure their whispers could be heard.

A little mountain range of yellowleg fried chicken ran down the tables, with peaks of roast turkey, goose and guinea, meat loaf, roast beef, mutton legs and veal and ham —even fresh ham, which was an extravagance in summer. There was so much that it vexed you to run up and down the tables and take a snippet of everything.

We had corn relish and chow-chow and artichokes and pickled red, yellow and green peppers, sweet and dill cucumber pickle and brandied peaches, pears, crab apples and cherries, pickled tomatoes; kraut and lye hominy and crocks of baked beans and bowls of string beans, and corn cooked with side meat or with small potatoes. There were tubfuls of corn off the cob, and whippoorwill peas, crowder peas and black-eyes. Deviled eggs were piled up like snowballs.

The Indians had bean bread, and there were fresh loaves of white and whole wheat, rolls, corn bread and biscuits. Little children had fly swishes made of newspaper strips on sticks, and they pretty much congregated where the pies were. There was almost every kind of pie in the world: molasses, grape, potato, egg custard and buttermilk custard, brown sugar, pecan, prune, elderberry—besides the usual ones. They had so many cakes that nobody could have tasted them all.

Tootsy Kinnamon had brought a Lady Baltimore cake as big as the bottom of a washtub, with nuts and raisins stuck in pink icing.

Tootsy was the only Bad Woman we ever heard about in our township. She lived spang on the line between North Carolina and Virginia, where she drove law officers crazy,

shuffling back and forth through her house to move moonshine out of their reach, into another state. Some white men
went there to spend nights with Toots and her two biggest
girls, and some said even with the little ones, Dumpling and
Muscadine. They were all bright-colored mulattoes erected
like women ought to be, with hair as black as a crow's wing
and the whitest teeth you ever saw. They had long thick
lashes that made their eyes look like they had been put in
the faces with a sooty finger. They smiled at everybody and
you'd think they had never seen a stranger.

It was a little surprising to see them at the Picnic.

Toots Kinnamon didn't look a day older than her big
girls, except that she was about twice as big around. Mama
said Toots was just putting on airs with that cake, and that it
was likely dirty, and as much out of place at the Picnic as the
Kinnamons were. But the men ate the cake in a wink, and
hardly ever took their eyes off those buckskin women.

While we were eating, Jess Sixkiller and Pembroke came
through the crowd, their faces as long as broom handles,
shouldering people aside until they came to our family. Pem
had slung his hunting rifle over Lydia's back in a scabbard
and the butt worked back and forth at every step. I couldn't
watch the Indians for looking at that gunstock. Jess walked
to Jimroe, but Pem butted in. "You n-n-never said she was
blind, wh-wh-white boy."

"He never asked me."

I was surprised at how loose Jimroe stood, chewing on a
chicken leg. He shook his head and grinned. Pem raised his
voice. "You going to let him do you thataway, J-j-jess?"

"Why didn't you tell me she was blind, boy?" Jess said.

"Hell, I thought it was a secret. Nobody told *me* when I
bought her."

The crowd laughed, and Jess looked up like he hadn't
noticed the people before. He laughed, too, but his voice
was mean. "Well, Big Britches, I'll take back my mule." He
held out Lydia Pinkham's halter.

Jimroe tried to stall him, and chattered about how pretty the mare moved and how awkward the mule was. Pem kept telling Jess not to let a white baby cheat him, and Jess saw men in the crowd grinning at him.

"I don't care a happy damn what you say. Gimme my mule."

"You're damn tootin', Jess. I never wanted you to have her atall—but you wouldn't have no for an answer."

Jess made a fist.

"I tell you what," Jimroe said. "If you'll swap back without making me break my great-grandaddy's rule, it's a trade."

Jess gave him a look. His eyes were red from drinking. "Whut you mean?"

"Just a little to boot, Jess. Give me a five-dollar bill and we're even. I've got to have some boot or it's no swap."

A dark vein swelled in Jess's neck and he looked sour. I thought Pembroke was going to hit Jimroe. But Tootsyroll Kinnamon pushed between them, laughing.

"Fair's fair," she said. "You crazy boys. A man won't go back on his word, Jess, trade or no trade."

"We ain't talking about men," Pembroke said. "We're talking about them damn Starlings."

There was a good deal of laughing and talking in the crowd and Jimroe kept yapping at Jess, and before we knew it Jess had forked over another five dollars and was stalking off with his mule. Pem walked beside him, yelling as if he wanted to eat him up alive. Jimroe put the bill in his pocket, like he did that every day and it meant nothing to him that he still had his blind horse and Jess had his mule but was out about a month's wages.

People went back to eating, and for half an hour it was quiet. Everybody hurried to eat their fill before the women folded the cloths over the leavings, to save something in case they wanted to nibble for supper before they went home.

Our family's food got away fast, but it was the tarts we

had to fight for. Mama always baked five dozen chess tarts for the Picnic, made from puff pastry so flaky that they never lasted long. It took her half a day to make the crust, mixing in the butter and putting the dough in the ice pit to cool between times. Goodloe and Fate Turlington, two old bachelors, came to the Picnic every year for no other reason than those tarts. They were about seventy and lived alone, and starved on their own cooking. They couldn't get enough chess tarts. Mama spread everything else on the table but kept the tarts in a basket, with one of the girls to guard them against the Turlington boys.

Goodloe reached in the basket and Cornelia jumped him. "No, sir, Goody. You've done had two. Let somebody else have some." He giggled and went away, but when Cornelia took a rest and Ivy guarded the basket, Goodloe sneaked up and got him another tart. That's about all those two had to eat that day.

Other people had brought some loaded melons this year, too, but old friends still flocked around Papa when he put his big babies on the table. The dark melons had spent the night in Grandpa's icehouse and were sweating with the chill.

Papa's knife was worn to a thin curved blade, and honed keen. The melons shivered and rumbled a little as he stroked the knife through, with a crack inching just ahead of the blade. The smell and the juicy red color when the halves split open made the people catch their breath and a long *"Ahhhhhhh"* went through the grove. The grown people went to work on them and Papa made sure that no young ones could sneak even a tiny piece, especially Jimroe. Papa ate three or four pieces and Mama kept looking him over as he got flushed in the face, laughing and talking with his friends and cramming in the loaded melon. The smell of whiskey was very faint.

Grandpa was one of the first to quit. He went with Aunt Lumbie to where Cousin Tree and his wife sat on a red carpet under a tree, and the old man sank down and yelled at Papa, "Ah, Hence—you and that primed melon are a cloud moving in the sight of the Lord. Noble fruit, noble fruit."

Papa scoffed. "Why, Pap, it's the selfsame old seed I always plant."

"Yes, but by God, Hence, it rests on the belly like the prayer of a maiden at twilight."

Tree's wife was a crinkly-haired little woman named Zelda who had a whispering voice when she was out among company. She looked as if she never got enough to eat. Her four-year-old, a boy they called Freck, was crawling over her.

The baby was husky but hadn't been weaned, and he kept reaching in his mama's loose dress to pull out her breast. Zelda elbowed him out of the way and tried to turn from Tree because it made him sore and embarrassed. Freck crawled to the other side and yanked out a skinny, leathery breast and pulled it under his mama's arm to hide from Tree. She elbowed him in the face again, so hard that Freck cried. Tree whispered, "Zel, you've got to wean that plagued youngun."

"I know I ought, Tree, and I'd like to the most in the world. I try and try. But he cusses me, and I'm afeard of him."

Tree popped the baby on the bottom and stuck a piece of chicken in his mouth when he started crying. Grandpa laughed and told Zelda she was a mighty handsome woman, from what he could see, and she blushed.

Judge Bucktarrel, who was our music man, strummed his tuning fork and got the hymns rolling, and Aunt Ly Sue broke out in the lead. She sang something like a peahen in trouble. Some of the younger ones played horseshoes and baseball. We could see the loaded melon taking hold on Papa. He bore down so hard with the hymn singers that he went red in the face and even on his ears, just squalling:

"Looooove lifted meeeeee—even mmmmeeeee.
When nothing else would help, loooove lif-ted meeee."

First I heard heavy running and then saw Jimroe dive under the table. Jess Sixkiller went over the table on one hand and caught Jimroe. They tumbled for a second or so, and then Jess held Jimroe like a rag doll, whipping him across the mouth with the back of his hand. Pembroke was yelling, to egg him on.

My brothers jostled around to the table and Papa got in the middle of them with his hands out like wings. "Wait! Wait!" People yelled at Jess and Papa yelled too, but the big Indian didn't stop for a minute. He huffed hard breaths when he hit Jimroe, and then took him by the shoulders with both hands and whammed him against a tree. Jimroe held still and blood came from his cut eyebrow and mouth. The men hemmed Jess away from him and Jess calmed down.

Cousin Tree walked close to Jess and looked him in the face without a word. Jess snapped at him, "I'll not have them Starlings treat me like I was a nothing. He used me like I had been gully dirt. Ten damn dollars!"

"You fool. You ain't got a soul to blame but yourself. You ain't got the brains it takes to grease a gimlet."

"I ain't at least no damn half-white man. I'd as soon be as black as the ace as to be a damn Poindexter."

"Keep talking. You're just begging to die young."

Pembroke was right behind Jess, but Tree didn't even trouble to look at him. Judge Bucktarrel stepped beside Tree. "Why, Jess," the Judge said. "I'm surprised at you."

It sobered Jess to see Judge Bucktarrel because he was the one who had sent him up for his time, and the Judge was a man who had never meant maybe in his life. Pem Sixkiller eased off backward and left Jess standing alone.

All the Negro Starlings watched the white men and the Indians with careful faces, as if they knew it was none of their business, but their hands were clenched.

While the Judge talked to him, Jess dropped his head like the starch had gone out of him, and when Tree asked him to help Jimroe to our wagon, Jess handled him as carefully as if he'd been a baby. Papa went to doctor on Jimroe. The rest of us watched Jess. He was a little sulkish at first but then began joking with Pem and some other Hockaways about his horse trade, and acted like he had forgotten all about Jimroe.

Papa came back to the table and warned my brothers not to bother that Indian. Mama was white around the lips the way she got when she tried hard to hold on to herself. She whispered, "Don't you dare do some fool thing, Hence Starling. Don't let me see bloodshed."

Papa patted her shoulder and helped himself to more of the loaded watermelon. He was just in time; the people were eating the last of it. Papa ate a big slice in a hurry.

The next thing we knew he was on the church steps, talking to a knot of men. Papa said he was going to preach a little sermon. He spouted a lot of Bible talk, and lit in on Jess Sixkiller for being a bully and a moral coward, and once pointed his finger at Jess and told him the Lord would have his way with him. Jess glowered and worked his hands together at his sides. People cheered, but not those near Jess. Others came from around the grove. Mama froze when she saw what was going on. I thought she might yank him down by the shirttail, but she didn't dare. Papa harangued the hide off Jess, then came down. Jess stopped him. The Indian was as red in the face as a turkey gobbler. "I heard you out, Hence. Now git ready. I'm agoing to whale you."

"I just gave you the Gospel, Jess, and I'm not half your size. How come you want to fight?"

"It's too late for begging, Hence. You're going to get it."

My brothers moved in close. "Step back," Papa said to them. "I'm twisting this monkey's tail." Then he turned to

Jess. "Well, then, Mister Sixkiller, could I have time to say a prayer before I take my thrashing?"

Jess began to look uncertain. "Yeah, pray if you want, but it's got to be short and sweet."

Papa took off his hat and some of the other men did, too, even Judge Bucktarrel. Papa bowed his head and began to call in a voice I had never heard him use before. There was something laughable about it, but nobody smiled.

"Oh, Lord God Almighty, Thou knowest that when I killed Shep Rouse and Cecil Houck I fought in self-defense. And when I cut out the black heart of Will Pyne and strewed the ground with his blood, that I did the deed with agony of soul—but Lord, Thou knowest that he drove me to it."

Men looked at each other and Jess gaped at Papa. Nobody looked like they even guessed Papa was lying about his killings.

"And Lord, lay Thy hand upon the sons of my loins and bid them stand aside and commit no lynching, for Thou knowest that Thee and Thy servant, Henderson Starling, will punish this wayward youth.

"Now, Lord, I call upon Thee to care for the soul of this poor wretch who has assailed me on Thy holy ground, hard by Thy tabernacle—and who is about to compel me to lay him in his coffin. Lord, care for the widow and orphan children and his poor old ma when he has gone. In the name of our Redeemer, Amen."

Jess was studying the ground. Somebody went tipping away in the sandy path behind. It was Pembroke, getting along from there.

Papa unfolded the long blade of his knife and whetted it on the sole of his shoe, and as he straightened, broke out singing in a high voice:

"Ye living man come view the ground
Where ye must shortly lie."

There was a scuffle in the crowd, and when Papa turned to find Jess, the big Indian was dusting along the road, trying to gain on Pembroke. He shouldered among the hitched horses and mules, hopped into his saddle and left. Mama looked at Papa and began crying, like relief was flowing in her. The crowd broke up in a laugh, and people beat Papa's back and said he was a good man and a brave one, but there was some nervousness because there was no telling what Jess would do next.

The big boys were so proud of Papa that I thought they would stay all night, taking it in. But I was scared and wanted to leave. I knew that Jess wouldn't rest until he got even with Papa, and with Jimroe too. I wanted to tell Tree about it.

The crowd parted a little and Tree spoke to Papa. "I was ready to help you out. My old rifle's there in the carpet. He was as good as covered all the time."

"I wish you'd let me know, now, Tree. Me and the Lord felt mighty lonesome before that big hooligan."

"Old Hence."

"How'd I know whose side you'd be on anyway, you red Indian?"

Tree laughed, showing the gaps in his teeth. "So long's you're loading melon, Hence, I reckon you know where I stand."

I went to Tree and tried to talk to him, and he took me around the neck so that his fingers almost met around it. He leaned over to listen, but I couldn't say anything because Papa and my brothers and the rest of them stayed so close, so I said that I would see him later, and he shook me a little and let me go.

I hitched up and went along with Grandpa before dark, and drove Ladylove while the old man snoozed. He stirred once.

"Boy, was you mixed up in all that flummoxing around

out there today? Did that damn Indian try to steal some of Hence's watermillions?"

"Steamer!" I yelled, and pulled Ladylove off into a cornfield until a car had passed.

"I don't hold with it," Grandpa said. "People have started mixing in too much with them Indians. I say no good will come of it. You watch."

By the time I was back in the road, Grandpa was asleep.

Afterward we called that day the Ten-Dollar Picnic.

8

Hard Times Coming

We got home from the Picnic after midnight and found Frank in a swivet about the tobacco. He said that it was already ripening mighty fast. He and Papa and Creed went into the patch with a lantern and looked at the color of the bottom leaves, and sent us in all directions to scare up some help for the next day, because they meant to pull the first batch of leaf. Papa was sizzling like it was our fault that the crop had sneaked up on him.

"If we don't start priming in the morning we'll never live long enough to catch up," he said. "I'll work that whole patch tomorrow if it harelips this nation."

The first priming would be especially hard work. It meant

harvesting the lowest leaves on the tobacco stalks before
they were scorched. You don't have to be long in a tobacco
field before you find out where the real heat is. The tops of
the plants are coolest, even in full sun, since the air can stir
up there—but down against the ground it's like an oven, and
hell on tobacco and farm hands, too.

They gave me the easy run, and I went to Cousin Tree's
cabin and made him promise to bring two of his boys. Nobody else found a soul because it was the same story at every
Corona farm—tobacco was beginning to turn all at once, so
that people had to pull their own leaf or perish next winter,
and had no time to help one another the way they always
had. When he heard about that, Papa went in the sitting
room, pried a hearthstone from the fireplace and took out his
money jug, a fruit jar half full of bills and change. He sat on
the sofa, and spread the bills and counted the change while
Mama stood behind him.

"Why, Beau, it's more than a hundred dollars."

Papa shook his head. "It's every last cash nickel I've got in
the world."

"It isn't like we were beggars, Henderson. Don't carry on
so."

"None of you ever listen to me," Papa said. "I'm telling
you, this little handful of chicken feed is all that stands between us and share cropping."

"Oh, Beau."

"Well, what else?"

"For a body who's always after us about worrying over
trifles, you're the biggest worrywart in the world."

"I'm damned if I want to be the first Starling who's ever
worked another man's land."

Mama laughed, but Papa still looked glum. He counted
nine dollars and divided it between Frank and Creed and
Damon like it was the last of his hoard. We had hired farm
labor before, but not this way. We usually swapped work
with our neighbors.

"See if you can get some of the Hockaways or Red-shanks," Papa said. "I'll pay half a dollar a day. Get anybody you can."

"Even-down Sixkillers?" Creed asked.

"Bring anybody who can find his ears with both hands, drunk or sober, red, white, black or green. It's root hog or die for us now."

He and the older boys worked all night to get ready and he rousted me and Jimroe before four o'clock, and made us cut branches of oak leaves to thatch a shed roof on a tobacco barn so that the women could have shade where they worked. I was so sleepy that I kept nodding off at breakfast and snoozed with my mouth full of food. There was no time for rest. At sunup we went to war with that tobacco.

The sun hung just over our heads by ten o'clock, and made me hop every time I set a bare foot on a rock in the red earth. The heat made us miserable, but some of the crowd sang now and then. Nobody had ever seen such fine to-bacco, and we were thinking about all the good things it would buy.

It was midmorning before our paid hands came to work, and they turned out to be only Sixkillers and Kinnamons. There was Jess with three of his younguns and his wife, acting like the scrap at the Picnic had never happened, and Tootsy Kinnamon with her girls. Papa shook hands. He got a little loud when he spoke to Jess. "I guess folks have got to get along, no matter how the wind blows when they're out larking."

"Hell's fire," Jess said. "I never thought hard of you, Hence."

Mama looked like she wasn't so sure.

My throat beat fast for a while, and I kept watching the path, afraid that Pembroke Sixkiller was coming, too. Nobody else came.

Jimroe and I worked with tobacco slides, and he followed the Kinnamon girls. He was sly, but Tree took heed and

teased him. The Kinnamon girls acted like they didn't mind
Jimroe watching their pretty legs when they stooped. They
wore tight dresses, with nothing on underneath.

People in the field pulled leaves, and the slides went down
the rows behind mules, to get the tobacco and take it to the
barn. The slides were homemade sleds on pine-plank runners, with high sides of fertilizer sacks tacked around.

All the women strung tobacco at the barn, and even
Grandpa, who had come home with us, tried to help. He
never quit talking to himself, rambling on about people who
had been dead for fifty years. The women paid him no attention. He turned to the pile of tobacco sticks in the shed
and rattled down an armload beside the stringing table,
where the women could reach them. They were straight-
grained pine sticks, an inch square and exactly four and a
half feet long. The women worked with them like they were
fighting fire.

The sticks fitted into notches in the stringing horses—the
horses were just two upright boards in a frame—and the
women held balls of twine to wrap tobacco leaves along
the sticks. They snatched three leaves at a time, wrapped the
stems a couple of turns, lashed the bundle to the stick, then
dropped back two or three inches on the stick and put a
fresh bundle on the opposite side. It took twenty-eight to
thirty of these hands of tobacco to fill a stick, and that meant
about ninety leaves in all. The women were so fast that you
could hardly see their fingers; they had strung tobacco all
their lives.

Close to noon, Wash Strawn drove up to the barn in his
buggy with the mail. He gave Papa some mail and some news.
"Hence, I hope you ain't wasting breath and money both, is
all I hope."

Papa looked to see if Wash was sober, and stopped his
work. "I reckon not. I can't say I ever put in better tobacco,
or more of it."

"That there's your trouble."

"I can stand a lot of that kind of trouble."

"Yeah. That's what they all thought, down the way." Wash gave Papa a knowing look.

"What who thought?"

"Why, every fool man that's raised tobacco this summer, clean down into South Carolina. The same story every place. Wherever the markets have been open, farmers have gone bust, just from all of them having such leaf as yours. The crop's too damn good."

Papa heard him out. He tried to respect the old man, since he and Grandpa had gone to war together. Wash kept on about how bad tobacco prices were going to be, and said we'd better not count on anything for the fall and winter. He was making Papa impatient. We knew that Wash did all kinds of things for Biscoe Allen, and that Biscoe kept the tobacco market of Corona in his back pocket. He was half owner of our warehouse and of the one in Randolph, too, and the tobacco companies trusted him to buy the crops for them as cheap as he could, every year.

"Well, they've spilt blood over it, whether it makes sense to you or not, Brother Starling." Wash was testy. "The big companies have got you by the short hair."

"We're mighty busy today, Mister Wash."

"You'd better take time to listen. Most every red-dirt grubber in this country has got just as big and fine a crop as you have, Hence."

"We ought to be thankful."

"So's the Tobacco Trust. There's so durn much tobacco to pick and choose from that prices will amount to nothing. They know they've got you, because you've got to get rid of it. It'll be hell."

"We've seen no trouble over it yet."

"You will. The mobs have burnt tobacco barns and warehouses down south. It's a fact. Farmers had done sold, for next to nothing, and then went haywire and burnt them up, just out of spite."

Papa said he expected we would be all right, and that he'd dealt with the Reynolds company in Winston ever since he could remember.

"I never got the dirty end of the stick yet," he said. "And I can't picture a mob in John Virden County."

He took his mail from Wash and said nothing more, but he looked worried until Wash was out of sight.

"What do you reckon?" Papa said.

"I expect somebody's trying to beat down prices for this fall," Tree said.

Grandpa piped up. "Don't you mind Wash Strawn. That peckerwood ain't got the truth in him. He's been jealous of Starlings ever since they elected me lieutenant in the Sixth North Carolina, back yonder after Chancellorsville."

"I expect Brother Biscoe Allen's up to something," Papa said.

"If he ain't, he's sick," Tree said.

"I tell you another thing," Grandpa said. "Wash Strawn never lost his leg in no damn charge. He was out robbing bodies of a night, and a burial party cracked down on him."

Papa and Tree talked no more, because Jess and the others were getting too interested, edging up close. We ate dinner under the shed and rested for an hour while Papa and Jess and Tree and a few others snored in the shade. Grandpa unrolled the Randolph newspaper that Papa had got in the mail, and held it like he was reading. Dumpling Kinnamon laughed. "You've got the paper upside down, Mister Grant."

"I reckon I know it," Grandpa said. He kept going over the paper upside down, almost touching it with his nose. The set of his mouth showed how mad he was with Dumpling. He was as proud as Lucifer, and it irked him for people to know his eyes had failed. Mama felt sorry for him and took the paper away so slick he never knew it wasn't his own idea, and she read to him. She soon stopped. "Why, the new schoolteacher's coming next month!"

The women and girls squealed to find out who it was and Mama said it was somebody we didn't know. She pushed the paper out to me. "Here, Faxie, you read it for us."

So I read, "It says, 'Miss Cassandra Carson, from Hustler, Virginia, a graduate of Rappahannock Female Institute and daughter of Mrs. Rich Prior Carson and the late Mr. Carson, who was a leading livestock dealer of the State of Virginia.' "

There was more about her winning a literary prize and some blue ribbons at the 1915 Pippin County Fair and I read it all, trying to think of what she must look like.

"She'll be a catbird," Papa said, "if she's anything in the line of old Rich Carson. He was the sharpest horse trader this side a Gypsy."

"I just hope she's a fine strong Christian woman," Mama said. "Lord knows we need some sainted somebody to help raise up this community."

Mama was always talking about improving our folks and saying they were sinful. Papa spoke up. "Damnation, Lin. There's no way on earth to help folks be what they don't want to be of their own accord."

Mama grinned. "I'm strong for trying it out, in some instances I can name."

Papa rumbled like summer thunder. "The only thing you'll get out of uplifting sorry folks is a strained back."

"Hush talking like that in front of the children, Beau—or they'll grow up not believing in the Good Book."

When I handed the paper back to Grandpa, my sister Ivy begged to go to the creek and play with Muscadine Kinnamon, who was her own age. For all her talk about loving everybody, Mama wasn't crazy about us playing with Tootsy's girls. She said they were dirty, to say the least. Before she let Ivy go, she took her aside and pretended to tie her dress sash and whispered, "You can go to the creek with Musky—but you be sure you stay on the upstream side of her. You hear me, now?"

They tagged off with the other little girls but were soon back, deviling Grandpa to tell them tales. Grandpa loved children so that he couldn't keep his hands off them, and they all got in his lap and he told them outlandish yarns. Grandma, who was his second wife, got watery eyes watching him entertain the children. "He always loved the least ones so. He'll not be with us much longer, but it'll be the children he'll hate most to leave behind. You know, he was away over fifty when I married him, and we had five quick babies in a row—just blip, blip, blip. And he always took a baby to bed with him every night for years and years. When we finally ran out of babies he had trouble. He couldn't sleep of a night until I poured a pitcher of warm water over him." We laughed with Aunt Lumbie and went back to work. Grandpa didn't even look up from his storytelling.

Grandpa soon began carrying on with Tootsyroll Kinnamon. Aunt Lumbie tried to hush him, but Toots egged him on.

"I remember your mama was the most woman who ever walked these parts," he said. "I don't say she was quite so full in the chest as yourself, but, ah, that Brown Sugar was something on a stick."

"Sug was my grandma, Mister Grant."

"Well, whoever she was, I recollect the day she came here, traveling with a tent show, and everybody in the county crowded into Randolph to see her. A right stout woman, big as a wagon wheel around her saddle joint, and had little bitty bird legs—she looked like a sack of broken hammers in that half-dress—and had a voice like the mating call of a rasping file. But sister, if she couldn't shimmy and shake! She did the wickedest hootchy-cootchy of any female ever I saw."

The other women pretended they couldn't hear him, but Jess Sixkiller and Tree and the others hung around Grandpa hoping he would get better.

"I remember I was in there with a crowd of fool boys,"

Grandpa said, "hollering at Sug and trying to get her goat while she did her belly dance. She just barked at me once. She said, 'Sonny, when they circumcised you they throwed away the wrong piece.' She broke up the show. Ah my, she was a warm something to take hold of, that Sug Kinnamon. All the boys got to know her."

It was the first time I had heard such talk around our women, but since it was Grandpa, there was no help for it and nobody gave it much thought.

When he was ready to put the tobacco into the barn, Papa took me and Jimroe off the slides and made us climb the tier poles inside. It was a job they always wished off on boys who could skin up the poles and hold on while they worked up high, and we were supposed to be proud of it. But as Papa would say, anybody with good sense would sooner be in hell with his back broke than under a tobacco barn roof in the July sun. The barn was a mud-chinked log house that had no windows. We climbed a frame of logs that was built into the barn, five rows of poles high and four rows wide. Those logs made a kind of rack in the barn for hanging to-bacco sticks; we called them tier poles.

We scrambled onto the highest poles and hung tobacco sticks as they were passed to us. The sticks were just long enough to hang between the tier poles and we shoved them close together until the top of the barn was full. It must have been over a hundred degrees up there and seemed worse in the heavy waves of green tobacco smell that made it hard to catch your breath. Once in a while we dropped down to where it was cooler and took a rest. Once when we were loafing we heard Mama and Papa arguing out under the shed. Jimroe and the Indians grinned at me but nobody said anything to me.

"I expect Fax would just as lief you'd not make him read like that, out in front of folks," Papa said.

"Law, I'd like to know why not. He's proud, and ought to be. It wouldn't hurt the rest of them if they did as well."

"Damned if you'd have caught me reading when I was his age, with men and boys around."

Mama laughed. "He looks enough like you to have been picked out of your hide with a splinter—but you and Fax are two different animals, if you didn't know it."

Papa talked about how fine school was, but said that we all had plenty of time to suffer when we were grown-up. Mama switched him off pretty sharp and he shut up and went on with the work. Jimroe winked at me in such a friendly way that I almost forgot who he was.

We had to watch our balance on the tier poles because every stick of green tobacco weighed about thirty pounds and was awkward to handle up there; when it had dried in the curing barn it would weigh only a pound or so, and be nothing to handle, but now it was a pain. We worked there for hours in the afternoon, with the Indians pouring sticks up to me and Jimroe and Damon until the top of the barn was so full that we couldn't squeeze in another leaf. It was an oversized barn and we would hang more than eight hundred sticks in it.

While we were at it, the sticks stopped coming. We heard a buggy come across rocky ground, and somebody called out. "Hence. Miss Linden. How you do?"

Papa's voice was a little frosty. "Pretty straight."

It was Biscoe Allen who had come up. We eased down from the tier poles up in the barn and went to the doorway. Biscoe was staying in his buggy, with his long legs crossed so that we saw his good boots.

"Well," Mama said. "This is an unexpected pleasure. Won't you light and come to the house with us?"

Biscoe Allen had courted Mama long before she married Papa, and sometimes Papa teased her about it, but pretty gingerly.

Biscoe said he wouldn't get down. He was going out of his way to be pleasant, but he didn't stir from his seat.

"You seen old man Wash?" he asked Papa.

"Yeah. He was by with the morning mail."

"I thought so. I can't seem to catch up with him. Well . . ."

"He was full of tales about bad tobacco markets, and how we're all fixing to starve."

"Damn his time. The old man's gone foolish. I've got to hush him up."

"We thought maybe he'd been sent."

Biscoe showed his gums when he laughed. "You ought to know me better than that, Hence. I can wait for trouble till it finds me."

"We wondered."

"Well, don't. You're the last man I'd want to leave in doubt about where I stood."

"You looking for a poor market, Biscoe?"

"Well, you can see that nobody could buy all the tobacco there is to be bought—not at a decent price."

"What'll we do?"

"Do like we always do in hard times—share and share alike."

Tree laughed. "Listen to him. He means 'share' for Biscoe and 'alike' for the rest of us, whatever's left."

"That leaves out the Poindexters," Biscoe said. "They've got their own ways of doing."

"You mighty right," Tree said. He winked at Biscoe, but nobody smiled.

"Hence, if it's got you worried," Biscoe said, "why, I might be able to think of something."

"I suppose it's up to the Lord."

"Maybe not. What did you average for your crop last fall?"

Papa waited a second. "Around thirty-eight cents a pound."

"Would you rest easier if I was to guarantee you twenty-five, here and now, for every pound you weighed in?"

Papa stared. "I never heard of such a thing."

"Nobody else. But suppose I'm fool enough to chance it."

Papa started thinking out loud, trying to follow Biscoe. "Who else are you dickering with?"

"There's not many I'd gamble on. Maybe Billy Lufler and Slim Poindexter."

"What'd they say?"

"You're the first I've asked."

"Well, that would give you the pick of the prime tobacco on the ridge."

"Yeah."

"And suppose prices go all to pieces between now and market opening. Where would you be?"

"They're already shot to hell, Hence. The market might's well never open this year. I could save you all that fuss and worry at market time."

"Why would mine be worth—"

"You know the tobacco companies ain't going to let a season go by without taking in some leaf from every market on the belt."

"I guess not."

"We can't close up shop for good—there's going to come another season."

"You mean to tell me you'd just buy a few crops off the big farms, and let everybody else go hang?"

"How else would you do it?"

"Hell. It wouldn't be an hour before every man, woman and child in Corona would know about it—and would be hating the ground we walk on."

"Well, it's just a notion, Hence. Somebody's got to make a move. If you change your mind, let me know."

Biscoe turned his buggy and went up the lane in a hurry. Mama frowned after him. "Why, Beau, that was generous of Biscoe to come to us. I don't see why . . ."

Papa put his arm around her. His hand trembled just a little. "We ain't going to worry about tobacco, remember?"

"I'll bet if it was anybody else Biscoe had asked, they'd be mighty quick to take him up," Mama said. "They wouldn't stop to think twice."

"We've got work to do," Tree said. "No matter what."

Papa went to the house with Mama, trying to calm her down, but all of us knew something was bad wrong. Nobody had ever heard of tobacco being bought like that in advance, outside the warehouse.

Papa had left Tree in charge at the barn because Tree knew more about curing tobacco before breakfast than the rest of the county would know in a month of Sundays. We fired the barn with two field-stone furnaces built into the logwork, and heat passed through a stovepipe that ran around on the dirt floor inside the barn. Tree built such big fires in the furnaces that the heat was enough to make us dizzy.

Papa kept a thermometer but Tree never used it. He waited an hour or so, then stuck a hand inside the barn to feel the heat and said, "Well, she's getting around to right." He would keep the heat low for a day or so, between ninety and a hundred and ten degrees, since he wanted to dry the tobacco to a clear lemon color. If he hurried the leaf it would turn black, but if the heat was too slow, tobacco would turn out red and leathery. After two days Tree would raise the heat about ten degrees an hour until it got near two hundred and then, when the color suited him, he would stop.

We were lying out under the tobacco barn shed late that night, until Tree and I were the only ones awake. Papa came and looked in the barn without saying much. Tree knew he was nervous.

"You might as well forget Biscoe," Tree said. "If you're trying to figure out what's in that head of his, there's a long line ahead of you."

"I don't much care. I've made up my mind to go about my own business."

"That's right. You've got a prime crop, come what may— and you've knocked Biscoe's little scheme in the head. I know that much. If you say no, then you know durn well Lufler and Slim won't go along with him."

"I just wish I knew what Allen is up to."

"Well, you can bet it ain't your hide he's worrying about. He ain't doing a thing but trying to wiggle out of trouble before it comes. When we have a bad tobacco market this fall, he don't want it to look like he was trying to steal tobacco from every farmer in Corona. He can already see that they'll be as mad as wet hens."

Papa soon went away.

Jess woke up and made steady work on the fruit jar and blew mean tunes on his mouth harp. Once he spat close to Jimroe, who was asleep.

"Damn his sorry time," Jess said. "If he was to look at me cross-eyed just once, I'd grab down his throat and take his tailbone and snap him wrong side out."

"Go get us another jar," Tree said. "You asked for everything he did to you—naw, you begged for it."

Jess prowled off in the dark underbrush. Tree dropped his voice. "You want to watch yourself with old Jess, Fax. Jimroe and your daddy got him as sore as a boiled owl at the Picnic. When the Wild Indian rises in that boy he gets red all over, and it's hell to pay."

"Pembroke too," I said.

"Naw. You could handle Pem yourself, with one hand tied behind you. But Jess is another breed of cat. He's more dangerous than the rest of the whole tribe."

Jess came back to the fire and we settled for a tobacco watch. I went to sleep watching Jess, thinking of Pem Six-killer and Biscoe Allen and Papa's tobacco crop and wondering what would happen to us.

9

A Night in the Wrong House

Grandpa hung around the first barn of tobacco we cured, every minute he could sneak away from the house. He lay on old quilts and told yarns without stopping, Jess Sixkiller blew his mouth organ and Tree ran things. They tasted the fruit jars now and then. Jimroe and I stayed with them, pretending that we were helping with the work. We stayed there night and day, because curing tobacco had to be watched.

Nobody thought of what day was which, until it dawned

on Jess while Grandpa was telling about the Kinnamon cat house and things that had happened there in his day.

"I'm talking about back there when men were men and women were glad of it," Grandpa said. "I remember when Sug Kinnamon was eighty-three years old and her old man was eighty-six, and she went down to Doc Kiger and told him the old man was losing interest in her and wouldn't play sex no more, and said she needed medicine to cure him. Doc asked her when she first noticed it and she said, 'Why, the first time was last night—but it happened again this morning.' "

"Goddlemighty," Jess said. "Here it is Saturday evening and I've got to go to town and get drunk, and I sure do dread it."

"Pshaw, if it was me I'd go to Tootsy's instead," Grandpa said. "You don't see many of them tasty quarter-ton women these days."

Tree guyed Jess about the time he had gone on a spree to Richmond, Virginia, and spent two or three weeks in cat houses up there. "It's a wonder to me a ragged-tailed Indian tobacco farmer could afford that."

"Hell," Jess said. "It never cost me a dime. We was all kinfolks."

"Balls of fire," Grandpa said. "I don't see why you don't tomcat on over to Tootsy's. I wish by God I was young enough. I sure wouldn't be studying no Richmond City."

"Me neither," Tree said. "You've about put me in the notion to go stalking, Mister Grant. And that jug's got me seeing double and feeling single."

Tree took another drink and pulled logs from the furnaces to get the fires down and asked Grandpa if he would keep an eye on the barn for him, provided he could get Damon to stay and help with the wood. It tickled the old man.

"By George, boys, I'm sending you forth like missionaries unto the heathen shore. Go on. Go on."

"What's the almighty hurry?" Tree said.

"Hell, you won't be young twice, boys. I'll tell you that. You've got to keep crowding in all the women you can."

Jess Sixkiller meowed.

"Yes," Grandpa said. "And you take notice of everything that happens. I want to hear of it when you get back."

Tree looked around for Lize and remembered that his boys had already taken her home. He grinned at Jimroe. "I'll trade with you. If you'll let us take Lydia Pinkham, you can sneak off to Tootsy's with us—and I'll keep Jess off your back, too."

Before Tree could get his mouth closed good, Jimroe was back from the stable with the mare. They still had an argument about how they would ride. The mare couldn't carry Tree and Jess and Jimroe all at once, and they didn't dare ask Papa for the wagon—so we wound up hitching Lydia to my tobacco slide. Tree and Jess took a couple more drinks, and I told Tree he would damn well not take off a tobacco slide I'd built myself unless he took me along. So we climbed in and Jimroe walked alongside driving, and we went off. Grandpa laughed so hard at the sight of two grown men and a nearly grown boy riding a tobacco slide to a cat house that we could hear him for almost a mile, cackling like a guinea.

Tree tried to make me go back home but I wouldn't budge. He gave up pretty easy.

"I don't want an iota of trouble out of you two sprigginses then," Tree said. "You stay out of our way and don't give me any sass, or you'll get a thick lip out of it."

We promised to do anything he said so long as he let us go to the Kinnamon place. We couldn't imagine what it would be like, for all the tales we'd heard of it as long as we'd lived. That was one place that we were forbidden.

"And the first one of you I catch messing around with Tootsy's baby girls, I aim to cut him up for catfish bait," Tree said. "I mean that thing."

"He's saving the little ones for seed," Jimroe said.

That made Jess laugh, and he threw an arm about Jimroe like they had been as thick as runaway slaves all their lives. Jimroe gave him a look out of slitted eyes, but didn't move. Jess played his mouth harp with one hand, pumping out tunes until Jimroe loosened up and began singing to them.

When we passed the fork of a road, Tree and Jess began to study the ruts ahead of us and saw fresh tracks of a rubber-tired buggy. Both of them could read the ground like it was a newspaper—better, for Jess couldn't read or write a lick and Tree wasn't much to brag on.

"It's old Wash Strawn," Tree said. "He's gone over to play Mama and Papa with Tootsy."

Jess groaned. "That lets us out. It'll take that old cooter till Monday morning."

Jess talked about the horse Wash was driving. We listened because we knew that Indian could tell everything worth knowing about the horse that had left those tracks.

"It's an old plug he got off Al Kemper," he said. "A nag that must be about twenty years old, and except for being windbroke he's not bad. His daddy raced for prizes."

Jimroe perked up. "Maybe Wash has sort of forgot about Lydia Pinkham, and I could trade her back to him."

"Fat chance. He could draw you a picture of every nag he's traded in his life and not leave off a hair. He'd have heard about how you cheated me, too, you devil, and ain't slept a wink since—if it's anything he hates to hear about, it's another good cheat in a horse trade. You might make him swap with you, but boy, keep an eye open." Jess went on like he'd never had a minute's trouble with Jimroe.

Tree said, "Watch him, Jamesroe. It'd not surprise me if old Jess had part interest in that plug of Strawn's." They all laughed.

We had rough going on that road. Toots lived on the tip of a peninsula that pooched out into the Redwine River and almost touched Virginia. The state line between us and Virginia was supposed to run down the middle of the river, and

Tootsy's house stuck out there so far, where she could almost step to the Virginia shore, that folks said that the line cut her place in two and left her kitchen in Virginia and her other room in North Carolina. Everybody had jokes about it, especially about the liquor officers who kept trying to hem up Toots, and about the men who went tomcatting there and would reach clean across into another state to hug their women.

We rattled on toward the river through plum-tree thickets and blackjack-oak scrub, and the land got sorrier as we went. The only things growing there were jimson weed and briars and poison ivy and cow-itch vine.

"It ain't hard to tell when you're coming close to Virginia," Tree said. "All you've got to do is go north till you can smell it, and then east till you step in it."

Our Carolina people told that kind of joke all the time, and it was a common saying that a man's spectacles would fog up from the miasmas when he got to the Virginia border. We knew that people on the other side talked even worse about us; Virginians thought it was downhill from their state in all directions, even to heaven. They said that Tarheels never learned a thing in school but the three R's—Reading, Riting and Road to Virginia.

We forded a creek and came up into honeysuckle scent thick enough to eat with a spoon. It came from Tootsy's. Her homeplace was like an island in the dusty underbrush and behind her honeysuckle fence everything was as green as money.

We could hardly see the porch for morning-glory vines and plants. The steps were almost covered with lard cans and crocks full of flowers. I knew Mama would have a conniption if she could see how much better Tootsyroll could grow things than we could. Vines ran over the porch roof, full of bees and hummingbirds.

"Mighty homey," Jess said.

"Don't mention home to me," Tree said. "If you ask me, the three most overrated things in this world are home cooking, home loving, and the State of Virginia."

"Well, how about it? We going to stay the night?"

"It'd cost you and me five dollars a head," Tree said.

"Suits me to a T. Let's go."

The house wasn't much. It was like dozens of thrownaway places in the county. The ridgepole sagged and the shingles were so old that they were white and curled. The house was two cabins with an open hall between, of the kind we called a dog run, but Tootsy had had the run closed in and had nailed up some old stained-glass windows from an abandoned church. There was a white figure of the Lord in the middle, with sunlight burning through and throwing purple and black and blue and yellow over Tootsy's plants, like nothing anybody had ever seen before. It looked mighty rich in there. We heard music in the dog run, a gramophone. It was a woman singing a hymn:

"Whissss! Whiss-per-ing hope!"

Somebody lumbered out a door, snapping a gallus over a shoulder, and sure enough, it was old Wash Strawn. He tried to make us think he had come to raid the place.

"I would like the most in the world to help you, Miz Kinnamon," Wash said, "but I've done and drawn up the indictment, and Judge Bucktarrel said the full majesty of the law was going to roll on this case if it took us across hell and half of Georgia."

Toots came out all dressed up like a sore finger, in a new orange wrapper exactly like the ones Mama and our big girls had. I thought for a second that I'd have to tell Mama about that, then I remembered where I was.

Toots yawned at Wash and showed half a dozen gold teeth.

"This here's mighty serious business," Wash said. "Bad enough to be moonshining, without trafficking the favors of

Southern womanhood. But don't worry. I'm goin' to try and
shake Judge Bucktarrel a little for you."

"You do that, now, Shurf," Toots said in a careless way.
She waved a fat yellow arm to Tree and Jess.

"Well, hidy, boys."

Then Wash pretended that he had caught sight of us for
the first time and invited the men to drink with him.

"I was just fixing to have a dollop of Miz Kinnamon's
Blink-Eye," Wash said, "being as my work's all done here.
How about having a snifter with me, boys?"

"Yeah, snifter," Toots said.

Wash did a quick dance on his wooden leg and Toots
slapped his back. "Boys," she said, "this damn one-leg tub
can hold more likker than my wash kettle."

"Why, Miz Kinnamon . . ."

"Boys, the last time this old boar hog was here he got so
drunk he lost his false teeth in the periwinkle. So I just taken
a string and soaked it in corn likker and drug it through the
brush, and by God them teeth came snapping up and
caught on. Wouldn't you know it?"

They joked until Wash spied Jimroe in the yard, looking
over his windbroken horse. Wash pegged out.

They talked loud so that they could hear over the rumbling of the horse's breathing. He sounded like a furnace
bellows.

"Ain't this the little mare I gave you one time, son?"

"*Gave?* I'm still bleeding from that time, Mister Wash."

"Why, I heard you did right well on her, renting her out
to the whole countryside. Don't I remember that this mare's
blind as a bat?"

"Well, her eyesight ain't what it once was, but I think it's
improving."

"Unh, hunh."

"Just some little blemish in one eye, I guess."

"Likely."

"Of course, it might clear up."

"Might, might."

"And this old windbroke thing of yours, I reckon, is so far gone he can't walk half a mile."

Wash blew his whiskey breath over us. "I wouldn't say that if I was you. That's the gamest horse I know. I wouldn't be surprised if he couldn't run many a five-year-old into the ground."

Wash talked about how fine his horse was until it was ridiculous, hearing the old thing pant and wheeze at every breath, like his throat had been cut. He looked as poor as a razorback hog, too.

"Young man," Wash said, "I come from too proud a line of folks to take advantage of any one of Grant Starling's tribe—at least twice in a row. All I want out of my steed is some little something to pay my debts with. The blind mare ain't quite enough."

Jimroe wouldn't be talked into giving any cash. Wash said it would have to be even Stephen then, at worst. Jimroe was bullheaded and stood out for Wash to give him something, even if it was only a dime, so that he could say he hadn't traded without cash to boot. They argued until it looked like no swap, then Tree butted in. He whispered to Jimroe, "Go on and trade, you fool. You can't be hurt no worse."

Wash overheard him and rolled his eyes like he was about to rue back on his trade, but he shook Jimroe by the hand and took the blind mare. He went off with Lydia pulling his buggy.

Jimroe rattled the old nag's ribs with his hand. "I'll feed him up and turn a dollar or two. You can always find some fool to trade horses with."

"Ah, that's the spirit," Tree said. "The real religion of this country is: 'Git all you can, and keep all you git.'"

"You said a mouthful," Tootsy said. "That's the way to get ahead in this life."

One of Tootsy's girls changed the record on the gramophone and played "Gimme That Old-Time Religion." Tree

grabbed Toots and sashayed her around, both of them barefoot in the yard sand. They looked like a brace of trained
bears, for they weighed about two hundred pounds each.
Then Jess danced with Roxy and Fan Kinnamon, both at
once, and Dumpling caught Jimroe and they all loped
around like people who had gone out of their heads.

Soon Tree and Jess and Tootsy and the big girls went in
the house and left us alone. Jimroe and I sat on the porch
with the little girls on some old bedsprings, and until it got
dark we helped the girls think up a name for Roxy's new
baby. We thought of them and Dumpling wrote them
down. She used all of her school tablet and then wrote on
the wall of the house. We thought of everything we could
put our minds to, but nothing struck them right until Jimroe
dug up a good long one.

Muscadine broke in the room where Tootsy and Tree
were hiding, yelling, "Mama, Mama! We got it. How about
General Lee Garden of Eden Heavenly Trulove Kinnamon?
Ain't it beautiful?"

They threw something at her, and she scrambled across
the dog run to the other door and squealed again. On the
way back she wound the gramophone afresh and kept wind-
ing it every few minutes until one of her sisters yelled out
of the dark, "For God's sakes, let's hear something else for a
while."

Dumpling played "When the Roll Is Called Up Yonder"
for an hour or so, and during that time Tootsy crossed the
porch and saw Jimroe and Dumpling close together on the
springs. She picked up Dumpling by the neck and shook
them apart. She laughed. "Here you ain't as big as a washing
of soap, little gal, and already at it. Be ashamed."

When Toots was gone, Jimroe and Dumpling went off
the porch and I sat beside Muscadine. She leaned hard
against me wherever I moved, and held my hand until it
was wet. She gave me a little kiss on the mouth and I
didn't know what to do about it and held still. Jimroe and

Dumpling came back and Jimroe bragged about what they had been doing, but I thought he talked too much to have done a whole lot. We got sleepy. The gramophone finally ran down, and it was quiet. The moon came up and mockingbirds sang and the breeze from the Redwine washed the smell of flowers over us. I thought that nothing would ever happen there, when I heard Toots and Tree talking in their room.

"What's old man Wash up to with his tobacco foolishness?"

"Beats me," Tree said.

"Something about Hence Starling."

Tree wanted to know what it was about.

"I didn't make head nor tail of it. He kept saying Hence had better watch out, or he'd get nothing for his big crop."

"Talk's cheap."

"Yeah, but he said that Starling farm would go up for debt, one way or another—and that one day a Strawn might live there and boss Starlings around. He wants to see them stiff-necks bowed down."

"Never happen."

"Well, the biggest fool thing he said was that if he had it to do, he could find folks who'd teach Hence a lesson he wouldn't forget."

"The old fool."

"Well, it's no skin off my rumpus. But don't say old Toot never told you. If you care about your white folks, keep an eye open. I'd hate to see harm come to old Hence; he never treated us no way but decent."

"Hell, I never come to jaw all night. Where's another jug?"

Their door squeaked open and I started to run. I couldn't bear to have Tree know I'd heard them. I felt like I couldn't talk about it. I was down the steps when Tree came out.

"Where the devil you think you're going?"

"Home."

He came down to me. "By God, you won't. I'll not have you scaling up that rope this time of night, getting caught and telling Linden Starling you've been off here with me."

I got loose but he caught me again.

"What's wrong, boy? You don't want to put my tail in a split stick like that. We'll be going home before long. Tell you what. Me and Jess will take you coon hunting this week."

"Damned if I'll go anywhere with a Sixkiller."

But when Tree kept after me I went back and lay on the springs and waited. I made up my mind not to fall asleep, but when they shook me awake it was daylight. The yawning women were on the porch and Wash's old horse was hitched to my tobacco slide.

Tree pulled out his purse to pay Tootsy.

"Naw, sir, Tree," Jess said. "Here's one place your money won't spend. This is all on me. I'm a paying for everything."

He pulled a check wallet from his pocket and had Toots fetch him a pencil. Tree gaped while Jess sat on the bed springs between the two little girls, who were sound asleep. Jess didn't know one side of a check from the other, let alone how to write one, but he scratched all over one of them like he knew what he was about, and handed the check to Toots.

"I guess that'll take care of it, and then some."

Toots wasn't right sure about it. "I don't never get checks. How do I know they's money behind this thing?"

"Every nickel in the Randolph bank is behind it."

"Says you and who else?"

"Law, woman, I've got money in there that's already rusty."

"What would I do with this paper?"

"Why, spend it like any other money. Don't skin your ignorance. Anybody around here will turn it to cash. It's the way big folks do all the time."

She looked at Tree. "Would you take it if you was in my shoes?"

"I never did know him to give out a bad one."

Tootsy folded the check between her breasts. "All right, boys. You're durn good old boys, even if you do wear folks to a frazzle everywhere you go. You come back, hear?"

She grabbed me and hugged me against her big bosom until I thought smother I would. She was as strong as an ox, and held me no matter how I wiggled. "I'm going to keep this'un for little Musky," she said. "This is the very one she wants, out of all the chaps she's ever seen. Wouldn't you think she'd have picked out a pretty one?"

I kicked and clawed to get loose, afraid that I would cry. I was thinking of her in the room with Tree all night and was half sick by the time I got away from her. All of them laughed at me and I managed to laugh back.

We left while the little girls were still asleep on the porch with their mouths puckered open like rosebuds. When we were thumping down the road in the slide, Tree got after Jess about his check. "Dadburn your time. If we had had you here in fourteen and ninety-two the white folks never would have taken hold in this country. You're the slickest thief I ever laid my two eyes on—and here we've been thinking you hadn't the sense to get in out of a shower."

"You can't hardly beat education."

"Amen, brother."

I knew that our Indians would fight like fury one minute and be the best of friends the next, but it made me uneasy to see Tree buddy up with Jess. They stood in the back of the slide with arms around each other, not quite steady, bellowing a song in Indian language. They laughed about Tootsy and the check and wondered what she would do with it.

"Tain't no good no-way," Jess said. "I never wrote on there what it was for."

"Hell, you couldn't have spelt it even if you could write."

"I feel like, if I could write ary word atall, I could write that one."

They almost turned the slide over laughing. Tree whooped, "A check in a cat house. Great day in the morning, how you ever dreamed up a thing like that. A head on you like a five-cent watermelon, and you thought up that one."

"It may be that I ain't such a fool as you taken me for," Jess said. "It may be I'm coming up in the world."

"Not likely," Tree said. "All a man needs to keep him down is a drop of the wrong kind of blood. Sometimes I wish I never had a pinch of white man in me—so I wouldn't give a damn."

It was the first time I ever heard Tree say anything like that, and the only time I knew him to talk with a thick tongue.

When we got back to the tobacco barn, Grandpa stared like he couldn't remember who we were. Our ride to Tootsy's had gone clean out of his head. He was thinking about dying. He called to Tree. "I've been going over my funeral arrangements. I had you on the right side of the coffin, at Pall Number One, but I don't like you there. Suppose you've been nipping a little that day and was to stumble. I don't want to be jostled on my way to Glory. I've done moved you around to the left side, in the back, where you'll not have to be plumb sober."

Tree slapped Grandpa on the back. "Hell, you're too mean to turn up your toes. You old Starlings never die—you just harden into whetstones."

"Naw," Grandpa said. "I'm on my way up Yonder. You'll like the left side better, Trevilian. Over there you'll pass the family and you can see if any of them ain't mourning the way he ought to."

Grandpa rambled until he thought of Tootsy's house, and then got after me about it. "Buddy, that's a thing I ought to tell you before you get to running with women. Sex, they call it. Sex, hell. That's one business the Lord made a mess of. I don't know if he made men and women too much alike, or too different, but he did it wrong. More people have complaints of that trouble than anything else in the world."

I thought Grandpa had dozed off then, but he was playing possum, lying in his quilts and cutting his eyes at Jess Six-killer. He had never had much use for Jess, but now he lay there and watched him like a hawk. When the Indian stepped into the bushes for a minute, Grandpa whispered, "Boys, I caught the women trying to poison me."

Tree laughed.

"It's the God's truth. That Linden Poindexter told me to my face she'd do it the first time she found one of my jugs at her house. I know she did it, boys. Look here." He pulled a gallon jar from his quilts. "See how curious it looks? It's got some kind of stain in there. Looks mean enough to kill you off."

Tree said it looked and smelled good to him, but Grandpa wouldn't have it. "They poisoned it, all right. I know it in my bones. Don't you boys say nothing, now. I've got an idea. That damn Indian might come in handy for something, after all."

When Jess Sixkiller came back, Grandpa grinned at him. "Old Jess, how'd you like something real to taste?"

Jess gave him a surprised look. The old man hadn't spoken a friendly word to him in a year or so, though they were always around each other. Jess could see the jug. "Why, I don't mind if I do, Mister Grant."

Grandpa uncorked the jug and Jess took a long pull. He grinned and wiped his mouth and said it was fit drinking liquor. Grandpa kept a close watch, and for the next half hour didn't take his eyes off Jess, to see if he was poisoned. Then he began to fidget. "Jess, I'd be proud for you to have another touch."

Jess didn't argue. He took a longer drink, and paid no mind when Tree and Grandpa didn't drink with him. After a while Grandpa couldn't stand it any longer.

"How you feel?"

Jess said he was feeling better every minute.

"Lemme see your tongue."

He looked in Jess's mouth and eyes, and fell into a pet and cussed Jess.

"Damn your time, you likker-hog Indian. They ain't one damn thing wrong with that jug. That's some of the best corn ever stilled in this county. Poison, hell! I expect you put me in that notion, somehow or other, just so you could lay your lip to my jar. Damned if you'll ever suck it again."

He carried on for a minute with Jess staring at him, and then the old man quit in the middle of his talk and fell asleep on the quilts.

10

The Teacher Comes

By the end of July, when we were curing our sixth barn of tobacco and still hadn't finished, Papa was edgier than ever. The leaf was about to run us out of house and home, with the pack house and corncrib and barn loft and buggy shed full, and the porches of the house piled with it.

Once, at night, Papa stopped work and looked down from our ridge to see winking fires on other farms, where people were curing the big crop. "I'm mighty nigh afraid Biscoe's right," he said. "The crop's too big to bring us top dollar,

even for prime leaf. I wonder what we're going to do." He
hated to think of all those barns on other farms, where they
were curing tobacco that would be going after the same
dollars we wanted.

But it only made him drive us harder. He shook his head
when he heard of the farmers' union out west, or tales of
warehouse burnings to the south. Some of our neighbors
would say that the tobacco companies had better watch how
far they pushed honest working people, but Papa wouldn't
listen to that talk. He told us that it was just a case of making
five or ten pounds of tobacco do the job of one pound of
leaf in a good year, and that we'd have to step. "Anybody
worth the powder to blow him up has always been able to
make a living here," he said, "and I guess those that try
always will."

"I wouldn't be too sure," Tree said. "You know how the
old folks tell about the time everybody in the country went
across the river to sell tobacco in Virginia, and had a mutiny
against our warehouses."

"Old folks," Papa said. "They'll be the ruin of us yet."

"I wonder if you'd speak up so rank if your pap was
here."

Papa grinned and went back to work.

Our last barn was a big one that held fifteen hundred
sticks, almost enough for us to live on in a normal year.
Cousin Tree cut down the heat for the last two days of
curing, when moisture was going out of the leaf, and not
long after daylight one morning he propped open the door.
We heard the tiny crackling of dry leaves; they were cured
so bright that the golden light shone out of the door on the
faces of Papa and Tree. The smell was perfect.

"She's tight as a fiddle string," Tree said. "I expect this is
the best-cured barn I ever saw in my life. I hate to think how
much money it'd bring in sensible times."

Every leaf was so brittle that the lightest touch would
have broken it to smithereens, so that it would have to be

steamed a little in the ordering barn and then put somewhere safe until sale time. It looked like we might have it on hand until Christmas or later, trying to find a decent market.

While we stood around we saw dust on the road and somebody turned in at our lane. It was Shad Starling, the Negro who drove for our Aunt Ly Sue Poindexter, and he had come from town in Judge Bucktarrel's phaeton. Aunt Ly Sue was great-aunt to Mama and Tree and about a thousand others, and was the only one in the family who put on any side. She lived in the biggest house in Corona Crossroads, almost hidden behind overgrown box bushes, and she kept Shad to drive for her.

We most often saw Aunt Ly Sue in a string hammock on her porch, fanning herself, with Shad's wife Poll to wait on her, and sometimes Judge Bucktarrel beside her, plinking his mandolin. Once when I had gone on her porch Aunt Ly Sue hugged me and she smelled of vanilla extract. I told Jimroe and he said she tippled all the time, but I couldn't be sure he wasn't making it up.

We waited at the barn and wondered what was going on, because it was a rare day that Shad came to our house. Mama sent Ivy down to us and she came out of breath.

"The schoolmarm's coming!"

Papa looked like he had heard better news in his day.

"Mama says you'll have to send for her."

"She picked a fine time. Why don't Shad fetch her?"

"Because Aunt Ly Sue is tailfeathers over teakettle, trying to get things ready for her—and you'll have to send. Mama said so."

"Of course, tobacco don't matter. Making a living is just some foolishness menfolks thought up. We've all got to go off to school and learn to spell cat." Papa was warming up in what Mama called his sourcastic vein, but he reined himself in and hugged Ivy. "All right, Sugarfoot. Where do we get her?"

"It's the noon train, and hurry."

Papa took a quick look to see who he could spare, and told Jimroe to go. My mouth popped open before I knew it and I wailed, "Papa."

He didn't say a word but knew what was wrong with me, and waved me on despite his itch to keep every hand at work every minute until the crop was finished. He yelled after us, "Take the buggy. She'll have a ton of traps and tricks. You'll have to squeeze 'em in."

Papa meant for us to hurry back as fast as we could, without wasting time. We had to cross the river and meet the train and take the teacher to Aunt Ly Sue's house in town. It was a long ride, but hers was the only place for a teacher to stay. The place was so big that the old lady and Shad and Poll rattled around in it, and Aunt Ly Sue was about the only woman in Corona with enough learning to make her decent for a schoolteacher to talk to. She had been off to school before her daddy died and left her all his money, a long time before. There was a story that some little girl had asked her once why she never got married, and Aunt Ly Sue said, "I was spoiled by Mr. Milton. I read *Paradise Lost* when I was young, and fell in love with the Devil and never found a man half so fascinating. I'm looking yet. Furnifold Bucktarrel comes close, but don't quite fill the bill." It was a tale Mama told sometimes.

Jimroe groused all the way to the river, where we left his old horse and the buggy. We got a free trip on the ferry with one of Tree's little boys.

"I ain't got all day to hang around for a fool schoolteacher," Jimroe said.

"Suppose she's prettier than Dumpling Kinnamon," I said.

"Shoot. She'll be as old as Methuselah and ugly as homemade sin. All them durn Virginia women are long in the nose and big in the foot."

We hung around the Atlantic & Redwine depot in Osmond until the noon train came, but there was no schoolteacher. We had only one other chance, the evening train, and we waited. The teacher was aboard. There was no trouble spotting her.

The conductor and brakeman came first, squabbling over who would set out her baggage for her. Then she came out, a woman about the size of a well-fed twelve-year-old, wearing a blue serge skirt that swept the gravel. She leaned on a steamer trunk while the old men worked. She was so pretty that she made me want to pin back her ears and swallow her whole.

We went up to say that we'd come after her, but she beat us to it and took both our hands. "I'm Cassie Carson. I've come to Corona School, and I expect you're some of my innocent victims."

Her blue eyes were the color of chicory flowers and as steady as the muzzle of a shotgun. Around the eyes she looked like she might be ready to laugh any second.

Jimroe pretended to be too busy to notice her. I tried to tell her about my reading and how fast I went in school and how hard I was going to study, but I made such a mess of it that she could hardly understand me. She smiled.

The trainmen called the livery-stable hack to carry her things the hundred yards to the ferry landing and the train captain paid the hacker himself. Miss Cassie blew the captain a kiss and the old man barked his shins climbing back into his train. The train puffed off in the dark.

The livery boy piled her bags around us at the shore. I thought we'd have trouble crossing, since Cousin Tree would be working with Papa and his boys might be helling around—they hated to work the ferry at night. But Jimroe jangled the bell and whistled and soon a lantern bobbed down to the ferry, and Tree came over, with the chain wailing every time he yanked. Tree welcomed Miss Cassie like she was anybody else he could squeeze for an extra penny. He stopped the ferry a few feet out in the river, and held the lantern to see who was there so that he could dicker for the passage.

Tree's character was perfect for coon hunting or most anything else, but when he stepped aboard the ferry he could be as cross-grained as any man who ever wore shoe leather.

"Who's there?" Tree said.

Jimroe went out in the lantern light with the bags.

"Great balls of blue mud," Tree said. "Here I get one night away from Hence Starling to catch a little shut-eye, and who rouses me but you two."

"We've got a lady, Tree."

"How much truck has she got?"

"Two boxes and a bag of hats and a trunk."

"Well, Sport, I'll have to get a quarter for all that."

"Come on, Tree," I said. "These little old boxes—and it hardly dark yet? You know the fare's fifteen cents."

Tree poled a few feet back into the river. "I don't give a hoot. Anybody who ain't got but fifteen cents, it don't matter what side the river she's on, anyway."

"Come back. You're already over here now. It won't cost you a cent to take her back with you."

I knew from Tree's voice that he had been drinking and had forgotten that the schoolteacher was coming.

Miss Cassie called. "Come back, sir. I'm the schoolmistress."

Tree held for a minute, and then banged the scow into shore. He was sullen at first, grumbling about schoolmarms. "Why in thunder couldn't you say so, Fax?" Then he saw her. "By God, nobody can say Trevilian Poindexter ain't a friend to education. I spend half my days trying to make something out of these Starling boys. Hop right on, miss. Set you over in a jiffy." He popped his fingers at me to hurry her bags aboard.

Butter wouldn't have melted in Tree's mouth. When she opened her purse to pay him, he acted like she had insulted his family on both sides back to the Year One. He went so far as to bring out Zelda and had her speak to the new teacher, and to let Miss Cassie hold their wild little young one, Freck. Tree kept watch to see that Freck didn't grab the teacher the way he did his mama, and there was some danger, too, because Miss Cassie had a noticeable bosom for such a little trick.

Miss Cassie looked out into the dark, listening. "If I didn't know better," she said, "I'd say one of you had an old wind-broken horse."

Jimroe took her to see the nag and she glanced at him in the light of the lantern and squatted, hitching up her skirts, and gave a quick look back through the horse's legs like an old-time horseman.

"Uh, oh," Tree said. "It ain't the first time she ever did that."

She went over the horse in a wink, and it was easy to see that she knew what she was doing. "What on earth are you doing with this poor thing?"

Jimroe didn't have much to say, but Tree explained how Wash Strawn had cheated Jimroe in one trade and then put the old horse over on him, too. Miss Cassie wanted to know more about Wash when she heard that he was the slickest trader in the county.

She took another look at the old horse. "That thing has running blood in him, or some of his line did. Are you sure he didn't come out of the old Gunmetal stock, over in Virginia?"

Jimroe said, "We know he's something good, out of a racing line. He's worth money, sorry as he sounds."

The teacher said the old horse was ten years overdue at the glue factory, and she wouldn't let us ride in the buggy behind him on the way when we went uphill. She made us walk alongside when the going was hard. Tree was so taken with Miss Cassie and her sense about horses that he went along too.

"I've been trying to drum up some way for old Jimroe to get his money back," Tree said. "We ought not to let him be slicked like that."

Miss Cassie said she would think about it. "I wish I had paid more attention to my daddy when I was a child. He could have fixed it in a wink. He used to say that he had traded for every horse in Virginia at least twice, and never got the wrong end of the bargain."

"He'd have made a good yoke-mate for Wash Strawn," Tree said.

"Come to think of it," Miss Cassie said, "I know he used to trade off windbroken horses. He had some way of passing them off so they seemed as sound as new. A man like you ought to know how."

She said no more about horse trading, and when we passed our lane on the way to town, Jimroe hopped off and went home. Tree and I took the teacher to Aunt Ly Sue's.

I knew why Jimroe had left us; he couldn't bear to have a woman knowing more about horses than he did, especially a teacher. He would have died before he would let her know that he was on fire to learn her idea about how he could cheat Wash Strawn.

All the lights were burning at Aunt Ly Sue's house, and people were scuttling around. "Looks like they've put the big pot in the little one for you," Tree said. You could smell almost anything there was to eat when you stepped in the house. Shad and Poll were so dressed up that I hardly knew them, and Judge Bucktarrel was there all combed and curried. The hall was full of old-fashioned roses from the garden.

Aunt Ly Sue was a raw-boned old lady, and when she leaned over Miss Cassie she was like a setting hen billing her chick. Without taking a deep breath she began telling Miss

Cassie who was who and who wasn't and where all the bodies were buried in Corona, and what families weren't speaking. Judge Bucktarrel tried to flag her with a joke and Miss Cassie smiled and tried to help, but Aunt Ly Sue rolled on. Shad took Miss Cassie and her things up the stairs and Aunt Ly Sue walked at her heels up and back, still talking as fast as she could.

"And I want you to know, dear, that you'll hear not one word of gossip underneath this roof, but there's some facts of life a woman's got to know—obliged to, coming to a strange town. They say the gossips are bad in this place. Law, if the Angel Gabriel came to Corona they wouldn't leave a feather in his wings. But the Lord knows I'm not that kind."

Poll had been sipping behind Aunt Ly Sue's back and she grumbled. "Oh, Lord knows. Old Ly Sue ain't no hand to gossip—why else does she fetch in all these schoolmarms for me to fuss over?"

Aunt Ly Sue shooed us off because company was coming to see Miss Cassie and she didn't want us standing around there in dirty overalls like country come to town. Tree and I went out, and Miss Cassie came to the porch and yelled after us, "Don't forget, Mister Poindexter. Put your thinking cap on, and find us a way to make that old stallion pass muster." Aunt Ly Sue looked at her like she had spoken in the Tongues.

Tree whistled on the way home.

"Sport, there's been nothing like that little woman to cross this county since Halley's Comet."

"She'll be the best schoolteacher of all."

"Hell, I clean forgot she come to teach. You wait. She's too pretty for comfort. Even her dimples have dimples. And that head of hers is full of gray matter. You watch out she don't use it on you."

"Ain't it funny she's just the age of Jimroe—and her the

teacher and been to college? Just going on eighteen."

"Age is no matter. She'll be pure unshirted hell in the schoolhouse, and don't you think she won't."

Tree climbed out of the buggy when we came to our place, and walked home in the pitch dark by himself. I led Jimroe's old horse up our hill, along the lane between the ruts, holding the nag by the cheek strap. When I'd gone halfway to our house I smelled one of Frank's homemade cigarettes. Frank was squatting in sassafras brush beside the lane with a rifle across his knees. I stopped.

"Get," he said.

"What's the matter?"

"If you don't get on . . ." His voice was hard. I pulled the horse along and tied him in the yard. The only light in the house was in the kitchen, where Mama had Cornelia and Ivy and the little ones at the table. Cornelia was reading aloud from *Grit*. Millers and all kinds of other moths flapped around the hanging lamp. When I stepped on the porch they looked toward the door. Mama whispered, "Don't worry, Faxie. It's all right."

Jimroe was upstairs by our window with my .22 and his shotgun.

"Hell to pay," he said.

"What're they doing?"

"Watching for burners. They got about half of our big barn of tobacco."

"Who did?"

"How would we know?"

"When was it?"

"Just as it got dust-dark."

"Maybe wasn't burnt on purpose."

"Hell, don't you know doodlesquat about anything? They drug out a big pile of our best leaf and lit it outside the barn. Papa found burnt corncobs that had been soaked in kerosene."

"What did Papa say?"

"He won't guess, and said he'd not have us guessing. He wants to make good and sure."

Jimroe pointed over the ridge to where the corncrib was and I saw sparks streaking up and smelled burned tobacco. He said that Damon and Creed were lying out in the dark by the lower barns, and that whoever saw somebody sneaking around would give a turkey yelp so that they could close in on the burners.

"Jimroe, who would want to burn us out?"

"Some fool halfbreed or other."

For a second I thought Jimroe knew something. "I'm going out tomorrow and see," I said.

"Precious lot you could tell."

"Was it somebody we know, you reckon?"

"All I know is, they'd better not show up here again, if they want to live and do well." Jimroe sounded like he wished somebody would come so that he could shoot. The little boys came up, big-eyed, and went to bed without a word. I sat with Jimroe.

"What would Papa do if we caught 'em?"

"Somebody wouldn't live to see the sun come up."

I wondered if I could tell Jimroe about Pem Sixkiller—but I knew in a flash that he'd tell Papa, and it was too late for that. If I told now, they would blame me for the burnt tobacco and everything.

I woke up under the window in the morning. Jimroe was still there, yawning over his shotgun. It took me a minute to remember where I was and what I was going to do.

Nobody said much at breakfast, and Papa pretended that nothing had happened, so as not to scare the girls. "We're in no danger," he said. "Somebody warned us—I don't know just why. We never treated our neighbors common, that I know of. But if they'd wanted to burn us out, they would have fired all the barns last night, and not that little pile."

Half a dozen men came during the morning to talk with Papa in the yard and poke in the ashes at the corncrib. I

watched my chance, and when nobody noticed I eased into
the woods and went along our ridge toward the river, hunting for tracks. It was where Pem would have had to come if
he walked from his place to our tobacco barns. The path
was rocky except for a low saddle, where the dust lay deep.

I found two sets of tracks there, going and coming. They
were pretty fresh. One big man and a smaller one, both
barefoot. I studied them as carefully as I could, the way
Tree had taught me, and made up my mind. It had to be
Pem and his boy Jiggs. I knew it as well as if they'd been
standing there in the tracks.

I went a ways toward their house, going slow, bent so far
down that I could almost smell the tracks. I was poking
along like that, about to lose the prints on the leaves and
rocks, when I saw two big bare feet. I jumped. It was Tree.

"Nice morning," he said.

"Oh, Lord."

"Well, boy, I didn't go to jar you out of a year's growth
—I thought I'd taught you to watch where you were
going."

"I was trailing."

"I know. I saw you come. You worked 'em good."

"Then you know it's the Sixkillers."

"What is?"

"You know. They hate us. It was them burnt the tobacco
last night. They're going to burn us out."

Tree stopped me. "How long has all this been going on?"

So I told him about the tobacco that had been burned in
the night, and how Papa and the big boys had stood guard. I
told him what Pem had threatened, that day by our springhouse, and what Jess had said.

Tree gave a little whistle. "Just when did you hear that
ugly talk?"

I told him, and he thought for a minute. "What did your
papa say?"

"He don't know, and I can't tell him now."

"I expect he'd want to know."

"Naw, sir. Not yet. Not after all this time of not telling him. Not when I could have stopped all our trouble."

"All right, boy. You needn't be so toucheous with me."

"Tree, I wanted to tell you before."

"It makes me proud that you told me at all. I knew something had ailed you lately. I thought maybe it was the Schoolmarm Fever."

I poked him in the ribs and he laughed. "And don't let the Sixkillers worry you. We can handle 'em when the time comes, if it does." He was looking sober in the face again. "And if we're going to take care of it ourselves, just try and let it blow over, if it will."

That made me more comfortable.

"And for God's sake, don't tell your papa right now. He wouldn't wait to ask questions."

"All right," I said. "Some day I've got to tell. I'm bound to."

"Some day's soon enough."

11

A Lesson for Wash

Jimroe thought he was going to lose his old horse the first week. He couldn't make him eat. He tried him on cracked corn and oats and even bran, but the nag was so far gone that he could do nothing but make a noise in the trough. He sounded like death when he snuffled, sucking air through his head. He couldn't swallow a mouthful until Tree came to show Jimroe how.

Tree came early, before Papa and the big boys had come in from the tobacco barn watch. He woke us by thumping shot against the window, and called Jimroe down.

"I finally thought of what to do," he said. "I'm going to

doctor your old bag of bones so that you can trade him back where he belongs."

He took Jimroe to the barn and made a mush of corn meal and fed the nag by hand to get him started; the two of them kept at it like they were working over a sick baby, and Jimroe was in the barn half the next night, feeding the horse every time he could make him eat. By morning the old thing was almost lively and had begun to swell in the belly.

Jimroe was surprised, but Tree said, "You ain't seen any-thing yet. I've got another bait or two for Wash Strawn. We'll teach him to go preying on little boys for his horse swapping."

Jimroe said he was no damn little boy but he was in a hurry to see what other crookedness Tree had thought of. Tree pulled out a little yellow sponge, the kind he used to oil his guns; we knew he meant business, if he would part with that. He cut two small circles from the sponge and tied a short piece of string to each one. Then Tree had Jimroe and me truss the horse's head in a halter and bind him against a barn post, so that he couldn't move.

"Watch now," Tree said. He took a thin stick and pushed a sponge up each nostril of the old horse, as gently as he could. The horse kicked once and was still. When he had the sponges way up the horse's nose, with the strings dangling down inside where they could be reached, Tree untied the nag. The old thing snorted, but the sponges stayed in place. We couldn't hear the windy breathing any more. Tree had turned him off until he was quiet as any horse could be.

Jimroe wanted to run right over to try a trade, but Tree held him back. "It'll fool Wash blind, I expect—it's mighty nigh the world's oldest horse trick, and that's the best kind. But you wait."

Tree said the horse needed more. "He already passes for ten years younger, without that bellows pumping, but we can do better. And to think I'd never have got these notions if it hadn't been for that schoolteacher. She's an inspiration to anybody who's got to cheat to keep body and soul together."

Tree cut tiny slits in the horse's loose skin where it sagged in hollows under his eyes. Then he found a goose quill, cut it short, and puffed in the hollows until they were swelled out smooth and plump. He rubbed axle grease into the cuts and you couldn't tell a thing. The horse had lost the gaunt look in his face. Tree said he was ready.

He told us to take him into town and find Wash. "Hurry. You can't be all day about it. In an hour or so the air will work out of his head, and Lord knows how long the sponges will hold."

Jimroe thought Wash might catch on. "You know good and well he'll spot the old thing as soon as he lays eyes on him."

"Sure he will," Tree said. "He'll know him at a glance. That's what makes it so rich. He'll be wild to know what you've done to the old thing. If you fool Wash, he'll buy him all over again."

We went slowly past the Boneyard, hoping for a sight of Wash. He wasn't there, and we trailed down the side road to his house. We saw the old man by the creek with a fishing pole and Jimroe led the nag up close, near enough so that Wash wouldn't miss a thing. We clambered down to the creek.

"I reckon you think I'm afishing," Wash said.

"Seems like, your line in the water and all."

Wash jerked his head toward his cabin. "My old woman's on the porch keeping watch. I can't touch one drop of liquor if she knows it." He eased up his fishing line and a pint whiskey bottle came out of the water. He turned his back, took a quick gurgle, and let it down into the creek. "She don't mind my fishing. She says it's good to steady me down, somehow."

Wash yapped at Jimroe, "Well, hoss trader, what's on your mind?" He was full of himself.

"I just come to see if we were still friends, Sheriff."

"None closer and none truer, son."

"Then how come you to tell me that old horse was just a weensy bit windbroke?"

"Ah, son. Just a manner of speaking." Wash jammed his fishing pole in the mud and put his hands around our shoulders, like a preacher passing out blessings. He was so proud of beating Jimroe in another trade that he was about to pop. "What I *meant* was, he ain't more than a touch windbroke—like you hear of women being just a leetle bit pregnant." Wash laughed.

"I believe I gave you more of the truth than you gave me, Mister Wash."

"Not enough wasted to hurt, on either side," Wash said. "You know, son, I had trouble getting rid of your blind mare yesterday—I never made but a twelve-dollar profit on her."

He dropped his voice and dug Jimroe with his elbow to rub it in. "Don't tell nobody, son, but I skinned my man with the same trick I used on you when I traded you that blind mare. I just dropped a little grain sugar in her eyes and it cut that cloudy film off in a wink. The fellow that bought her never dreamed she was blind—any more than you did. Remember that, son, if you are ever forced to cheat a fellow mortal in a trade. What they don't know won't hurt 'em."

Jimroe stalked up the path pretending to be sore. Wash yelled after him, "Now, son, I was only aiming to teach you. If you're going to live by your wits in this evil world and trade horses and all, you've got to look sharp."

Wash was so cocksure over having cheated Jimroe that he hadn't troubled to look at the old horse until that instant—and then he saw how different the nag was in the face, younger and stronger. It broke over him all at once that he hadn't heard the horse fighting to get his breath. Wash gave a low whistle. I looked back as we walked toward town and saw him rubbing his chin. He looked a little hacked.

We had to wait when we got to Biscoe's store. Toots Kinnamon was ahead of us and was taking her time. We sat on sugar bags while Tootsy pawed through things, because we had to buy something for Mama. Jimroe wanted to give Wash time to come along and see the old horse, too.

Red Dowd was trying to wait on Tootsy and wasn't bright enough to see that she only wanted to talk with Biscoe Allen. Biscoe was in back of the store with his wife, arguing. She was after money and Biscoe was giving her down in the country for being wasteful. He was the richest man in the county, and as Papa said, it wasn't by accident.

"What's lemons worth, Red?" Tootsy said.

"The devil with lemons. We don't keep 'em no more. Soon as I get 'em in, you fool women buy 'em up and they hardly last the week. What's the good of stocking stuff like that?"

"You ain't got the sense God promised a jaybird. Why the hell do you want stuff in here unless it's to sell?"

Red said he didn't hire out to cater to the whim of every idiot woman who could think up some way to waste his time, and that he would go on being stock clerk in that store till Biscoe cut off his pay, and that he would buy what he damn well pleased to buy.

Tootsy kept walking along the counter, talking to Red but keeping an eye on Biscoe. She finally ordered. "Gimme a dime's worth of assy-fettity and a root of ginseng, and about three bales of Sweetpea Snuff—and if you've got something for the All-Overs, Mister Red, I'm feeling right peaked, this weather."

Red was bundling up her stuff, yanking twine from his beehive holder with one end of the string in his mouth, when

Tootsy laid down the check Jess Sixkiller had given her. Red cut his eyes at her to see if she was trying to pull something.

"What in hell's that supposed to be?"

"Why, a check. The Randolph Bank. Ain't you ever seen a check?"

"How much is it supposed to be for?"

"Now, I never asked the gentleman. At least ten-twelve dollars. Red Dowd, can't you read—and you aclerking in a damn store?"

That was an insult. Everybody knew Red had been reading law in Judge Bucktarrel's office for months before he took a regular job.

"Ah, Toots, that's no check. Who in Tophet gave it to you?"

Biscoe Allen and his wife snapped up their heads and looked toward Tootsy and fell quiet. Tootsy hesitated.

"This ain't even writing on here," Red said. "Just hen tracks. Can't you remember who it was gave it to you?"

"I'll tell you this much. It was somebody I damn well thought could write his name ten dollars' worth."

"Well, I never," Red said.

"You don't mean you won't cash it for me, Dowd?"

"It ain't worth the paper it's written on."

"Have you took over this country—telling folks what's money and what ain't? You're a regular Mister Know-It-All."

"I know enough to stay away from that pigpen place you keep."

"Who you think you're atalking to, Dowd?"

"You think folks don't know what goes on over there—Indians and Redshanks and God knows what sneaking in on one side of the clock and white folks on the other? One of these days you're going to blow things in this county sky-high, and then we'll see how far your downcome will be."

"You're one piece of white trash won't be there when she blows," Tootsy said. "I reckon Mister Biscoe would want to cash this check for me." Biscoe straightened like he had been tickled with a bull whip from behind. "Won't you cash my check for me, Mister Biscoe?"

Biscoe came, squeezing out a measly smile, looking over his spectacles at the check. His wife watched him. He traced a finger over Jess's scratchings and moved his lips, pretending to read. He mumbled, "Ah, Miss Tootsyroll Kinnamon. Ah. Twelve dollars—no, I see that's a ten. Ah . . ." He spoke to Red Dowd. "Well, Mister Dowd. I think it's all right. I feel like I know who wrote this. I do. I believe I can collect it for Tootsy if we have to." He shoved the check in his pocket in a hurry.

"I sure hoped you would, Mister Biscoe, good a customer as I am, and all."

Tootsy held her palm to Red Dowd and took her change. When she went out, Biscoe's wife flashed a look at the fat legs Tootsy showed over her brogans.

Red Dowd started to wait on us, but Biscoe stepped in front of him and barked like he was glad to change the subject.

"What's for you, boys?"

While he got up things we wanted for Mama, Biscoe's wife opened his cash drawer and took a ten-dollar bill and waved it at Biscoe.

"I'm agoing to Randolph and get me that new frock right now," she said. "I guess it's all right, ain't it?"

"I never said it wasn't. I've been thinking how nice you'd look in a new getup."

"I bet so, *Mis*ter Biscoe. I just bet you have."

Biscoe's face looked like he could cloud up and rain.

We went outside and there was Wash Strawn, fooling around the old horse.

"All right, boys," Wash said. "Tell me what in thunderation you done to him. I admit you've got me skinned."

"He just had a little case of the glimpses, Mister Wash," Jimroe said.

"That's a new one on me. What kind of ailment is it?"

"Why, he could glimpse that good food, but never could get none of it."

"Ah, talk sense, boy. What'd you do to him?"

"We fed him, you old skinflint."

"Like hell. He couldn't bite a biscuit."

Jimroe had brought some corn meal, and dipped a handful of water from one of Biscoe's rain barrels to make a mush. He held it in his hand and the poor nag gulped it, rumbling in the belly. Wash scratched his head. He went around the horse, putting his head against the bony ribs to listen; there wasn't a sound of the old windbroken bellows. Wash stared in the horse's face. "I don't believe it. Nothing alive could eat enough mush in two days to make the difference. It's some damn Starling trick—or worse, Poindexter."

Jimroe held up his right hand and dared the Lord to strike him dead on the spot if he wasn't telling the truth about the horse eating mush like a baby. "Mister Wash, I give you my word he's been sucking in that mush day and night."

"Yeah, and what else have you devils fed him, to stop his windiness just like that?" He popped his fingers.

"Not a thing, I tell you."

"I know," Wash said. "You used strychnine. I ought to have known. They say strychnine will cure the windbreak for a day or two."

Jimroe yelped so that Wash almost believed him. "Naw, sir, Mister Wash. I never heard of that stuff, whatever it is, let alone fed it to a horse. This horse ain't taken in one single solitary thing but mush since we've had him—unless you want to count some good, clean, healthy John Virden County air. Ain't it so, Fax?"

Jimroe said that I was famous for never having told a lie in my life, and I looked as honest as I could on short notice and held up my hand and swore to it.

Wash began to lean. "All right then, sir. I'll just give him my little windbroken test, and if he's sound, who knows? I just might want to take him off your hands—if the price got down to right."

Wash took the horse's bridle and ran as hard as he could go on his short wooden leg, pumping up and down in the dusty road. He went almost out of sight, then came humping back, trotting the horse. When he stopped he leaned again to listen for the telltale sucking of air. He couldn't hear a thing. Wash was puffing and blowing.

"By George, I believe I'm more windbroke than he is. I don't know, son. I'm a fool, I reckon, but I want to chance him. How'd you trade?"

"I'd hate to do it, Mister Wash," Jimroe said. "No disrespect or nothing—but you wouldn't have time to tend this old fellow like he ought to be tended."

"You trying to tell me how to care for stock, you young strip?"

"All I know is, Mister Wash, somebody had to be up feeding him nights to get him back to life."

"Boy, I was trading horseflesh before your daddy was born, when he was just a wicked gleam in old Grant Starling's eye. What'd you say you'd take for this nag?"

"Since it's you, Mister Wash, and old family friends and all, I've cut him down to twenty dollars."

Wash squalled and stomped his peg leg and said the horse hadn't brought that much when he was sold five years before. They hassled, but Wash had gone crazy to have the horse back, and in the end Jimroe took twelve dollars from him and gave Wash the old thing. He asked Wash not to let folks know how cheap he had let him go.

"What they don't know won't hurt 'em, will it, Mister Wash?"

Wash made a face. He couldn't get used to the way Jimroe spoke up to him in a trade, like a grown man, even if he did look like a half-grown boy.

We worried all the way home over Wash coming back on Jimroe about the old horse, but Tree laughed when we told him.

"You needn't worry. Old Wash will never peep. In a few hours the nag will snort out them sponges, or Wash will find 'em, and will be so shamed of having been fooled that he'll never crawl you about it. He'll snoop until he finds out how we tricked him on the nag's face, too, and if he's right bright he'll use the sponges on somebody else, and get him some goose quills to boot."

Jimroe got airy about it. "Ah, hell," he said. "It wasn't a thing but one or two old Indian tricks that any fool could have thought up. You might know tricks, all right, but it takes something else to get in there and talk Wash Strawn out of hard cash."

Tree winked at me. "That's right," he said. "You're a big man, and we ain't anything but hired hands—and the lady who put that bug in my ear is only a schoolmarm. I doubt she'll last long around here."

Jimroe strutted in the house to supper, hoping that somebody would ask him about his trade, and finally had to tell it himself. I would sooner have swallowed my tongue than helped him out.

12

New Broom in the Schoolhouse

It was only early fall, but it was like ending one year and beginning a new one when we had to quit fooling with tobacco for a while and go back to school. A gaggle of the least kids from our end of the county went by our house not long after sunup one morning, and we fell in with them. We trailed along pretty fast, thinking that we would get there before the teacher and play ball and get used to being on the school grounds again before we had to face her.

Miss Cassie was standing in the door. The room had been

swept and there was fresh water in the bucket with a new dipper floating there. She was ready to go.

Our building was what we called an Old Field School-house, a shack perched on stilts on the mountainside with a fairly level yard around it, rough and weedy and surrounded by woods. Hunters often came by the door, chasing game. We couldn't see the village of Corona Crossroads because of the woods, but if we climbed the bell tower we could have looked down the hill a mile or so away to see Biscoe Allen's store and the tobacco warehouse and the black-smith's and the few houses in town. Corona Crossroads was so little that Tree said, "Town, hell. You'd poke it with a stick before you ever saw it."

We had one room and about forty children in our school, and we ran from the First to the Sixth Readers—all with Miss Cassie to teach us. Some were only five years old, and the worst boys ran up to more than twenty—but they didn't come at first. From our family, only Trout and Ivy and Cornelia and I went to school the first few days, because we could be spared from the work. Jimroe and the others couldn't come until later.

In the middle of the schoolhouse an iron stove squatted in a sandbox, where the big boys would spit their tobacco juice. Girls sat on one side of the room, with boys on the other, and we had homemade benches and desks. Up front was the water stand, and Miss Cassie sat at a table with a blackboard slate. There were two windows and only one door, and cracks in the walls wide enough to fling a cat through. Our necessary houses were outdoors at the edge of the woods, with boys' and girls' about a hundred yards apart.

We read our lessons all at once, and until you got used to it the racket was fierce. Little five-year-old girls squeaked and the oldest boys growled like bumblebees in tar buckets. Miss Cassie sat as straight as an ironing board without touch-

ing her back to the chair, and took turns hearing our lessons
while the other children hummed on. Her hair was pulled
hard across her head and done up in little balls over her ears,
about the size of biscuits and just the color of butter.

We opened with a Bible reading and everybody had to
take a turn, so we passed the Bible around. Then we sang
"The Star-Spangled Banner" and pledged allegiance to the
flag—but without a flag in the room. When she caught one
of us whispering or fiddling around, Miss Cassie popped him
on the hand with her ruler, sounding like she was swatting a
mosquito. When we miscalled words in the reading, we had
to look them up in a big Page's Dictionary on her table and
all of us tried to learn to spell them. None of us knew what
they meant.

Miss Cassie began the first day to see how far she could go
with us. "Children, what would you say if I asked you if
you wanted to go home early today?"

"Yase, ma'am!"

She made my sister Ivy stand up.

"Did you say 'Yes, ma'am'?"

"Yase'm."

"Would you come up and write the word 'yase' on the
slate? "

Ivy wrote it out for her, y-e-s, and Miss Cassie said that
Ivy was a crackerjack speller.

"I guess it's a surprise to you children, but this word is
pronounced *yes* just about everywhere else in the country.
We don't say *yase*—and we don't say *naw* for *no*, either. If
you went to other places and talked like that, people would
laugh at you."

While we tried to get that down, she said that there were
places in the world where people didn't say *ma'am* every
time they opened their mouths around a grown lady. She
went on with the lessons, taking all of us in turn, and it was
dinnertime before we knew it. We snatched our dinner pails

and went out to eat and play. I went back in for a dipper of water and saw Miss Cassie open her lunch at the table.

Aunt Ly Sue was known to be stingy and the sorriest cook in Corona, and I could tell she had put up Miss Cassie's dinner herself. When the teacher opened the pail she had nothing but two hunks of light bread with a canned tomato slapped between, so that it was just a handful of pink sog. Miss Cassie made a tight little mouth and sent me to Biscoe Allen's store with a quarter, and I got her some potted meat and sardines and soda crackers. Afterward she stopped at Biscoe's every morning on her way to school and got something for her dinner. I was sorry she didn't let me run that errand for her so that I could be alone with her in the schoolhouse for a minute or two; she smelled like lemon verbena when you got near her.

I forgot about *yase'm* and *naw*, but the next day one of the little ones hobbled to school and told Miss Cassie that his papa had licked him for putting on airs and said it was none of the teacher's damned business what he learned at home. We heard no more of that from Miss Cassie, except that as an example she talked like she wanted us to talk—but sometimes, in the heat of playing ball, she slipped and said *yase* herself.

We thought she must have noticed our smell in school. She kept somebody opening our windows even after cold weather came, and sometimes when she could no longer stand us she broke in on our lessons and turned us out for recess, no matter what the weather. Once or twice I saw her pat a little perfume under her chin when she finished eating, and I thought it might be so that she couldn't tell what all of us smelled like in there. At recess she was always getting out a little mirror and primping her hair, too.

At home Mama began teasing me when nobody else was around. I was getting up earlier every morning and hustling through my chores before the others stirred, and went into the kitchen for breakfast. Mama would say, "Where you off to in such a rush, boy? I know you're not old enough for a sweetheart." I would gobble corn mush and milk without waiting for bacon and eggs, and go to school. When I took the short cut through the woods I usually beat Miss Cassie there.

I did the sweeping then, or got fresh water, and lots of times did extra studying, and left my work on the slate so that she would notice. Then I went outside quick, before any of the others came and caught me.

When all of us went inside after Miss Cassie rang the bell, and we had finished the Bible reading and prayer, I watched to see who she would notice first in the crowd. I hated any other boy she looked at first, or called on to do his lesson before me.

But when Jimroe and the other big boys finally came to school, everything changed. Jimroe and I had begun to get away from each other at home, too. I hardly ever found him around. He worked with Papa and my older brothers, keeping watch over our tobacco and sometimes going to town with Papa to talk about the opening of the tobacco market. Jimroe was out late at night, and finally moved out of our big bed into the room with Creed and Damon. He had begun to dress in Damon's old clothes when he went into town, and wore his hair slicked down. Once before he went to school, Jimroe asked me lots of questions about Miss Cassie, but pretended to pay no attention to what I said about her.

It was late when the big boys came to school, for they wouldn't go until the very last minute, when they had run out of excuses. None of them would even talk about going until tobacco curing was over. But most of all they waited until they got baseball out of their systems for the year. Most of them played on our county league team, and Corona usually won the league, and people like our ballplayers didn't bother much with school. Baseball was played until late fall, since we had no other games. It didn't matter; we had no grades in school, and every year each one went as far as he could in the Readers, and took up in the place where he had left off when the next year came.

The big boys came to school for the first time one rainy, cold morning, about ten of them in a bunch, and we knew they had been up to something. They crowded around the stove and took the warmest seats. Jimroe was one of the first to fall asleep by the hot stove. Then I knew what made him look peculiar. They had been drinking. I knew it wouldn't take much to do him in, because he wasn't used to it.

Miss Cassie had a careful eye on all the big boys, and especially on Jimroe. She had heard how Jimroe had clonked our old teacher on the head with a baseball bat the year before—but she didn't know that it wasn't really Jimroe's fault. Miss Mary B. Smitherman had tried to break up a baseball argument in the yard and had walked under Jimroe's bat while he was flailing it around. She had got her scalp laid open the width of your hand, and had to be sewed up by a doctor. The grown folks didn't forgive Jimroe and he got a stout licking for it at home. It had finished Miss Smitherman. So Miss Cassie kept an eye on Jimroe like she was thinking of that but wasn't afraid of him. She just watched.

Miss Cassie was hearing the Third Reader people when Jimroe fell out of his seat. He fell on his face beside the stove and didn't stir, lying there with a foolish smile. Miss Cassie was over him in a flash, trying to give him artificial respiration. When she found she couldn't push hard enough she put one of the other boys to work.

"Open the window," she said. Her hair was beginning to string down in her face.

Jimroe didn't move. When the kids saw what she was trying to do, they couldn't hold in any longer. The little ones tittered and the big boys broke out in a roar and beat at each other and almost tore the place down. They fell on the floor holding their bellies, or staggered around laughing.

Miss Cassie finally shook Ivy to her senses. "What on earth's the matter? What's wrong with Jimroe?"

"He's . . . he's drunk." And we bawled again.

She had him dragged outside until he came to. Miss Cassie got after me.

"What has he been drinking?"

"Just cider wine."

"What on earth?"

We explained that it was only hard cider with the juice poured off after it had been frozen, and then poured off again after another freeze, and then kept for a year or so until it was mellow. When Jimroe came to himself she said nothing to him, but he knew that he had better not try that again. She kept the big boys after school that day. Some of us listened under the schoolhouse.

"Boys, I came to teach you a little something and not to run a circus. You're bigger than I am and lots of you are older, but I'm paid to handle the school and so long as I'm here, I'll do it."

They were quiet and she chirped again. "Some day it might come over you just how overgrown and ignorant you are. Maybe you'll have the grace to be ashamed of yourselves. But yes or no, you'll not break up school for the young ones who want to learn. You behave, or you're going home."

One of them growled and she shushed him. "You needn't treat me like I hadn't a grain of sense. I know we have some silly rules, but I didn't make them.

"For one thing, we'll have no smoking on the school grounds. It's against the state law. It may be foolish, but the state doesn't know that. They keep thinking about the little ones. I don't care how much you smoke, if you're out of my sight, but if I see you at it, you'll go home."

After that Miss Cassie paid more attention to Jimroe. She loaded things on him, so that he hardly had time for devilment. She made him captain of the lightard knot brigade, and about half of every day he had a crew of us in the woods hunting up old pine knots so full of resin that they would explode when you lit them in the school stove. They were the kindling for our fires.

That wasn't enough, so Jimroe had to fetch the water from a spring about a quarter of a mile away. He soon had that worked out so that he could boss, and two little kids lugged the buckets. When Jimroe fidgeted she sent him alone for water, even if the bucket was almost full.

I had to find new things to do in the early mornings before the teacher came. For a while I worked on handwriting. Papa said I already wrote like a girl, I had worked on it so much, but I kept practicing, and one morning Miss Cassie helped me. I was writing on the slate at my desk: "Raleigh is the capital of North Carolina," and all about Sir Walter Raleigh, from my Reader, when she leaned over my shoulder and touched me in several places without realizing it. The lemon smell was all around us and she covered my hand with hers and helped me make my letters smoother, straighter up and down. The other children came in while we were working and she moved her hand off, but it was a long time before the warmth of her palm went away, and I thought I could feel her pulse beating. During recess, when I took a dipper of water from the bucket, I got another whiff of her lemon perfume, because I had drunk just after her. The water had a different taste to me. Every time I saw her take a drink from the dipper I had to keep myself from running to be next to drink, for fear the kids would notice.

She worked to keep the rest of them busy and I helped her. When I had finished my Reader for the day, I would go into a corner with some of the youngest ones and help teach them. Once she bragged on me about that before the others, and that made me shy away for a few days.

Miss Cassie paired the smart ones with the dull ones and

mixed the Indians with the whites on both sides of the room, and got even the worst Indians interested by making them stand up and tell things about the way their people lived— almost anything she could think of. And so we got on together.

One day we found out Miss Cassie wasn't afraid of any of us, or anybody else.

Two of the roughest Indian boys, Perry Poindexter and Dock Sixkiller, decided to take over her school for the term. Perry was a pure Hockaway and Dock was Pembroke Sixkiller's son, a Redshank, so that their people had little to do with each other. But those two had run together most of their lives and were as close as brothers. They put on a fight in the schoolyard.

They smacked each other with open palms and hopped around kicking dust, cussing and making what they thought were Indian war whoops until lots of us had circled them. We could see that they were only playing, but all of us thought that Miss Cassie would think somebody was going to be killed.

The Indians planned to make her run out there, and have her give them a sissy lecture and tell them to be good boys and an example to the little ones, and then they could turn on the rest of us and slap us around and do as they pleased. Miss Cassie came out and watched a minute until she saw what they were up to.

"All right," she said. "You're both Indians, and old enough to be warriors. No Indian is a coward. Now take off your coats and fight until one of you has enough, and let's get it over with. The winner will be our Indian champion."

They were sheepish at first, but when Perry's fist caught Dock under the ribs and got him in the short breath, things began to happen. Fists cracked on jawbones and skulls and they elbowed and kicked and butted and got more vicious all the time. They remembered the differences between Hockaways and Redshanks and all the old insults their families had thrown at each other. It was a kind of tribe war.

Blood from Perry's nose spattered both of them and made them fight harder. They shuffled and hit until Perry fell. He was up in a hurry and dragged Dock down by the knees and they went together like boar weasels, pulling hair and gouging eyes and kneeing in the groin and playing hell. Miss Cassie let them go on until Perry quit. He was panting and had blood all over him, and one sprained wrist was puffing. They called it off with bitter half-grins, because they knew that Miss Cassie had put one over on them. It was the last trouble they gave her.

13

Everybody Whips Me

Almost all of us in school scribbled on our skin with ink when we did our writing lessons. We had a way of drawing faces in our palms, with the eyes across the big lines, so that we could hold up our hands and make the little faces wink at other people across the room. Some wrote the names or initials of their sweethearts on their hands and arms.

One afternoon when I was fooling like that, without thinking of what I was doing I put Miss Cassie's initials on my wrist in big black letters—C C—and drew a heart around them. When it was dry I buttoned my sleeve so that nobody would see it, and then forgot it.

We went home in the usual way that evening, strung out in the road like a flock of geese. The little ones went first, with the boys in one crowd and the girls in another, with a lot of pushing and squealing and giggling. The older ones came behind—and away in the rear, so far that they wouldn't have to be seen with us, the big boys.

We had a game of follow-the-leader that day, with everybody in it except the big boys. We hopped across the road on one foot, jumped a branch, ran along logs, and things like that, until we came to an old beech tree beside a creek. A long limb hung out over the water. Talfourd Kemper was the leader, and he swung on the limb until he was far out, then hung down and skinned the cat and made a jump for the bank of the creek. He missed and fell at the edge of the water. There was a lot of whooping, and all the boys in the crowd had to try his trick.

When my turn came and I was hanging down from the limb, my sleeve ran up my arm and everybody saw the initials on my wrist. I saw them when my head skinned through my arms as I turned, but couldn't stop. I hung there for what seemed a long time, with that big "C C" showing. Somebody under me went "*Whoooooey!*" and they tried guessing who my sweetheart was—and then some girl guessed: "Fax loves Teacher. Fax looooooooooves Teacher."

I came out of the knot on the limb so hard that I made the creek bank, the first one to land there, and I was the leader then. I gave a half-hearted run at one or two of the others to try and make them shut up, but I knew better than to fight about it, because they would only yell louder and then the big boys would catch on and come to help tease me, and it would be more than I could stand. So I pretended that nothing was wrong. I wanted to run to the creek and wash off my wrist, but instead I went on playing leader as hard as I could.

I started throwing rocks because I knew that nobody else could keep up with me. I threw one in an old woodpecker hole about fifty feet up a locust tree, the first try, and hung around waiting for the others to follow. Nobody could, and so we went on. I walked a snake rail fence for a few yards and they came after me, and it wasn't long before they stopped singing about Miss Cassie. But then, when I lost my place as leader, trying to walk backward on the fence, some of them started again:

"Faaaax loves Teacher! Faxie has a sweetiepie. Oooh, you fast Fax!"

I was about to run for home when some of them began saying, "Shhhhh. Here she comes."

Miss Cassie was coming through the big boys in the road behind us, walking fast. Jimroe was with her, carrying her things and looking like she had him captive. She passed us nodding and smiling, and didn't hear them chanting at me. Jimroe didn't give us a look.

When she had gone ahead the children began all over again, but I didn't care much then. I half wished that she had heard them. I was jealous of Jimroe, walking with her.

It was that day that Dock Sixkiller's little brother, Jiggs, began picking on me. He was the loudest on the singsong and said lots of things about me and the teacher. He had never looked straight at me before, but for some reason was after me now.

The next week, when we went back to school, Jiggs hopped on me while we were playing in the yard. We were playing Gully Keeper, a game we had made up; all the kids got on one side of a ravine and ran down and scrambled up the far side, before the keeper, down in the bottom, could catch them. Jiggs was about my age and size, but rougher than any fifteen-year-old I ever saw. He wore smelly clothes cut down from the worn-out work clothes of his family, and homemade rawhide brogans so old that they had split in the back and were tied on him with string. He would fight like a hungry gamecock, and had whipped lots of the big boys in school.

Jiggs pretended to be sore because I caught him playing Gully Keeper, and jumped on me from the top of the gully and mauled me before I could get hold of him. He hit hard and fast and knocked me down two or three times. When I got up he cussed me. "Yeah, your daddy's a damn money hog, thinks he'll get all the tobaccer money. If he keeps on cheating folks, all your damn barns will get burnt."

He made me so mad that tears scalded my eyes and I couldn't see to hit him, and he finally ran me into the school-house. Then I was surer than ever that those tracks I had found on our ridge were made by Jiggs and his daddy, and that they had it in for us for good. I knew that it wasn't just Pembroke alone.

When school was out for the day, Jiggs ran and I couldn't catch him. I walked home through the woods and tried to spruce up a little. At supper there was some talk. Some of the kids had told Papa about my fight. The table got quiet while Papa talked to me, because he wasn't like we had seen him before. His eye was like a snake's, looking over some little bird.

"I heard you got a whipping."

"I guess I did."

"No guessing about it, is there?"

"Naw . . ."

"Naw, *sir*."

"Naw, sir. But he fell on me . . ."

"I don't give a hoot if he shot you with a cannon ball. Don't you ever back off."

"I'll get him."

"I don't want to hear more about it. Never let me hear of you picking a fight, but if you have to fight, fight to win."

"You don't know what it was he said."

"No, and don't care. You've got lickings coming all your life, one way or another. But if I hear of you taking one from a boy your own size, you'd better not come home. You'll get twice the thrashing when you get here."

I knew he meant business.

I laid for Jiggs Sixkiller the next afternoon. It was all too easy. He had set a trap for me. I ran after him when Miss Cassie turned us loose, and there he was at the edge of the woods, just out of the teacher's sight, with two of his cronies. They looked around pretty sharp to see if Jimroe was in sight because they knew that even if we did fight among ourselves, it would be too bad for them if Jimroe caught them ganging up on me. Jiggs squared off with his fists. "All right, ninnyboy. Come git some more."

We jigged around for a while, punching at each other's face. He hissed "White boy!" at me, like he thought that was the most low-down thing on earth. He said it with a lifted lip, as if it was too nasty for his mouth. Then he got me with a child's trick. His buddy Skin Chalk slipped behind me and got down on hands and knees so close to me that when Jiggs gave me a shove, I went over in a flip and hit the ground like a sack of meal. Jiggs lit on me and pounded away. Every time I turned him off, Skin and the other boy caught my feet and whirled me under. The harder I fought, the more they laughed. Jiggs didn't hurt me much, but I broke out bawling. I couldn't do a thing.

They ran when they were tired of playing with me. I just hoped that not too many people had seen us. I got home all right and it looked like I might have got away with it. There was no sign of trouble at supper. We had been asleep for half an hour when Papa yanked me out of the bed, lifting me by an arm and a leg so easy that the others barely stirred. He waltzed me into the yard by one arm. He didn't ask questions.

Papa kept a switch on the back porch, a crooked buck-berry limb that cut like barbed wire, and for a minute or two he drew the blood from my legs so that I could hardly bear it. I wanted to tell him the whole straight of the fight and the things that Jiggs had said about him—and even about Pembroke. But I was damned if I would beg. He made me dance with pain and I still wouldn't peep. I made up my mind that I wouldn't let him see me cry either. I could feel the blood on my hide and knew there would be wicked welts under the nightshirt.

When he was through I looked him in the face, like I would make him see the truth without telling him, but he turned and got a bucketful of water.

"Turn around. Lift your shirt." He sloshed icy water over my bottom and legs. It took my breath. "As soon's you dry off, get back in the bed." He went in the house.

I had lost my place in the bed and holed up on the edge, tugging for a share of quilt, blubbering and mumbling to the last, "The old fool. Old fool. Damn such as he is. I don't care if they do burn him out." I wondered how I could get even with Papa—and even thought for an instant that it might be true that he was trying to trick the Indian families and take most of the tobacco money. I thought that maybe they had a right to be jealous of him and his good crop. Then I was ashamed of myself. I went to sleep wondering how much Jiggs knew about us and what his daddy had told him.

There was more when we got back to school the next day. Miss Cassie made me shake hands with Jiggs in front of everybody and said that would be the end of fighting, any fighting, on her school grounds, even if she had to break up the whole term to stop it. She talked about how you could fight until you were blue in the face and still not settle anything worthwhile. Jiggs and I said we understood, and so did the other kids, and we sat down.

I didn't forget. Every time I saw Jiggs I knew that I had something to do to help Papa out; it made me feel better to think that Papa didn't even know it. So I studied Jiggs like I was going to murder him. I looked for every chance to get at him, and swore that I'd fix him if it was the last thing I did on earth. It took a while, it turned out.

14

Jimroe Goes Too Far

Jimroe couldn't leave Miss Cassie alone to save his life. He was forever pestering her in school. He could see that there wasn't much chance he could fool her about anything, but he never quit trying.

Once, when he came to school late and she asked him why, he gave her a smart-aleck tale that he had learned from Tree.

"I'm late because Roller has a cold nose."

"What's that got to do with coming in at noon?"

"Well, Roller's our best hound. Last night something got into the hen house and raised a fuss and Papa went out with his shotgun to see about it. He had on his nightshirt, and was stooped down on hands and knees by the hen house when old Roller came up behind him and touched him just right with his cold nose. Papa had his finger on the trigger, so I've been picking chickens all morning."

Miss Cassie took it good-naturedly, but she doubled Jimroe's work for the day and made him spell new words until he was sweating.

The next time, he dragged me into trouble with him. It came time for our best milk cow to go and see a bull, and Papa had spoken to Billy Lufler on the next farm, and made plans to send the cow to his prize Holstein bull. It was my chore. I hated to see the love season come on. The first sign was that the cow would be hard to milk, giving ropy cream into the bucket. She would hang around the fence all day, and moo and knock down posts trying to get out. She frisked until Papa told me it was time to take her to the Gentleman Cow.

It embarrassed me to lead her. I went along, fighting her every time we passed a fenced pasture or another cow, yanking at her when she saw a dog, or just anything that moved. I passed women working at a tobacco barn and had to walk close by them, feeling like I had been born with my skin wrongside out. The women didn't look at the cow, as if I was standing there with nothing at all on the end of my rope—but they kept me talking, about the weather and crops and just anything that came to mind. I was about to sink into the ground when they let me go. I heard them laughing behind me.

Then I had to pass Lufler's wife just as I went into their barn lot. She stood with an apronful of fresh eggs, looking at me, and I couldn't think of a thing to say. I couldn't tell her I'd come to have the cow serviced, so I just broke open the gate and went through. The cow saw the bull in the pasture and dragged me halfway there before I could turn her loose. I got her free and climbed a tree while they gallivanted

around, lowing and butting and chasing each other for half
an hour before anything happened—and then I had to run
her down in the woods and yank her home. I got to school
away up in the morning, and Miss Cassie lit in on me.

"Fax, where on earth have you been? Do your folks know
you played hooky?"

"Yes'm. I had to take the cow . . ."

She understood me, but wouldn't stop. "Couldn't your
papa have done it?"

Jimroe laughed. "Hell, Miss Cassie. Papa ain't even regis-
tered."

Miss Cassie didn't laugh with us, and Jimroe had to stay in
school until dark, and she never said a word to him.

It was then that she seemed to make up her mind to do
something about Jimroe.

One morning Jimroe came to school smoking a handmade
cigar from some of our own tobacco—a thing eight inches
long that he had made to show off, rolled in the pink outside
papers from a *Police Gazette* and packed with crumbled leaf
as strong as red pepper.

Miss Cassie caught him at the door. "Do you think that's
good for your health, young man?"

"I don't smoke 'em for my health."

She gave him a look but it didn't take.

"For that, I drink cider wine and run after women."

She sent him home like she had promised and he went off
as if he didn't care, but the next morning it was different.
Miss Cassie had a rule that when she sent you home you
couldn't come back to school unless your parents came to
get you in—both of them. Papa wasn't at home. He'd gone
with Billy Lufler and Slim Poindexter down to Winston to
talk about the tobacco trouble.

Jimroe came to school by himself that morning, with a
note. Miss Cassie made the rest of us stay outside while she
talked to him. We listened.

I knew what was in Jimroe's note, because Mama had

raised such a ruckus about it the night before that the whole household was in an uproar. The note said that Papa was away and that Miss Cassie should for the Lord's sake keep Jimroe in school; Mama didn't want him at home with Papa gone, and she couldn't give him the licking he deserved.

Miss Cassie was quiet for a while, like she was reading the note, and then said, "Well, I don't see what I can do about this. You know the rule. I've got to send you home."

Jimroe wasn't talking so big and I knew what was wrong. He was afraid of what would happen when Papa got home.

"What Mama wants you to do is written there on the back," Jimroe said.

I knew that note, too. It said, "Please give him a whipping for me."

"Jimroe, you know good and well I can't give you a whipping—and you almost a grown man."

"Yes'm, you can. Sure you can."

"Does your mother have any idea what size woman I am?"

"No'm, I guess not, but it don't matter. I'd appreciate it if you would beat me and get it over with, and not take it up with Papa or anything."

"All right, sir. If that's what you'll have. Go get me a switch."

Jimroe came back from the woods with a stick bigger around than his thumb and she sent him out again. "You know I can't handle that big thing. Bring me a little hickory branch, just a limber withe."

When Jimroe came back she made him roll up his britches legs and bend over.

"Go ahead," he said.

Miss Cassie waited. "In Colonial times they gave prisoners thirty-nine lashes," she said. "How many do you think would be fair for you?"

"I guess I could stand about ten."

She hesitated. "Now, Jimroe, don't forget your dreadful

temper. Don't lose your head and do something you'd be sorry for."

"No'm. I won't. Go ahead."

"Now, if you have had all you can stand when I get to five or six—you yell for me to stop."

"All right'm."

Half a dozen of us crawled from under the schoolhouse to the windows and watched. Jimroe was bent down, holding his ankles, with his britches legs rolled up. He flinched at the first lick and we knew she had surprised him. She went on, hitting as hard as she could flail, until she got to ten. Jimroe breathed fast when he stood up.

"Thank you, ma'am. You did a lot better than I thought you would."

On the way home that evening Jimroe showed us where she had broken skin on his legs. He had five or six little welts with beads of blood on them. Jimroe was proud of Miss Cassie.

The teacher had marched away from school like she would be glad to whip Jimroe any time she could, but the next day we found out the truth. Aunt Ly Sue told Tree about it.

"The poor thing," Aunt Ly Sue said. "She came home and cried half the night over having to flog that smart aleck. I don't see that he's worth it."

"Don't sell him short," Tree told her. "As uppity as he is, he can make a mighty pretty mouth over things when he wants to. He'll draw women like flies to a molasses barrel some day."

A few days later Mama went to a box social at Aunt Ly Sue's house with the Women's Bible Class and found Miss Cassie. "Can you tell me where I would find the lady who teaches Jimroe Starling?"

"I teach him."

"Not you. I'm looking for the one who gave him such a thrashing."

"I'm the one."

"I can't believe it. I've not been able to flog him in years myself."

"Well, I'm just sorry it had to happen."

"Oh, I'm so grateful to you. How on earth did you manage it?"

All Mama got out of her was a smile; Miss Cassie said that was a secret between her and Jimroe and that she was sure Mama would understand. We knew all about it, because Mama came home with her head full of notions about Miss Cassie, and how she was going to have her help the women straighten out the township—Mama said she was going to put the Women's Bible Class to work right away.

"We're sick and tired of you men fighting over that dratted tobacco, so that honest people can't sleep. And having that rumpot old man Strawn for a law officer."

Papa moaned. "We ain't in shape to stand much of your salvation, Little Bit. I've got enough to worry over with the tobacco crop. We'll be lucky to save enough to pay for the last bill of fertilizer."

"That's something we'll tend to right away. You think more of your old tobacco than you do of your own women and children."

"Who do you think we raise the damn stuff for?"

"Well, at least we're going to put a stop to this foolishness of night riding and burning and barn watching before somebody gets hurt."

"Oh, Lord."

That time with Miss Cassie changed Jimroe, and it was only a few days later that she got him—hook, line and sinker. It was about trading horses, again.

Jimroe's money had been burning a hole in his pocket. He pretended that it never crossed his mind that he had more cash than lots of grown men in the township, but I knew

better. The money was never out of his mind. He was apt to
size up everybody he met, wondering if they had as much as
twenty-two dollars to their name. Jimroe carried his money
folded in a rag, and by day it was pinned in the breast
pocket of his overalls. Damon said he slept with it under the
bolster every night, and the first thing that woke them up
every morning was Jimroe scratching around for his money-
bag.

It wasn't like him to show his cash to anybody, but one
morning when we were up before the others, Jimroe squatted on the kitchen floor and spread his money and whispered
about it. He smoothed the bills and stacked his change in
piles. "Here's what I trimmed off old Wash, that first time
. . . And this is Jess's ten—and here's old Wash again."

He looked like he could have eaten that money, and he
talked to it like it was human. "Some day I'm going to have
me a hundred for every one of you—no, a thousand. They
ain't no telling how rich I'm going to be."

He folded it into his rag and said he was going to start
trading horses again. We went to town, where crowds were
bigger every day, with the tobacco market ready to open.
He stopped at the Boneyard and went looking for a horse.

The line of stock wound far up on the side of the mountain, but in all that crowd there was only one string of good-
looking horses. It was Biscoe Allen's stock, and Wash
Strawn was handling it.

Jimroe knew better than to try Wash, of all people. We
knew that any lively horse he had might have been rubbed
with pepper under the tail, or fed arsenic or strychnine or
something. But the horses that caught Jimroe's eye were too
good for those tricks. He liked the fat shiny stock that Biscoe's partners had sent over from Randolph, in case people
had any new tobacco-crop money to spend. We hung
around, watching, before Wash spoke to Jimroe.

"It'll do you no good to slobber over that string. They're

all forty and fifty dollars a head. I do have one bargain. I've been holding him out for you."

Jimroe laughed, but he had to know what Wash was trying to pull on him. Wash slapped the oldest horse of the lot. It was the nag that Wash and Jimroe had been passing between them, that Cousin Tree had used sponges on and pumped with air under the eyes. Jimroe looked up in the horse's nostrils and saw the strings hanging down. He snorted. "I've done been there. Find you some other fool."

"Not so fast, now, son."

"I've got a little sense. I want something alive."

"I mean to give you trading bait, boy. Something you can take and turn into a piece of money. Now, you know all about the poor thing, and just how to handle him right. You know I gave you twelve dollars—you know everything there is to be known about him. Now, then . . ."

"I can't help it that you bit on him."

"No matter, boy. No matter. No hard feelings. How you prettied him up and fooled me is your own secret."

"I don't care what you say. I don't want him. I wouldn't have him on a Christmas tree."

"You can have him for four dollars."

Jimroe shot him a quick look. "How come?" He stalked around trying to see if the nag had something worse about him than usual. Wash whittled and let him have a look.

"Well," Jimroe said. "If I can't make money on him at that price, I ought not to be off from home by myself."

"Yes, sir. You curry that thing up a little and you'll double your money in the snap of a finger."

Jimroe paid Wash the money and they shook hands.

"Now, son. It's all over. We've done cheated one another long enough. We can be friends so long as we're both swapping horseflesh, and I'll do you another good turn any time I can."

Jimroe led the old nag and we went down the road toward Aunt Ly Sue's house. Miss Cassie came off the porch. "What are you doing with that old thing?"

Jimroe told her about the trade and she shook her head. "If he lives a week, it'll surprise me. He's sold you a funeral."

"You'll see," Jimroe said. "I'm going to swap him off tomorrow, and roll my money into some good horse before tobacco market is over."

Miss Cassie went back to the porch laughing, where she was hemmed in by about a dozen men, ranging from big boys from school to white-haired widowers—all of them come courting. She had to sit with them every Saturday and Sunday, because she was the only woman between sixteen and thirty in Corona who wasn't spoken for. Aunt Ly Sue was always bragging about how Miss Cassie got proposals in her parlor and pressed flowers in the mail, and sometimes even second-hand wedding rings.

Jimroe and I went to the barn lot, where Shad Starling put the old horse inside and said he would keep an eye on him for the night.

"Don't bother about feeding him," Jimroe said. "I'm going to trade him off first thing in the morning."

We got back early the next day and walked around to Shad's shack by the stable. He came out shaking his head. "Good thing you never wasted feed on him," he said. "Mister Wash oughtn't to treat you like that, and him sheriff and all."

The old horse was dead, lying stiff-legged beside the fence. Jimroe hung there, looking at him, swallowing hard. Miss ssie came out to see. "Well, Jimroe, it isn't the end of the ld. Maybe we can do something."

'm. The time to do it was yesterday. I was a fool."

, you find Tree Poindexter, and we'll see. Between

us, we ought to be old enough and mean enough to think of something. If I wanted to find some other way to skin a cat, I couldn't think of a better man to help than Mr. Poindexter."

When Tree came, she just waved a hand at the horse like she was in school and sending him to the blackboard. "I knew you would know what to do," she said.

"Yes, ma'am. I wasn't raised to say no to a lady—but this is the first thing I ever had to bring back from the dead."

She stood there like she expected something to happen, and after he had looked about for a minute, Tree put us to work. Miss Cassie watched and enjoyed it.

"Raise him up," Tree said. "No. Lean him against the fence, lightly, just so he's barely touching."

We managed to get him up, but he wedged there on legs like boards, two of them off the ground, looking deader than ever.

"Hook his head over the fence," Miss Cassie said.

Tree helped us tug until we worked the head and neck over, and the horse was holding on by the top rail, looking toward the wood lot. All four feet were solid on the ground, and he was leaning so natural that if you didn't look close, he seemed to be as alive as ever.

Tree and Miss Cassie backed off and squinted at him. "He looks like he'd switch his tail and whinny any minute," she said.

"Then he'll do," Tree said. "If you think you could get Wash over here for us . . ."

"He'll never fall for that," Jimroe said.

"You wait, young man," Miss Cassie said. "If there's one thing I can do in this world, it's play schoolmarm."

Tree put Jimroe to work with a currycomb until he was satisfied with the way the horse looked, and Miss Cassie went after Wash. "It wouldn't surprise me," Tree said, "if we was to see some old Virginia horse swapping."

Miss Cassie found Wash in the Boneyard and was on him
like a duck on a junebug. "Sheriff, I'm ashamed of you. I had
hoped that you'd turned over a new leaf."

Wash eyed Jimroe, but he pretended that he didn't know
what she was talking about. Miss Cassie poured it on Wash,
all the talk she had heard from the Bible Class women, about
his drinking and swearing and cheating people. She backed
him up, step by step, across the road on the way to Aunt Ly
Sue's. People came out of the house to see what the matter
was. Judge Bucktarrel and Aunt Ly Sue were among
them.

By now Miss Cassie was whispering to Wash. "Now,
you're going to do what's right by that boy, aren't you?"

"Oh, no. I've done done it. He took that horse as is."

"Don't you 'as is' me, Wash Strawn. I won't have you
ruin a young boy, teaching him all those dirty tricks and
taking advantage of him while he's trying to be an honest
trader."

"Heh. He'd put a gypsy to shame. He'd steal my last
mouthful of bread if I didn't watch him."

"It's a pity about you."

Wash sneaked a look at the nag across the fence. "Why,
he's got him looking in better order already. He ain't got a
thing to complain of. Durned if I'll give him his money
back."

"Well, what will you do for him?"

"Nothing atall, I tell you. If you want to peck at somebody, peck at him, a hothead, headstrong youngun just
dying to cheat folks. A Starling to the marrowbone."

"Now, Wash, if you want to hear the end of this before
you die . . ."

Jimroe piped up. "Would you give me back part of my
money?"

Miss Cassie hushed him. "Here's what we'll do, now,
Wash. You give him back half of his money and the horse is
yours. You get the profit, and he gets the experience, and I

hope that next time he'll know better than to trade for such a thing."

She talked to him so hot and heavy that Wash couldn't look up and get a good eyeful of the nag. He looked once more out of the corner of his eye, and got a greedy twitch in his mouth. All he wanted was to see that the horse was still on its feet.

"It's a trade," Wash said. He fished two dollars for Jimroe from his pocket and told Miss Cassie that he hoped all parties were satisfied.

"We are if you are," she said. "Will you send somebody for him?"

Wash said he would lead the nag himself and pegged into the lot. He was within ten feet of the horse before he saw what was wrong. He went stiff, but only for a second. He took two or three more high, slow steps, swinging that peg leg like he had forgotten he had one. He didn't go close enough to touch the nag. He came back, hobbling fast, and gave Miss Cassie a sick grin.

"As is, hey?" He went by her out of the lot, saying over and over, "A woman. A durn woman. A goddurn woman from Virginia."

Jimroe took it harder than Wash did. You'd have thought Tree had nothing to do with saving his money for him. He followed the teacher to Aunt Ly Sue's porch like a pup at her heels, and sat with the other men and boys who hung around her, just as calf-eyed as the worst of them. It was like he had never really noticed her until he saw how easy it was for her to lead Wash Strawn around by the nose, without raising her voice.

They sat on the porch and drank lemonade that Aunt Ly Sue sent out to the crowd by Poll. Jimroe and Miss Cassie joked with each other about Wash and asked each other if everything was "as is," like there was nobody else on the porch with them. Miss Cassie was acting like somebody else entirely. I left them.

I hung around the warehouse for a while, watching Biscoe Allen's men cleaning up for the opening of the tobacco market, shoving baskets around and sweeping up the old dust left from the year before. I stayed where I could keep an eye on Aunt Ly Sue's house, and soon Miss Cassie and Jimroe went out the gate between the box bushes, holding hands. I felt like somebody had licked all the red off my candy.

I started home, going slow, mooning about Miss Cassie and the way she had paid me no attention, hardly watching where I was going. I got on the short cut through the woods to our farm.

When I came to our ridge, where I could see a long way in every direction, I saw a boy and a girl ahead of me on the hill pasture with their arms locked. He was carrying flowers.

It was Miss Cassie and Jimroe.

They stopped, and he put his arm around her and gave her a quick kiss. When he tried again she pushed him away but she was laughing. I couldn't hear what they said but I heard her laugh. She sounded like she might not push him away the next time.

I ducked out of sight and waited until they were on top of the hill, where I could just see them against the sky. It made me mad with Miss Cassie. I knew she had done me wrong somehow, but I didn't know just how. I knew she'd been talking nice to me just to make me study hard, and I'd done everything she said, like a fool. She didn't care a fig for anybody except Jimroe. I couldn't understand what she saw in him. I wished that I could tell her everything I knew about him. I hated them both.

15

A Make-Believe Tobacco Auction

Grandpa thought they couldn't open the Corona tobacco market without him, because he'd been going there every fall for eighty years except when he was off with the Confederate Army, whipping back the Yankees. He and Aunt Lumbie came to our house late in the night, but everybody was still up. Papa had us hunting Trout, who was the last one minus a haircut.

He caught all of us one at a time, even the big boys, and tied us in a porch chair with a dishtowel and ran his clippers over our heads, like he was shearing sheep and was behind-

time in his work. He left a rim of hair over our ears, strewing
nicks and bumps everywhere. Trout always hid at haircut
time, almost always in the same place, so we dragged him
from under the pack house by his heels while he bawled, and
took him, still keening, to the porch. Trout scrooched away
down with his head in his neck, and Papa had to shear him
harder than ever and made it worse. When it was over with
we had breakfast and went to town.

The tobacco wagons were ready.

We were all tired. We had spent most of the day before
packing those two wagons, the kind of aggravating women's
work that we hated. Finished tobacco had to be handled like
it was made of china, with each twist of the leaf laid in soft
and easy until you had even layers piled as high as the wagon
would stand; then we tied it in old quilts and canvas, tight
but gentle, and it was ready for market. Even with our
wagons stacked as high as we dared, we knew the leaf
wouldn't weigh much despite its bulk.

We carried the better part of two barns to town, maybe a
fifth of Papa's crop. It was the best we had. Everybody
knew that the first sale of the year would tell us about what
we could expect for the rest of the crop.

The buggy went ahead, with Grandpa and Aunt Lumbie
and Mama and two of the girls. As they went away we
could hear Grandpa singing. He was as happy as if we were
about to have a good market, with plenty of money for
everybody:

> "Oh, Nellie had a pair of shoes,
> She could wear 'em if she choose . . ."

He was still carrying on as long as we could hear him.

The rest of us walked, with Papa and Frank driving the
wagons. Papa took pains on the rough road; lots of other
wagons were going, too, because nobody would miss opening day at the market.

There was a long wait at the warehouse, with the line of

wagons reaching around the bend of the road out into the country. It was full daylight before our wagon came within sight of the loading platform. While they waited, Jimroe eased off to Aunt Ly Sue's house. He took me and Damon so that nobody would notice him hanging around Miss Cassie. Aunt Ly Sue was feeding all the tobacco company buyers at breakfast, and a good many others were there, too. Ly Sue and Miss Cassie enjoyed themselves by pecking at Wash Strawn. The old man didn't seem to mind, but went on eating and laughing while they lectured him and the buyers listened.

Wash would never had been deputy sheriff except for the moonshine crowd, who knew that he would never bother them but would keep the big sheriff from Randolph off their necks. Ly Sue scalded him about whiskey making and gambling and cussing in front of children.

Wash had been nipping, even before breakfast, and was loud. After breakfast they went on the porch and kept after Wash. He took off his big hat and slipped his tobacco cud into it, and turned it around and around in his hands while Miss Cassie and Aunt Ly Sue gave him Holy Moses. He didn't give them much satisfaction until Aunt Ly Sue sent Poll out with a glass of sweet milk and a wedge of her blue-ribbon poundcake. That moved Wash.

"I promise you good women one thing. You'll never have another whit of trouble out of me. I'll never touch another jar of likker as long as the Lord gives me breath."

Aunt Ly Sue reminded Wash about the last time he'd promised, and that very night had got his peg leg caught in a knothole in the wooden sidewalk and marched around in a circle half the night before somebody got him loose, cussing a blue streak all the time. Wash laughed.

"You've got no idea how wicked I would have been without your Christian help. I feel like I've cut down about fifty per cent on the meanness I ought to have done lately, just on account of you good women. Just try me once more again."

Other women came before Wash could get away. Biscoe Allen's wife and Mrs. Billy Lufler buzzed at him, wanting to know what he was going to do about all the sinning that was going on.

Aunt Ly Sue said, "Why is it, Sheriff, that those terrible things can go on at Tootsy's place, and nothing's to be done about it? The Kinnamons are an insult to every decent woman in this county."

"It ain't possible to stop 'em," Wash said. "I've turned two states loose on that woman, but she's too shifty for me. You'd never catch her at it. I go out there with my Carolina bunch and she shoves the likker over on the Virginia side of the house, and I can't touch her. And once I went through all that rigamarole with the Virginia deputy, and all she did was shift over to the Carolina side. They ain't nothing to be done about her."

"I think Miss Carson could tell you how," Aunt Ly Sue said. "Lord knows why somebody hasn't got onto you before now. She says all you've got to do is go out there with officers from both states at once."

Wash gave Miss Cassie a look like she might have two heads, and the other women took it up and yammered at Wash to make him promise that he would stop Tootsy's goings-on. He promised, just to get out of there, and looked hangdog while he was stumping down the steps, but went out of Aunt Ly Sue's gate humming "Nearer My God To Thee" as he headed for the tobacco warehouse. The town was ready for the market opening.

Two leftover banners were hung across the road, the same ones they had always used:

WELCOME TO THE WORLD'S BIGGEST LITTLE TOBACCO MARKET

And:

TOP DOLLAR EVERY TIME
THE FARMER'S FRIEND—B. ALLEN

It was too early for the auction, but the crowd was already drifting around and Corona Crossroads was full. Wagons were tied everywhere, and not just in the line of loaded ones at the warehouse. Nobody was spending money, with bad prices expected at the market, but everybody felt that they had to see the sale to know what to do about their money crop. Biscoe Allen had two men playing guitar in front of the Eat Well Café next to the warehouse, but nobody listened. They were waiting to see what would happen.

Biscoe came on the loading platform and made a talk, of the kind he always made every year. He was full of grins.

"Morning, neighbors. Old friends. I see all them good old familiar faces out there. You traders. I know you've come to pick my bones."

He tried his old trick that always brought laughs from the crowd—he put his hands over his head and made a funny face and expected them to hoot at him about his trading joke. But nobody said a word. Biscoe shook his head.

"All right, men. Let me talk business to you one minute. You know that my partners will try and do right by you if I won't. For if we don't, we won't be open here long. You know we can't help it the way the big crop has hurt prices. You know I can't make the boys buy tobacco high when they can get all they want cheap."

The men in front of him listened with set faces, like they were daring Biscoe to say something wrong.

"You know I can't pay more than we can get for tobacco on the other end, boys. I don't blame you for looking for a slow sale. It's slow all over, and you know it."

Grandpa kept mumbling half under his breath while Biscoe was talking, but Tree was about the only one who paid him any mind, as usual. "That young fool is more like old man Shirt Allen than his shadow. By God, I know he's first cousin to an eel. They don't come no slicker than an Allen. I'd see him in hell before I'd trade here, if it was me."

Biscoe was still going. "You come in and trust me for a while, boys. Give me just half a chance. Come on in and let's see what our buyers can do. We've got the best, and you'll not have to take Biscoe's word for a thing. You know they'll deal you fair. Hard, but fair."

The crowd went in behind him, but it was quiet, not like a tobacco market holiday had always been. I went in with Tree and Grandpa and Papa and my big brothers, and we found our piles of tobacco, six hampers of it, about twelve hundred pounds, all prime leaf. I knew it was prime, clean to the bottom, because Papa made such a point of putting the very best on the under side, bending over backward to be honest about it. We hadn't long to wait for the sale to reach us. Papa's leaf was on the second row.

Papa was proud, watching it come to him. All of us could see that the leaf ahead wasn't as pretty as ours, and shouldn't bring the price of Papa's. We were hoping we might get a few cents more than the market was bringing up to then.

Biscoe was leading the buyers around, just a step ahead of the auctioneer, stopping at each pile. Biscoe and all the rest were working like beavers.

"At least he's giving it a try," Papa said. "I never saw Biscoe go harder."

Biscoe was what we called the sales leader. He tried to lift prices as much as he could by bidding against company buyers. Every company buyer had a range he could offer for each grade of tobacco. He might start at twelve cents a pound for good leaf in that bad market, but could go as high as twenty and still satisfy his company. The sales leader had that spread to work with.

The auctioneer had come in from Winston, and was an old-timer and a good one. If you hadn't been brought up in tobacco country you hadn't a chance to follow what he was saying. He was as fast as lightning. When he went loud and fast on his chant, pointing to a pile of tobacco, a buyer would lift a finger, or wink, or waggle a pencil, or give some other sign, and the auctioneer would really sing:

"Oh, a twelve, twelve. Runnels says a big twelve. Who'll go a fif-teen, a fif-teen . . . Yes, yes, I hear my four-teen. Say that six-teen . . ."

For a while he was so fast that he sounded like he wouldn't catch another breath till noon, but they slowed him down. He had to stop longer at each pile until he thought he'd got out every penny. Biscoe kept on bidding for a while.

Since he was the warehouseman, he could bid against the companies, and if it was knocked down to him, he could sell the tobacco later, hoping to get a better price. Before he knew it, he had bought about half the first row of tobacco, and had the hampers pushed aside. He would have them repacked and try to sell them the next time.

Biscoe was trying every trick that day, but the buyers had him where it hurt, and when he came by us he was sweating.

All the big companies had buyers there, Reynolds and Laramie and Columbia and National. They were in a good humor, and looked like they wanted to help Biscoe stay in business, but had no choice but to keep prices low and take the very best of the leaf on the floor.

Biscoe started by trying to jump the buyers pretty high. When a Reynolds man said twelve cents a pound for a good pile, Biscoe yelled "Fifteen," so that all the farmers would see what he was doing; he was usually quiet with his signals. That worked once or twice, and a Laramie man went to sixteen on a pile when Biscoe forced him, and then Biscoe dropped out of the bidding—so everybody knew that the farmer had Biscoe to thank for boosting his price four cents a pound over the starting bid.

Biscoe had soon bought more tobacco than even a warehouseman ought to buy, with times so hard. When he came to us, Biscoe had bought a good many piles on our row for himself because the company men were hanging back. Then he began losing his nerve.

They came to Papa's pile and stopped.

The auctioneer took off a couple of hands of the best of our leaf and shook his head, grinning. "Oh, prime. Prime. You know it'd bring forty cents in good times. Don't I hear a sixteen?"

Papa looked unusually sober, like he wasn't noticing that they were talking about our tobacco.

A Reynolds man gave a sign, and the bidding went from sixteen to seventeen, and then Biscoe tried to add one more penny, and it stuck there at eighteen cents a pound. It was the highest bid yet. The auctioneer gobbled that figure for a while and stopped. Biscoe had bought our piles at eighteen cents a pound.

Jimroe was the first to have the big figure in his head. "Two hundred and sixteen dollars," he said.

Papa looked at him and took that in.

We knew that was the top price we could expect for any of our crop of tobacco—because what we had left at home wasn't as good as the piles we had brought. We had tried the very best. Papa looked like he had forgotten where he was for a minute. Of all the places we had to go during a year, the tobacco warehouse at opening sale was the one where we knew everybody would be watching to see how you took things. Papa was beyond thinking of that. His hands were crammed deep in his overalls pockets and his hat rode the back of his head. He looked out over the tobacco and didn't change his gaze when people passed in front of him. It was like the auctioneer had called off the price for our whole year's work—more, because several years of Papa's debts were tied up in our leaf. He would have next to nothing to pay for them with.

"Don't take it," Grandpa said. "I'm damned if I would let him treat me like a cur dog."

Behind the buyers, moving from pile to pile, came the ticket men, who stuck the price tickets on each pile of tobacco. Farmers didn't have to sell at the bid price unless they

were satisfied, and the first ticket man gave Papa a look
when he tied on the little red tags—they just said "18¢."
Papa looked to Tree and Frank, but they were looking at
the floor. Papa hesitated. They were waiting to see if he
would settle for the dirt-cheap price for our family's labor
all year long, because he had the top price for the day. Papa
waved to the ticket men.

"Pass me up," he said. "I'll tell you later."

After the ticket men came the pullers, who scrambled all
through the piles, looking for mouldy leaves or bad tobacco,
just in case somebody had tried to trick the buyers. They
went around ours when they saw Papa; they knew him, and
knew it was no use to hunt through. Papa liked that.

The sale crawled along the warehouse rows, pile by pile,
with things getting no better, and as they got near the end,
the buyers walked faster. They had almost quit bidding, and
they looked like they weren't sure what the crowd had in
mind. It was pretty quiet, and the buyers must have thought
of the ugly talk about riots and burning in the South. Near
the end the halfbreed Indian farmers had their tobacco all
together, and all of them looked mad enough to bite nails.
You could see in their faces what they were thinking: even
if there was only a penny or two to be made, it was going to
the white farmers, and none to the colored people.

Biscoe tried talking to the crowd again. He said he had
done his best, but that things couldn't be helped. "I just
want to ask you to stick with us, friends," he said. "If you'll
come back next week, maybe we'll do a little better. Old
Biscoe ain't through yet." He sounded like he knew they
wouldn't come back.

"Now, you can see I'm in this thing with you. I've got a
sight of tobacco on the floor if you take up my bids. And
I've got to sell, too. Let's work together, men. Don't take
your tobacco home."

Billy Lufler talked to Papa, and they tried to decide what
they should do. "Something's going on," Lufler said. "I

never knew him to stick that skinny neck out this far before."

Jess Sixkiller had come up beside them. "Hell, Biscoe's taking no chance," Jess said. "He knows good and well you folks ain't selling to him at that rate. Looks like to me all you big growers ought to be able to handle him."

Tree kept a close eye on Jess, and his neck was stiff with being suspicious. "You changed your tune mighty quick," he said. "Whose side are you on? Well, whatcha say, Jess?"

"Here's what I say, boys!" Jess yelled. He ran down the line ripping off the red tickets he found on the piles, flinging them to the floor. He raised a racket.

"What the devil's going on there?" Biscoe said. He climbed a stool to look across the tobacco piles to us.

"None of your damn business," Jess said. "Ain't you never heard of crossing the river? You think you got the onliest tobacco market there is on this earth? Come on, boys, don't you let him treat you like that. You ain't got to stand for it—don't you know we could all take our tobacco over the river? Hell, we can still try Danville, can't we?"

Then Jiggs Sixkiller and a couple of other halfbreed boys ran down the far rows, picking off the sales tickets, and others took it up, and people began laughing and talking. Things changed in the wink of an eye, and nobody paid any attention to Biscoe while he stood with a long face, calling, "Boys, boys. Don't go and leave me, boys. We've got to live together, hard times or good."

People were excited and lots of them kept saying, "We're crossing the river, and Biscoe be damned." It was as if they had never thought of such a thing before.

Some laughed like it was a joke on Biscoe, and hurried to get their wagons back into line to take tobacco from the platform. It would take hours for them to repack before they could go back home, and it might be days before they were ready to cross the river.

Lufler asked Papa, "Well, are we going?"

"I can't see what else we can do," Papa said. "It sounds like foolishness to me, but there's no place else to try."

"That damn Allen's got a cotton eye like his daddy," Grandpa said. "I've never seen one of that tribe would give you air if you were in a jug."

Tree took the old man out of the warehouse with him. Men were beginning to drink before we left town, and the Eat Well Café was as noisy as it had ever been in the good market years.

"And that ain't the worst of it," Grandpa said. "I don't like that half-honest look that come over that Indian's face. It don't become him. He looked like a sick calf, making that mealy mouth. I'm satisfied in my own mind that somebody put him up to it, and I bet his name was Allen."

Tree said that was about as near nothing as a tobacco market could be.

"It's nothing but one big horse trade," Grandpa said. "Bad times and good, they'll cheat you out of your eyeteeth, and it's devil take the hindmost. Always been thataway."

"Times have changed," Papa said.

"That's no lie," Grandpa said. "They get worse every few minutes. And you heed what I say, that Allen has got something in mind for you. He ain't through with you yet. He bribed that Indian for some dirty work. You wait and see."

16

The Smiting of the Sinners

Miss Cassie had me working so hard in school that I had forgotten what Tree had told me about the plans for the moonshine raid. I was boning in my Reader, some kind of geography, and kept hearing a turkey call in the woods. It went on for a long time, like a young hen saying *kee, kee, kee*, and I knew something was wrong, because you wouldn't hear one like that in the open country. Then I thought of Tree, who was the only man in the world who could call so much like a real turkey.

I studied the woods through the window until I found

him. He and Lize were waiting on the mountainside in a clearing. I knew he had come to take me to Tootsy's house, and that he was so leery of Miss Cassie that I'd have to run away.

I didn't stop to think of how to get out. I ran. When we had to go to the necessary house we were supposed to hold up a hand and say "Number One" if we were in a big hurry, and "Number Two" if we could wait a while, but I said nothing.

I thought of it when I was in the yard, and began a hobbled walk, like I had the "green-apple quicksteps." Miss Cassie sent Charlie B. Wade after me, and I yelled over my shoulder at him, "Number One. Nuuuuuumber One!" He ducked back inside and I sprinted past the outhouse into the woods.

Tree said it was as slick a runaway as he ever saw, and I must have strutted a little because he said, "Hell, don't be too sure she didn't see through you. We'd all have to get up mighty early of a morning to fool that little woman."

He said he wouldn't be surprised if she knew more about the raid on Tootsy Kinnamon than anybody guessed.

I didn't believe it.

"All right," Tree said. "But don't make the mistake of thinking she's got loose from somebody's church choir. She knows too much about horse trading for that.

"And I know one thing—she ain't got her heart in this Bible Class business of straightening up the world before breakfast. I expect it to turn out that she put Wash up to this foofooraw just to shut up those holy hens, and make 'em leave Tootsy alone for a while."

We went through the woods cross-country on Lize, without seeing a soul on the way.

We found a crowd at Tootsy's house. Jess Sixkiller and two of his boys were staking a line, running twine across a row of stobs, and tying hanks of cloth on the line so that you couldn't miss it. The string ran across Tootsy's neck of land and through the middle of the dog run between her two rooms. Jess had pecked a hole in the stained-glass window, and the Lord was holding the string in his hand. It was the state line between North Carolina and Virginia, all right. It made the place look solemn, like something in a history book.

Toots was squatting on the bedsprings, playing a game of setback with two of her girls and Red Dowd. Her skirt was hitched over her fat brown thighs and her underlip was full of snuff. She spit way out in the yard when she saw Tree.

"Light and come in," she said. "In little or no time every durn limb of the law in the U-damn-nited States of America will be here anyway."

"Don't get me mixed up with 'em," Tree said. "We just come to see that they gave you fair and square."

"Oh, I reckon I can see to that," Red Dowd said.

Toots sniggered. "My damn sorry lawyer. How you like my ten-dollar lawyer, Tree? Ain't he some kind of hell?"

Red acted like he practiced every day, and Tree didn't let on surprise.

"You never slipped up on me, Poindexter," Red said. "I guess my lookouts decided to take a chance on you."

Toots slapped down her cards. "Ah, dry up, Dowd. I want Tree to check my line."

They went down the line of stakes, and Toots told of how Jess had learned to run lines when he was in the pen and had gone out on road work gangs. Jess pointed up and down the river and showed us where the line split the place half in two. Tree said it made some sense to him. We squinted along the line until Toots got tired and took us back to the house and lifted a couple of floor planks on the porch, and there was a cache of corn liquor, row on row of quart jars stacked under the floor boards—all lined up just under the string. Tootsy and Red argued about the state line.

"I tell you, dammit, she's got to be wide enough to be

reasonable," Toots said, "or else it'd never be any good to anybody."

"Who's lawing this damn case? I tell you I studied it out, and the line ain't wide enough to cover that likker."

"I know in my bones it is. I've got the likker safe right down the middle, just where Jess said. How come me to spend all that measuring money if it ain't right?"

Jess took a gulp from one of the jars and all of them had a refreshment.

"Let's be sensible," Tree said. "That line varies. Some places it's got to be wide enough for a horse and wagon. Others, she ain't none too wide for a lizard to tip along a fence. But she's got to have some substance. How the hell else would you keep all them big states apart? Who wants to go around feeling like he's in two states at once?"

"Nawp," Red Dowd said. "It's just as thick as the edge on a razor blade. No more, no less. There's no way in God's world to stack likker on it. They'll snatch every drop of that stuff, sure as you're born."

"They've got to find it first," Toots said. She wrapped an arm around Red's neck until he gasped for breath. "I'll kiss your foot if it ain't at least a foot wide," she said. "Let's stack them jars again."

She made us help her move the liquor and string it out in an even narrower line, a single row of quarts, and then put the floor boards back, and had her little girls strew dust on the porch and sweep it around so that nobody could tell it had been touched. She dusted her hands together like she was satisfied and went out to see what else Jess had done. He had hidden her still up in the air; you could see it for a quarter of a mile in every direction, hanging by ropes over Jess's line, tied to trees on either side. It looked like somebody's big kitchen had blown up, with the kettle and some mash barrels and the coil worm dangling and turning up there.

Toots laughed. "I can't wait to see them fools try to figure out which air she's hanging in, Calina or Virginny."

Red Dowd told her she was crazy and would go to jail if she didn't hide the still in the woods and forget the state line.

Toots marched back to the porch and tore up the floor for a drink and made the girls sweep and dust again. Toots played the gramophone, band music: "Oh, the Monkey Wrapped His Tail Around the Flagpole," and they went under the porch again and again after liquor until they were all mellow and quit arguing about the state line. Red Dowd asked Toots if she would put the liquor in pint bottles and turn them sidewise on the line, just to be safe.

"The hound with it," Toots said. "I ain't got no blue billion pint bottles to devote to it. All the law in the world ain't got sense enough to find my likker. I don't know why I'm fool enough to worry over it."

Red thought they would check once more and he took up the planks again and drank, and the girls dusted and swept and Dowd said, "Fetch me a hammer and a nail. I don't like that durn loose board."

Toots watched, reeling over him while he hammered in the nail. It was new and shiny, the only new nail you could see on the place. "All right," Toots said. "Let the damn law come. I wouldn't care if it was to rain law."

One of the lookouts ran through the woods, yelling over the noise of the gramophone, "Here he comes! He's cleaning up both sides of the line."

The deputies drove the lookouts in front of them with hands in the air, and marched through the woods like an army until they hemmed us along the line. Wash Strawn yelled, "Everything here's under arrest. Every form thing. Even you little old boys." He pointed to me. "Yes, I mean everything, living or not." He confiscated the gramophone and said it was just such common music as a church man would expect to find in a den like that. Anybody would have thought that Wash had never set foot in the place.

Toots cussed him, but Red Dowd shushed her.

"All right, gentlemen," Red said. "To let you know before it's too late and you do something foolish, Miz Kinnamon is represented by counsel. We know our rights, our Commonwealth of Virginia rights and our State of North Carolina rights. And by God, we've got American rights to burn." Toots clapped.

Wash stumped to the porch and Red jumped beside him, flat-footed, from the ground.

"Hold on, sir. Don't put a foot on this premise until you show me your search warrant. You'll not treat good citizens this way. I'll appeal your ass straight to the Supreme Court of the United States, Washington, D.C., by God."

Wash slapped papers into his hands. They were search warrants from both states. Wash went in the house.

"No!" Red said. "You listen to me. You can't touch one bit of this woman's property unless it's necessary to the search. You can't rip one picture off her wall, or bust one stick of furniture. You can't pull one little bitty nail, not a single one. That's the law of the land, and it covers this troubled mother as it does ary other."

Toots began to cry. "By God, I know I'm getting my money's worth. That's the grandest little old lawyer in this county, and I don't care if he ain't got a licent."

Red yelped louder. "Don't pull one single durn nail, now, Sheriff." He shook a finger under Wash's nose. "The law plainly says—pull not ary nail."

Wash said he was worn out with it, and that they would cover the yard and the woods. Tootsy heaved a big sigh. Wash turned for a last look to see what she was sighing about and spied the new nail in the porch floor.

He looked it over and talked with the Virginia sheriff, Arch Davis. Arch handed him a hammer and a nail punch, and Wash went down on the porch on his bad knee and pounded in that nail so fast that Dowd could hardly see what he was up to.

"All right," Wash said. "We can't *pull* no nail, the lawyer man says, but there's sure God no law says we can't drive 'em—is it, lawyer?"

He drove the nail out of sight, whipped up the plank—and school was out. They emptied the cache in a wink. Wash and Arch Davis both laid a hand on every quart as it came out, to make it legal. They counted eighty-seven quarts and had them put in the wagon. You could have heard Toots all the way into town, yelling at Red. "Yeah, Dowd! You and your damn new nail. Loose board, he said. Oh, you simlinhead!"

She cussed him until he ran from her, and we got no quiet until Wash couldn't stand it. "Put her under hush-mouth arrest," he said. "If she don't shut up, gag her."

Toots yelped for Red to save her.

"What's the charge for this fool arrest, Sheriff? You can't arrest her twice," Red said.

"Hell I can't. I arrest her on suspicion."

"Suspicion? Suspicion of what?"

"Suspicion of being a damn nuisance to everybody, right here and now."

"Damned if I can argue that with you. Let the law run her course."

The officers had to hold Toots to keep her from tearing up Red Dowd.

Wash arrested all of us a second time, to put us to work—even me. I had to help them herd Tootsy and her girls into the back of Wash Strawn's wagon, and they wouldn't go until we put in a whole chance of dogs and cats that didn't want to be left behind. We finally got all of them in the wagon bed. They played the gramophone until Wash finished his search.

Wash didn't much want to seize the moonshine still, and pretended that he couldn't see it hanging up there, swinging in the breeze as big as a hogshead.

"Well," he said, "I guess there's no sense wasting half a

day helling through the woods to find her cooking still—
we'll just get along."

But about a dozen of the deputies yelled and pointed up to
the hanging still, and so Wash made them whop off the
ropes and when it all fell down atop Jess's string, Wash took
the worm—the part where the coil made the mash steam and
distill into whiskey—and put it in the wagon.

We trailed into town with officers straggling front and
rear, with Tootsy and her girls on straight chairs in the
wagon, and the little ones and dogs and cats spilling over the
pile of confiscated liquor jars. Jess Sixkiller was supposed to
keep watch over the liquor.

We had a dog fight or two, and once or twice the gramophone went *rowwwwwwrk worrrrrrk* on the cylinder, with
snatches of music between. As we came near town, people
came grinning to the side of the road. Toots yelled.

"That's right, white folks. Come and see old Tootie's
shame. Come one, come all. Tain't the first time your menfolks been hanging around old Toot." She caused a little
confusion.

I was near the tail end, riding behind Tree on Lize, where
we could see things livening up. Jess opened one of the jars
and passed it to people near him. He played "Birmingham
Jail" on his mouth harp and Toots sang. Wash and the Virginia sheriff looked like they wished we would dry up and
blow away.

We dragged up to Aunt Ly Sue's house. Judge Bucktarrel
was on the front porch with his mandolin. He had been
interrupted playing for Aunt Ly Sue and Miss Cassie and
looked at us as if he thought the Civil War had broken out
afresh. Aunt Ly Sue stayed in her hammock, fanning. Wash
went to the porch.

"Judge, this here's the evidence. I say no more." He pulled
out the worm from Tootsy's moonshine still and one jar of
liquor and put them at the Judge's feet.

The Judge said, "What in the pluperfect hell is all this?"

"The Strange Woman, Judge. I caught her red-handed and we've come for justice."

"The hell with that justice noise, Judge," Toots said. "We could stand a little mercy."

Some of the Bible Class women had come, and kept their mouths closed like bear traps. While the crowd laughed, the Judge eyed those women and said we could all get as deep in contempt of court out in that yard as we could in the biggest courtroom in North Carolina if we didn't shut up. The Judge called Tree. "Mister Poindexter, come on up here."

The Judge touched the liquor jar with his foot. "See what you find in this so-called evidence, sir. I know you've got a trained nose to dedicate to the cause."

Tree opened the liquor jar and sniffed deep. He shook his head.

"Your Honor, I can't smell a thing. If I don't miss my guess, this here is pure water."

Wash opened his mouth, but the Judge waved him aside and took up the jar himself. He gave it an even deeper sniff.

"By George," he said. "I can't find anything here that's incriminating to my nostrils."

"Yes, sir, Judge," Tree said. "It may be that somebody has made some white likker, but these jars are as innocent as babes. I expect they're just full of spring water."

Some of the Bible Class women muttered and shuffled their feet like they wanted to get after Tree and the Judge, and Biscoe Allen's wife yelled to Sheriff Strawn to watch out for tricks. The Judge frowned Wash back down the steps and said he was able to care for any business that came before him, even if it was just on a front porch. Then he gave the crowd another careful look and had Tree and Wash and the deputies carry the liquor jars from the wagon to the porch.

"Now, I don't want to be hasty about this matter," the Judge said. "We appear to have a difference of opinion over this thing. Just to lay the dust, suppose we go into this case here and now."

Wash said they didn't want a trial or anything, but only to put things in the hands of the Judge and get the township clean enough to suit folks. He was just about begging. Everybody said that was all they wanted, even Tootsy.

Red Dowd pushed out front. "Judge, Your Excellency, I call for habeas corpus."

"Who're you supposed to be?"

"Lawyer Dowd for defendant."

"I'll just be damned if you do. You'll have no jury, so we'll have no lawyering. The only trouble I have running court is messing with the dratted lawyers. If you'd leave us alone, me and the sinners would work out things mighty well between us."

"How about habeas corpus?"

"I ought to have known you'd make the nearest no lawyer I ever turned out, Dowd. Ain't you got the sense to see that all that town law don't apply out here in the country, and me high and dry without a jury? Dry up."

The Judge told Tootsy to step out in front of the crowd, and she stood there with the Judge in his rocking chair and Aunt Ly Sue in her hammock and Miss Cassie rocking behind them, trying to turn her smile inside out to keep it from showing. Poll and Shad had their noses against the screen door.

The Judge played the crowd a little. He looked at the Bible Class women. "I know of the miracles you have worked for the Christian folk of Corona, and it is a privilege to be a hand unto you." He rolled his eyes.

The Judge looked out at the rest of the crowd in the yard. "Now, it don't become us to judge our fellows. We've got to live together, like it or not, and we could use a drop of the milk of human kindness."

Biscoe Allen's wife went up the steps with Mrs. Billy

Lufler behind her. "I've had about enough of your bleating, Furn Bucktarrel," Mrs. Allen said. "I guess you don't mind if we see about this water you've got here."

"Now, ladies. That's in custody of the court."

"Well, it's going right out of custody this minute. I know you don't care if we water Miss Ly Sue's grass and her plants—not if this is nothing but spring water."

The Judge closed and opened his mouth, and the smell of liquor began floating through the crowd. People laughed, and several more women crowded up and began helping to empty the liquor bottles, enjoying themselves by splashing it all over the yard. The men in the crowd began to look sick.

When it was over the Judge managed a grin and said, "Well, it appears that somebody's been tampering with the evidence of this court, a serious matter. And perhaps Miz Kinnamon wasn't so falsely accused, after all. What have you got to say, ma'am?"

When he could get the people quiet, the Judge had Tootsy say her piece as she stood on the steps.

"I'm glad it all come up, Judge. I've been expecting it to blow, and I guess it would blow bigger yet if the whole truth was to come out." Tootsy got carried away and talked more than anybody had ever heard her talk in public. Near the end she said, "Now, I've got more sense than to think we're as good as other folks, and we don't want to be, neither. We were all born antigodlin, and my mama and grandma and I reckon those before 'em were old maids. But we do the best we can."

"All right, now, Miss Tootsy."

"Just a damn minute, Judge. They pulled me all the way in here and I want to say my say. All my people had a still before me, and everybody knows a hundred families around here have been moonshining since anybody can remember, and just because it's got to be against some damn new law lately is no reason to pop out with the sweats, is it, now?"

"You mean to confess you've been stilling liquor?"

"Judge, I never said it. We never had to touch it. It was on my place, all right, but the boys who come there to see me and the girls tend it."

"You can't remember any man who kept it, I suppose?"

"Naw, sir."

"That's not such good remembering."

"I can't help it if they come. Pretty near every man in Corona has come there. We were raised to let 'em come if they were good men and would do right. I tell you one thing, Judge, them old boys wouldn't come out to my place for lovin' if they was to be treated better at home."

"I guess that's about enough of that."

"Judge, you talk like this was more your trial than it is mine."

"What else is on your mind?"

"Well, I say that if the women of all the boys that come to my place was to leave here right now, we'd not have much of a crowd. I hear tales about some mighty cold sticks —and them churchwomen, too, Judge."

People fidgeted.

"Tootsy, I reckon that's all you've got to say, isn't it?"

"Yase, sir. Just let come down on me what's to come, Judge. I'm just like I've always been, and nobody ever held it against me till now. And Judge, I thank you. I appreciate it."

"Let's pray," somebody said.

The Judge stomped his foot. "Like hell we will. The Lord handles enough of our dirty business. We'll do some of it ourselves."

He motioned to Wash. "Mr. Sheriff, let me see that worm." The Judge turned the coil in his hands and saw that it was a good sound one, and hadn't been made of galvanized pipe or something that would poison people.

"Miz Kinnamon," the Judge said, "I sentence you to pay a fine of ten dollars and costs, and to serve sixty days in the county jail . . ."

"Fore God, Judge."

"Sentence suspended, but the fine to stand. Mr. Sheriff, see to it that the worm is returned to the defendant."

Even children in the crowd knew that the worm was the most expensive part of the still, and that when she got it back Tootsy could be making liquor again within a couple of days.

The Judge made a speech and shook hands with the Virginia officers and Wash Strawn, and told the Bible Class women how they had shamed Corona with their devotion, let alone their sharp noses, and that they were lights unto everybody's feet, and that we would all be the better for what they had done. Then he said, "Now, I've done the best I could with this case, and I propose that your class take this unfortunate woman under your watchcare. I know you could lift her with strong and loving arms. I commend her household to your care."

The women looked like that was something they hadn't expected, and court broke up in a buzzing, with people not knowing what to think.

17

The Day I Got Even

At school the next Monday, Miss Cassie acted like she'd
never heard of trouble. She played baseball with us, and for
a while we forgot that people at home were just waiting for
something to happen about the tobacco market.

We played mean baseball at school, and threw and hit like
demons, because the big boys were sprinkled around on each
team and everybody played for neck or nothing. Early in
the year the weeds were so bad that we had to play that you
could catch a man out on first bounce, but when we got the
field walked down pretty well, we opened up. We had a
stump for first base and planks for the others.

Our balls were made of string, wrapped tight around

rocks. They were mighty hard until the bats had beaten them for a few days. Good hitters used narrow bats, sticks about like the slats that hold wagon bodies, and for girls and other weak hitters we had paddles with handles trimmed out. Players ranged from knee-high to six and a half feet, girls and boys, too.

The woods were close, and when a ball was hit into them the fielders yelled, "Lost ball, stop!" and then the runners stopped in their tracks until somebody yelled "Found ball, go!" and they tore off again.

Sometimes one team stayed at bat for three or four days because we couldn't get it out—they kept on banging the ball and making runs. The catcher was the only one with a mitt or a glove, except when Miss Cassie played. She said she needed one for her tender hands. She couldn't hit one all the way to the woods, but shot them out of the infield every now and then. She was handy to have around, too, because when the ball went near the girls' toilet none of us would fetch it, and the girls would titter and say of course they couldn't go, with us watching. Miss Cassie would bring it out. A ball hit down there was always counted a home run. The only thing wrong with having Miss Cassie play was that one of the big boys would have to run the bases for her.

One day a state supervisor came to see if we were getting enough recreation in our school. He was a long drink of water, in tight pants, wearing spectacles and carrying a big ball—a dodge ball like they used in sissy games in town. When he saw the kind of rough-and-ready baseball we played, he hid the big ball and pretended he hadn't brought it. Miss Cassie was at bat when he came, and she hung one like a rope between shortstop and second base, and tore down toward first before she remembered she had to have a runner. The supervisor looked sheepish.

"Come on in, Mr. Simpson," Miss Cassie said. "The children want you to play. Jiggs, let Mr. Simpson take your turn at bat."

Jiggs and Mr. Simpson both hated the idea, but Mr. Simpson came to the plate and Miss Cassie called me to pitch to him. I didn't half try, but the ball zipped by him so fast that he hardly got the bat off his shoulder, and he struck out on four pitches and ended the inning. Miss Cassie said she was sorry that we were so far behind in our school recreation, but that the children didn't like dodge ball. Mr. Simpson took his ball away with him.

Miss Cassie had a way of taking each of us aside and trying to give us some kind of sly lesson now and then. It wasn't easy to understand her at first. She kept me in once after the others had left—to help her clean up, she said. She pretended to dust, and talked to me about how easy it was to grow up.

I felt myself getting my back up. Since I'd seen Jimroe hug her, she was different to me. I couldn't seem to look her in the face, and I kept thinking, I hate you. You think I'm nothing but a durn baby and I hate you.

"All grownups are really old children," she said.

"Yes'm."

"They have the same troubles with things that you do."

"Not the ones I know."

"Inside, they do. When things get bad enough, any one of us would like to go away and play and forget them—or just sit down and cry."

"I never saw Papa do it—or Cousin Tree."

"That's because they have to put a grown-up face on things. They're too proud to show it."

I made out that I didn't care what she was saying, and she took me by the chin and pulled up my head. She was pretty serious.

"What's wrong, Fax?"

"Nothing's wrong."

"Don't tell me that. We used to be such friends. You used

to talk to me. Sometimes now, you act like you never want to see me again."

"I can't help it."

She gave a deep breath and turned loose my chin. "Well, whatever it is, you'll outgrow it. All of us grow up without knowing it, and one day we have to do our part in running things."

I couldn't imagine knowing as much as Tree, or handling the farm and the family like Papa.

"It's coming over you right now, freckle by freckle. The beauty part is that it doesn't hurt, because you don't feel it until it's too late."

She said that when I grew a little more I wouldn't want to be fighting about things that didn't go just right, and that I'd have to find other ways around. Then she surprised me. "It's hardly ever worthwhile to fight about anything, I mean with your fists. But sometimes, of course, you can't help it . . . any boy with grit."

I wanted to talk to her about it, but I couldn't bring myself to do it, and when I left her my mouth was still poked out. I could see her in my mind, walking with Jimroe's arm around her, and Miss Cassie laughing and doing nothing to stop him. That made me feel sorrier for myself than ever, thinking of how Jimroe was always taking things away from me.

Once in a while, after the weather began getting cooler, we ran away from school. Miss Cassie seemed to know that we were going to do it, and after the first time she was ready for us. We had always been that way. If foxhounds ran near the schoolhouse, or we could hear hunters in the woods, blowing their cow horns, the bigger boys would jump up and run out the door.

Maybe Jimroe or one of the big Indian boys would be slouching away down in his bench, on his neck, with knees propped up in the air, when a hound yelped hot on a fox trail. The big boys would unlimber like the place was on fire and shoot out the door. The other boys would pile after them and we would be gone the rest of the day. We paid for the first one by staying in after school—just as long as we had missed the day before, to the minute.

"I don't blame you," Miss Cassie said. "If I could do it I might run off, too, but I can't. I'll warn you not to pull that stunt again. If you do, you must stay in school to make up your time. You decide in your own minds whether it's worth that."

We held back as long as we could, but once in a while it was too much for us and we ran away. When we had a little skift of snow on the ground we almost always tried Miss Cassie. We played a game of Fox at dinnertime and chased one of the big boys through the woods, howling after him like hounds, and it was usually an hour or so before we remembered to come back.

It was on one of those days when most of the school ran away that I got even with Jiggs Sixkiller. We were right at the edge of the woods, leaving the schoolyard, when Jiggs turned around in front of me and yelled, "Come on, ninny-boy. We're gonna burn down a white-folks' barn."

I ducked my head and butted him in the belly so hard that he went around and around on his heels, fighting to breathe and holding his middle with both arms. I followed him, hitting him in the face until he thought it was raining fists. He began backing away, looking sidewise to see if some of his buddies were around—but we were all alone.

I got two of his teeth loose and closed one of his eyes and had his nose oozing, when he seemed to get his second wind and began to stand me off for a while. For a minute or two it was a close fight, and he whacked me a pretty hard one now and then. But something got into me that made me feel twice his size. I couldn't seem to feel his licks any more, and I just gritted my teeth and whaled him. I was glad there was no-

body around to get in our way, so that I could fight him to
the finish and he'd never want to cross me again. I saw the
look on Jiggs' face change. He was scared. After a minute or
so of that kind of fighting he broke and ran. He headed for
the school, but I cut him off before he could reach the door,
and he went for a big white-oak tree that grew behind the
building. He beat me there by a few steps and went up like
a squirrel. I shinnied after him. He took off his heavy old
broken shoes and threw them at me. He missed with one,
but the other clipped me on the shoulder and numbed my
arm for a few minutes.

Jiggs went high in the tree and broke off a long switch,
and when I got close enough he slashed me in the face as
hard as he could. I couldn't stand that for long before I had
to back down. I slid to the ground and waited until it didn't
hurt so bad and I got up my nerve again, and then went
back.

Jiggs kept hissing at me through his teeth, "Come on,
white boy!"

The more I went up, the harder he cut me with his switch.
I was afraid that he would put out my eyes, so I closed them
tight and stayed up a long time before he whipped me down.

I went up a half-dozen times or more. He wasn't hissing at
me by then, and did nothing but hang there with his eyes
bugged, looking down at me, breathing hard and slapping at
my head when I came in range. It went on that way until it
was getting dark in the schoolyard, and sometimes I got
within a few inches of being able to grab him by the leg
before he whipped me away. Then I'd go down and sit, and
as the hurting eased I got madder and madder, thinking about
him, and would jump up and try the tree again. I hadn't said
a word all that time; the kids were long gone by now. It was
quiet in the yard. I waited and waited at the bottom of the
tree and didn't know what I ought to do. If I went home to
do my regular chores or to take a licking from Papa, then

Jiggs would get away—but I'd get a licking anyway if I didn't go home and do my work.

I tried Jiggs one more time, and hung just a foot or two under him while he caned the devil out of my face and head and shoulders until my eyes watered. I just hung by one arm and kept feeling up for him. Then I came down. It would be dark soon. I left him.

When I rounded the corner of the building I saw Miss Cassie. She was sitting, watching, inside the window in the half-dark. She waved me in. She had a note in her hand. For some reason I felt different about her right then. I didn't hate her and didn't love her. I thought she had been crying and I was sorry for her. When her hand touched mine it was damp.

"Fax, take this to your daddy. And leave Jiggs alone."

"Yes'm."

"And don't take things so hard. Remember what I told you about growing up, now. We'll soon be having our school Christmas party, won't we?"

"I guess so."

"We will that, and we'll have a big crowd from all over Corona, and I'll want to show off my prize pupil. You'll have to spell and read for them."

I turned out of the door, but she called me back.

"Fax."

"Yes'm."

"You're the bravest little boy I ever saw in my life."

I ran all the way home. I couldn't remember touching the ground on the way. I knew that Miss Cassie was the greatest woman in the world, and I didn't care how much Jimroe hugged her.

I washed up at the spring and went to the house and walked around on the porch, waiting for somebody to notice me. I had to keep my lips clamped so that I wouldn't yelp when I moved, because I was bruised all over and my face was cut up considerably. My knuckles throbbed where I had cut them on a tooth. I was too proud to hunt for Papa, but he soon came on the porch with a lantern, on his way to the barn.

He started to speak, but when he saw the mess my face was in, his mouth set hard. He looked at my puffed hand when I held out the note from Miss Cassie. He unfolded the paper and looked up at me with his eyes a little wet.

"You whipped him."

"Yase, sir."

"I don't care a damn, then, if you never go back to school."

Mama had come on the porch. "Now, Hence."

Papa steered me for the barn. I felt light in the head, like this was happening to somebody else and that I was just watching it.

He walked out of sight of the house and stopped to look at me. "Dog my buttons. Old Fax."

He slipped his black snapmouth leather purse from his pocket and shook money from the coin side, half a foot deep in the sack. He handed me a brand-new quarter. I rubbed it.

"You take care of money, boy, and it'll care for you some day. Money ain't everything, as they say—but it's way the hell ahead of whatever it is that's in second place."

We walked back to the house side by side, not with Papa in front as usual.

"I guess I don't know all I ought to know about that Miss Carson of yours," Papa said. "What description of woman is she?"

"Just a little old woman."

"Little, hell. It sounds like she ain't so much little as that she's just wound real tight."

"She's all right. Just an ordinary old woman—but she don't put on airs."

"I aim to have a better look at her."

He took me on the porch and touched me up with some of the medicine he used when he doctored people in the family or in the neighborhood. He daubed something on my face that stung like fury for a while.

I thought that Mama might pitch in and give us both Hail Columbia, but she went on like nothing had happened and didn't even frown when Papa sat at the kitchen table and said, "Hell's katoot, Little Bit, I'm so hungry I could eat a mule stuffed with firecrackers."

I felt better about Papa than I ever had.

18

The River Crossing

The next day was Sunday, and in the evening after supper, while we were in the parlor listening to Cornelia play the organ, Cousin Tree came sliding in. He motioned Papa outside and they went on the porch. Cornelia kept playing "Abide With Me" without missing a note. When I peeked outside I saw what was the matter.

Wagons were coming down Wildkitten road, what looked like hundreds of wagons, with the noses of one team almost touching the tail of the wagon in front. I knew they were tobacco wagons heading for Virginia—just about every farmer in our part of the county had joined the uprising against the warehouse in Corona and was going to sell his tobacco in Danville. I couldn't believe there were so many, more even than we had seen at the opening of the market.

The sky was getting dark and I could see each new wagon as it topped the rise, coming our way, when another lantern would bob into sight and join the string of lights snaking down the mountain, inching slowly along the three crooked miles from the ridge top to the river. Wagons backed up into our pasture until they filled the lower section, and then turned off on each side of the road until we were almost surrounded on the river side of our place.

Families in the wagons began making camp, and fires sprang up and people played fiddles and guitars and banjoes. A good many friends came to our house, and stayed late talking with Papa and Tree and Mama.

By morning it looked like a city of some kind had popped out of the ground, and nobody thought of our going to school that day.

The wagons had to wait because the river was high and there were no fords to use, and everything depended on the little ferry at Tree's house. It would take only one wagon at a time, and that pretty slow, with water foaming almost to the top of the side boards. The heaviest wagons had to be turned back, and a few men had them pulled over the river by swimming their horses, ruining half the tobacco in the water but going ahead anyhow. They kept up a stir at the crossing and it was exciting to watch. Jimroe and Damon and I and the little boys were there every minute we could get away from home.

People slept under the wagons and began cooking before daylight. There were lots of women and children along, and they were noisy, but it wasn't a lark. People were sore about the low tobacco prices in our county, and they blamed everybody they could think of: Biscoe Allen and his partners, the tobacco companies and other growers. The big growers blamed all the little farmers, for overplanting their few acres, and the little farmers said the big ones always rigged things their own way. They talked about almost nothing else around the wagons. Most of them seemed not to expect much from driving all the way to Danville, the nearest big market. They hoped prices would be better, but were afraid they would be the same. Most of the families were going because everybody else was going.

Some men knocked together a couple more little ferry scows so that they could hurry things, and pulled them back and forth on ropes, using mule teams on each side of the river. The mules lived hard, day and night, lashed by whips and scampering up the steep river banks to haul the ferries. But it was still slow, and the wagons that had crossed first were already strung out for miles on the long road to Danville.

The morning was nippy, about the coldest of the winter so far, and we ate breakfast early—or started early, because about half the county came in to have a bite with us, once the ham-and-egg and coffee smell blew down the lane.

Our big old Home Comfort range gulped armloads of hardwood chunks as fast as the little boys could bring them in. The stove chuffed up and down like a mad monkey, with its firebox roaring, and all nine stove lids glowed cherry-red, and the water reservoir steamed and sizzled at every crack. Mama had been cooking corn mush since four o'clock in black iron pots until the house was full of the smell of corn meal and butter and milk simmering. We ate it out of thick crockery bowls, with yellow cream and sorghum syrup.

The big girls stood over the stove, cooking and handing things, and nobody knew how many eggs and slices of ham they cooked; Mama had cleaned the pin-money basket of eggs and had the little kids scouring the yard and crawling under sheds to look for more, even to taking them from under hens they found cackling in the hayloft. People kept coming into the kitchen and the dishes got washed a dozen times before it was over; pans of biscuits kept coming out of the oven in puffs of fresh heat. We all thought that was the only way to treat neighbors.

Cousin Tree came in late, when only biscuits and coffee were left. Grandpa woke up then and spoke for the first time during breakfast. "I heard you was getting rich, Trevilian. All that ferrying going on."

Tree laughed. "It's no joke. You know I wouldn't dare to charge 'em, and they're about to tear up everything we've got. Well—looks different in here. Me out there, risking my life trying to direct 'em over the river and out of your way, and you living high up on the hog."

"No trouble?" Papa said.

Tree said it was the tamest crowd he ever saw. "But I'd hate to be the man to try and stop 'em going to Danville. They've got the bit in their teeth, I mean to tell you. They don't know what they're doing, but they're bound to do it."

"What else can we do but pack and go with 'em?" Papa said.

"Whichever way, the year's wasted," Tree said.

"It ain't the first time the damn river's been crossed with tobacco," Grandpa said, and started telling about the mutiny of the farmers before the Civil War. Papa lost his temper with Grandpa and surprised us all. "Tell us something new," Papa said, pretty sharp.

"You listen, sprout, and I'll do that thing," Grandpa said. "You get sick of hearing about the old times and the trouble they had crossing—you heard talk but you didn't hear enough. You never did know what they found out when they came back from Virginia that time, did you, now?"

Papa cooled off. "Naw, sir."

"They found out that the damn warehouseman had tricked 'em into going, to get 'em off his back. Yes, sir. All he had to do was spread the word on the sly that folks ought to go, thinking that they were spiting him, so that he wouldn't have to bear the blame of low prices and hard times. Nobody blinked wise until too late."

"The hell you preach," Tree said.

Tree and Papa looked at each other. "It's just childish enough to appeal to Allen," Tree said. "I wouldn't put it beyond him."

Mama came to the table with a dripping dishrag in her hand. "What's the matter?" she said.

"I know what I'm saying," Grandpa said, "and that hammerheaded Hence is too stubborn to listen. The Allens are trying to pocket this country."

"Not Biscoe, surely," Mama said.

"If he's Allen blood, he'd cheat himself if he could," Grandpa snorted. "Go on! Go if you're fool enough, Hence."

"By God," Tree said. "What if he's right?"

"Well, how do we get anything out of it if we sit here like bumps on a log?" Papa said. "If we cross, we'll at least get Danville prices."

"You'd meet the same old crowd of buyers," Tree said. "You ain't likely to pay for your trip."

"They might close the market in your face," Grandpa said. "It happened before."

"I can't believe it of him," Mama said. "I can't see him doing it."

"You ain't got the sense to listen to an old man," Grandpa said, "but the day'll come you'll wish you had kept your good crop and not gone traipsing off with all them fools."

"It almost sounds like sense to me," Tree said.

Mama wasn't sure. "Oh, Beau. Let's get rid of that crop. I'm tired of this night watching and fearing for our lives. I don't want to see more such times."

Papa took her out of the kitchen, and they all went to the wagons in the pasture and we tagged along. Papa watched the people and the mules at the ford, all working with the loaded wagons.

"I'll give old Biscoe this much," he said. "If he was of a

purpose to get their minds off his warehouse, he's done the job."

We found Judge Bucktarrel in his phaeton and he made us push Grandpa up to sit beside him. They argued with each other about the river crossing like it had something to do with the Civil War.

"It's a damn-Yankee Republican notion," Grandpa said. "I wouldn't bat an eye if they was all to drown, except for the pretty women."

The Judge bickered back and forth with him, but they soon gave out and the Judge put his arm around Grandpa. "The only trouble with this living forever," he said, "is that you've got to stand by and see every generation come along and make bigger fools of themselves."

"It ain't because they've not been told better," Grandpa said. "I have just tried to give that muley Hence the last lesson I aim to."

"I hope you gave him good true history, Grant," the Judge said. "The kind you know best."

"Damn you, Yank. If things I can remember don't suit me, why, I make 'em up afresh. Suits me better, anyway."

The Judge pulled a bottle of white liquor from his lap robe and the old men took turns sampling.

"God knows how younguns will get along when we're gone, Grant."

Grandpa sang one of his old Army songs, and the Judge drove away with him. People in the crowd grinned after them. Tootsy Kinnamon was there, and I heard her say, "There's as randy a brace of old billy goats as ever came my way. I wish I thought the young fry would turn out as good."

Tootsy had a load of tobacco going to Virginia. She had Red Dowd with her, and she laughed when Red talked about "our tobacco" and the money he thought it would bring.

Several Indian farmers spoke to Papa. "Why come you ain't going, Mister Hence?"

"Well, I expect you'd have all the money before I ever got into sight of Danville. I might go yet if you ever clear out and give me room."

"Damned if I wouldn't find me a way across if I had all that prime tobacco that's in your barns."

"Well, all tobacco's a chance and a gamble," Papa said. "I took the first risk when I burnt new ground for the plant bed last January."

The Indian laughed at Papa, and you could see that he thought Papa was a fool not to join in.

Mama and Papa went back home. Tree stayed by the river all day while the ferries sloshed back and forth, and Jimroe and I stayed as long as we could. The wagons kept pitching up the hill on the Virginia shore, one by one and out of sight, along the road to the northeast, up toward Danville.

Near sundown Tree came up to our house and he and Papa stood on the porch. Tree said that the river was falling and that they might begin fording in a day or so, and that the crowd could clear out.

"I'll be glad to see 'em go," Tree said. "There's too many empty bottles in that crowd tonight."

"We'll watch sharp," Papa said.

"Oh, nothing extra. Just make sure you don't go to sleep and leave things lying around loose."

Tree stretched. "Just about bullbat time," he said. He unfastened his collar and looked at Papa like he expected something. Papa slipped a jar from a cabinet on the porch and was unscrewing the top when Grandpa popped out.

"How the hell you think you can open a medicine bottle without me taking notice?" Grandpa said. He took a drink from Papa.

Tree told his worn-out story about bullbat time—about how gentlemen never drank until dusk, when the nighthawks were flying. Tree claimed he had known a man who'd been such a hard drinker that he had caught a bullbat and tamed him, and carried him in his shirt so that he could turn him loose any time of the day or night, and then take his drink and still be a gentleman. Grandpa popped Tree on the back and asked for another sip.

They stood on the porch for a while, watching the crowd down at the river until Mama called supper. Papa sent Frank and Damon and Creed and Jimroe to the barns to stand guard. They brought their guns without Mama noticing.

19

Tree and the Barn Burners

Papa had gone into the house, and Tree and I were on the porch by ourselves, washing, when we heard a wagon in the lane, rattling fast downhill. It was a little while before we could make out who was driving—it was Tootsy Kinnamon, alone.

She said she wouldn't have time to get out, then just sat there, moving from one side of her seat to the other like the plank was hot beneath her. "I've got something to say to you, Trevilian."

Tree stepped down in the yard. "You can speak up, it's just Fax."

Toots gave me a look and said, "Well, I expect it's too late already, Tree. Somebody's going after Hence's barns tonight."

"We'll be watching."

"I tell you, now—they don't mean maybe. They left the wagon camp a while ago."

"Who'd you say?"

"I never said."

"I thought we was friends."

"I'd as soon take off my tongue as to lay it to one of them names. You ought to know better than to ask me."

"We'll be down there in a jiffy then," Tree said.

Papa came on the porch and Toots stopped talking. Papa said he wished she would come in the house, but Toots said she had better hurry, and whipped her mule and left. Mama got to the door in time to see who it was, and looked to us, wondering.

Tree said, "I believe I'll have you fetch me a pail of coffee, Lin. I want to go down to the barns. Hence—you come when you're through."

Papa went in the house and Tree whispered to me, "Keep him away from down there as long as you can. Until I'm clean gone. Give me time. All they'd want is one good shot at him, where nobody'd ever know who did it."

I went in the kitchen and sat in front of Papa at the table and tried to slow him down, hoping they wouldn't notice how hard I was breathing. I talked about school and anything I could think of. Papa stayed for almost ten minutes, eating.

There was a rifle shot from the direction of the spring, near the lower tobacco barns. It echoed in the woods like several shots. Grandpa said, "Hell I reckon. Yankee bushwhackers." Papa jumped up and sloshed coffee on the oilcloth. Mama was standing, and dabbed at the spilled coffee with a rag, with her eyes big, saying, "I told you, Hence. Oh, Beau, didn't I say so?"

Papa went into the yard, yelling for her to have the little boys stay in the house, but for me to saddle a mule and follow him. Papa ran into Jimroe at the bottom of the steps, and they talked like that for a few seconds, holding on to each other with both arms, heads thrown back and yelling.

"What is it?"

"Barn burning. Indians."

"Come on," Papa said. He snatched his rifle on the porch. There was another shot from over the ridge. I saddled the mule and went down to the springhouse after Papa as quick as I could, but by the time I got there, he was crouched against the side of the first barn with the big boys. I heard fire crackling beyond, and could smell it.

"Step in here," Papa said. "Out of the light."

"Where's Tree?"

"Trailing, like a fool."

"We ought to go," Frank said. "They'll ambush him."

"Wait," Papa said. "He knows what he's up against."

"Yes," I said. "He's gone to get shot for you, Papa. He knows they laid for you, and he went instead so that he could save you."

They all looked at me and Papa looked the least surprised of any of them. He seemed as if light had broken on him the minute I opened my mouth.

"I know," I said. "He knew they'd get you, and he went. It's the Sixkillers."

They said nothing. Papa's teeth were gritted.

"I know all about it," I said.

"Who said so?"

"I just know. Toots came and told us they were coming— and I knew who it was all the time. I heard 'em say they'd burn us out, a long time ago. It's Pem and Jess, I tell you."

Papa took me hard by the shoulder. "I hope to hell you know what you're saying, son. Come on."

Another shot cracked in the dark while we were stumbling down the path. We went as fast as we could in the rutted trail, but it was steep and rocky and the shadows from the burning barn made it hard to see. We met Tree before we came to the creek bottom.

He was on Lize, but she was hanging her head and he held himself up with stiff arms against her shoulders. He was trailing blood from one shoe.

"Don't mess with me," he said. "Get back to the barns before they get 'em all."

Papa and I led him back and the others ran to the barns. Papa kept stumbling on the rocks, trying to hold Tree in the saddle with both arms while I pulled on Lize's bridle. Papa kept saying over and over, "Tree. Tree."

When we got to the house, Mama had settled down. She helped me and Papa get Tree off Lize and onto the porch.

We rested him a little there and then got him off a chair and upstairs to the girls' room. Tree made no sound, but was hurting. His breathing was slow and jerky. Papa went to work on him while Mama helped him in the kitchen. The girls brought up clean rags and hot water.

The first thing Tree said in bed sounded like a woman talking, with a kind of bubble in his voice: "See to Lize."

Papa said she was all right, and tried to get Tree to give up and let himself be doctored.

"Keep your boys back, Hence," Tree said. "Don't let 'em go tracking in the dark."

Papa straightened the bad leg while the rest of us tried to hold Tree down; he twisted and flailed us with his big arms, and Mama was punched around like a pillow, but she said, "Go ahead and cuss, Tree. Get it out of your system." He bit blood out of his lip and it swelled all at once like a little sausage. He had sweat over his face and in his hair, and it began to smell close in the room. When Papa turned the leg loose, Tree sagged.

Papa leaned over him.

"A little more and it'd have smashed the shinbone," Papa said. "The bullet's still there. We ought to have help."

He went on the porch and sawed a bed slat into three or four pieces and bound the leg tight with torn sheets. Mama sent Cornelia and Ivy to find Judge Bucktarrel and see if he would get a doctor from Randolph.

Papa got some of the strong medicine that he used when he doctored us or the stock, and it began to smell of carbolic acid upstairs. We went outside while Mama and Papa undressed Tree and washed him. Once I heard Tree half crying. He sounded like he was trying to cough up something dry from his throat.

"It was my fault, Hence. I'm a damn fool."

"Yeah," Papa said. "I know whose fault it was, all right. I'm late, but I know now."

"You hush," Mama said. "Both of you hush. He needs his rest."

When Mama came out of the room I begged her to let me go to the barns and help stand watch for the rest of the night, but she wouldn't have it.

"I'm not going to have all my little children shot too," she said.

I kept after her until she finally said, "All right, you can help them in daylight—one day. But not unless your papa says you can." She sounded like she was sure that Papa would never hear of it.

Nobody got much sleep that night. Once I tipped out in the hall and heard Tree and Papa.

"I could use another swallow of likker," Tree said.

"One more is all. You had enough. Get some rest now."

"I hate to be here, messing up Lin's bedclothes and all."

"Well, it can't be helped."

"If I'd had about half sense, I'd never have got knocked down."

"Who was it, Tree?"

"I ain't exactly sure."

"Like hell. It was Jess."

"Well."

"The son of a bitch. I expect I goaded him into it, fooling around with him last summer."

"Naw, it was just his natural meanness. He didn't burn your barn, though, Hence. He'd never do that. He was covering somebody."

Papa waited.

"There was somebody beyond him in that path and I got almost on top of them before Jess shot. I guess he felt like he had to stop me."

"Bushwhacking."

"He yelled first. I'll say that for him. He warned me back. I knew his voice, all right. It was almost like I knew who was going to yell before he opened his mouth. You know how me and Jess have always been close."

"Yeah."

"He's drinking hard. He'll sober up mighty sorry for it."

"Never mind. I'll deal with him."

"Naw, not you. This is just between me and Jess. It's got to be settled the Redshank way."

"It was you he shot, but it was us you were saving—me, I mean."

"I don't care what you say, Hence. He's mine."

"If he's drinking so hard, how'd he happen to wing you?"

"He broke the leg with his first shot, out of the dark. Then he punched me with the rifle and said, 'I'd as soon kill ye, Pinedexter, but you'd better get. This ain't your business.'

"I couldn't walk, but when he cocked that rifle, somehow it made the leg work pretty good and I crawled in the saddle."

It was quiet in the room.

"You did it for us, Tree. Knowing all the time . . ."

"Hell. You know better. I didn't stop to think who. I just went."

"I'll get him," Papa said. "I can do that much."

"Naw, sir. I tell you, he's my meat. He'll take to the brush and hide and I'll have him to hunt down. I'll take my time; I want him to fret over it while I make up my mind what I'll do to him."

"It's my worry. It was me you were helping."

"It don't matter about that. The man you've got to watch is still out there—and he ain't through."

"Pem."

Tree said he thought it might be—but he and Papa both knew who it was. "He won't rest, anyway, till he's fired every last barn you've got," Tree said.

"If he does burn 'em, he won't get just mine. One of the barns belongs to you, Tree."

"Why, damn your time."

"You ought to have more than that—I just wish it was so that it'd bring you some money. Right now, it looks like it ain't worth a dime."

"I can't take your tobacco."

"Ah, if it wasn't for you, we'd have no tobacco at all. Don't be that way."

"It ain't the tobacco. You don't fool me. I know you right down to your marrowbone. You've got to be a colored man to know a white man, Hence."

"Goddamn, Tree."

"I can tell by the cut of his eye, or the way he holds his head, or the hairs on the back of his neck, when a white man hates for me to come around him."

"You've got to get some rest."

"I'm going to have my say. You're the only white man that ever treated me like he never noticed what color I was, or cared. You've got no idea how rare you are. If you woke up some morning with a wrong-colored skin, you'd find out what I mean."

"Oh, come on, Tree."

"Hell, it's been boiling in me since I was old enough to

know B from Bullsfoot—and who is there you can tell? It's the thing that ails old Jess, too, and he hasn't the sense to know it."

"Tree."

"I know things ain't the way they used to be when we were chaps. Don't think I ain't got some sense."

Papa put his hand on the doorknob and I scooted. I was awake a long time, with Tree on my mind.

Doc Kiger was there when I woke up, washing his hands in a basin in the hall. He said that Papa had patched up Tree right well, and hadn't left much for him to do.

"He'll hobble for a while, but he's going to make it all right. A couple of weeks or so and he'll be on his feet a little."

Zelda came to see Tree that morning with all her kids and went in the room howling about Tree dying and leaving them alone with their troubles. Mama was having a fit to get them out, and in five minutes had hustled them into the yard. In the end they went away laughing, like Tree was just there on a visit.

Tree called me into his room and said he needed somebody to talk to, but while I sat there he slept, twitching his big hands like he was dreaming hard. Judge Bucktarrel came later in the day and he and Papa and Grandpa came in to see Tree.

The Judge had brought a bottle of red liquor from the store and Tree took a pull and straightened up.

"A little more of that kind of doctoring and I might take the notion to live," he said. "I was beginning to feel three years older than God."

Papa saw Grandpa working his lips and passed the bottle to him.

"I came to say," the Judge said, "that we're going to care for Zelda and the children, and see that they don't starve.

We're going to keep you in all the doctoring you need—
with plenty of this good medicine here. And we're going to
see that nothing more bad happens to Hence's people.
How's that strike you?"

Tree still felt like joking. "It puts me in mind of the fellow
who was running for President of Hell," he said. "He run on
the platform of cutting down the heat and establishing
water. Who in Hell wouldn't be for that?"

Papa and the Judge laughed enough to be polite, almost
enough so that Tree wouldn't know they'd heard it so many
times—but Grandpa carried on like he'd never heard it at all,
and they had a time stopping him laughing.

"I take it to heart," Grandpa said, "seeing's I'm damn soon
going to be down there, trying it out."

The Judge got back to Tree. "You didn't get a look at the
burner?"

"Not a peep—naw, sir."

"You think it was a Sixkiller."

"I never said that."

"I think we can assume it was. But it wouldn't make sense
to arrest anybody."

"Naw. It's no arresting matter. They've got to be stopped
when they come for the barns, and that's all. They mean to
burn or die."

"What got 'em all that stirred up?"

"Bad times to begin with, and living jealous. Then I expect Wash Strawn ran his mouth too hard, trying to help
Biscoe wiggle out of his market. You know you can't play
games with a Redshank. He don't follow you."

"You don't suspect old Biscoe."

"Naw, sir. He'd stoop to anything he could think of, if
there was any getting away with it—but he knows way
yonder better than to get caught in a burning scheme."

"Yeah. I reckon there's little to lay at his door," the
Judge said. "At least we know he'll find damn slight pleasure
in life. Mrs. Allen sees to that."

The Judge helped us carry Tree out of bed to the chamber pot, and it seemed to hurt him worse than the leg, to have to be lifted around like a baby. We had him out of his old clothes and into some of Papa's clean ones before he knew it. Tree said, "Dammitall, Hence, I didn't know you were so fleshy. I feel like a possum in a bearhide."

"You talk so damn much," Grandpa said. "Let me hold that bottle." He took a gurgle.

"All right," Papa said. "It's getting on toward noon. We'd better let Tree rest his bones."

Mama came in with some dinner for Tree just as Jimroe was working on Papa about guarding the barns. I couldn't believe my ears, but Jimroe was trying to get him to let me help stand guard. Mama stood with dishes drooping and her mouth open, looking at Jimroe.

"We need old Fax bad," Jimroe said.

"I'll be damned," Papa said.

"I mean it, now, Papa. If we had one more hand, we could have somebody at every barn, and have things covered right."

"We'll have to leave it to the men," Papa said, but he gave me a sidewise look.

Jimroe went up close to him and gave him his halfway smile. "What I mean, now, Papa, is that if you put him in just the right place, where things wouldn't go too hard on him . . . see. And you know how steady he is."

Papa looked at Mama's feet. "I'm half a mind to let him," he said. He looked up at Mama and went faster. "We do need him. We'd keep him just a night or so, and be careful where he was."

Mama put the dishes down hard in Tree's lap and spilled navy beans on the covers and went out, flapping her apron. She spoke like she hadn't heard Papa. "Come on down now, and get you something to eat."

I felt like hugging Jimroe.

20

Fire in the Night

Mama was molding butter on the kitchen table, slapping down the pale yellow chunks and popping them into the mold and taking them out stamped with her sheaf-of-wheat design, all beaded with cold water. She didn't look up while she told me what I was to do.

"I'm going to let you go down to the barns tonight like your papa said, because I promised—but just this once."

"Yes'm." I was busy eating dinner after everybody else had finished, and it was almost two o'clock. I hurried to the porch. "And, son, I don't mean for you to have a gun."

I howled about that, but she wouldn't budge. She just

said, "No gun, or it's no barn for you. You're not even sixteen years old. I won't have it."

So I went down to the barns, where Papa and the boys were getting ready for the night watch and told him what Mama had said and he just shook his head. Papa talked it over with Frank and they sent me to the biggest barn.

"I'm going to give you the money barn," Papa said, "because I know you'll keep an eye peeled, and are an old coon hunter, and won't do any fool thing to bring on trouble."

I knew what he meant, though. The big barn was the safest one, because it was surrounded by all the other barns on the low side. Any burner who came through the flat woods would have to pass by some of the others before he got to me. The only way anybody could get at me directly was down that steep ridge above the barns, and nobody would be able to come down the hill without making enough noise to wake the dead. So Papa thought he wouldn't have to worry over my getting hurt.

I went to the barn in the afternoon and fooled around to get ready, going over my throwing rocks. I had brought all the smooth river rocks from under my bed, the ones I had been saving for months. I thought that if I didn't get to shoot at somebody, I could at least knock off his noggin with a rock. I practiced a little, throwing at trees around the barn, and whacked everything right on the nose. Damon peeped around his barn to see what was pecking in the woods, and waved and said for God's sake to watch where I was chunking.

Papa came late in the afternoon to see that I was all right, and brought a quilt for me to wrap in after dark, because a fire would be dangerous in case somebody wanted to wing one of us. He said he would soon send me some corn bread and backbones to eat.

"I'm going to get some water up here," I said. "If I had a few buckets, and we did happen to get set afire . . ."

"Do that. You're the first to think of it. It's too bad we didn't have a schoolboy on the job before."

I got four buckets of water from the spring and put them under the shed of the barn. It was dark before I finished, and I was glad to see Ivy come with a plate of supper. The bread and meat were still hot and I ate so much that I could have popped a beetle on my belly.

I never did know whether or not I fell asleep, because what happened seemed like a dream. I was just below the top of the ridge. On the far side of the ridge, where the house was, it was pretty well lit up after dark by all the camp fires from the wagons. But the ridge cut that light off, and we were in dark that was as black as a cave. The air felt like rain and it was so quiet that I heard sounds from the wagons near the river crossing. Nothing stirred around me except an occasional breath of wind, when the dry leaves of the shed roof riffled over my head. I knew just where Papa was, and every one of my brothers, too. I had taken a good look in every direction just before the light faded, trying to memorize every tree so that I'd be ready for anything.

I had the feeling that time hung like that for a while, with hardly a sound, and nothing to be seen—when in the midst of it, so near that I knew something had gone wrong, I heard a footstep. It seemed to be high in the air, yet close to me.

There was a whisper. "G-g-god-dammit. St-st-strike fire!"

It scared me half to death. I wasn't even surprised to recognize Pem Sixkiller. I didn't stop to wonder how he had sneaked so far in there, past Papa and my brothers. I knew that he was coming for my barn.

I squatted inside the quilt and tried to think what I would do. I had my pockets full of the rocks, and two in my left hand and one in my right, ready to throw. The rocks were getting damp in my hands. I kept snapping my head around, one way and another, trying to see something, but everything was black. In my mind I kept seeing, over and over, old Pem Sixkiller as he had squatted by our spring branch with Jess, drinking whiskey, and then had struck his match on his trousers. Then I remembered Jiggs Sixkiller, too, the way he had been climbing the tree at school, popping his eyes at me and cutting away with his switch like he was killing a snake.

I thought that I should yell, but I couldn't. I kept thinking, *I'll see him. He's going to light a match and I'll see him.*

Then, like he had dropped from the sky and his head was floating in the night above me, Pem Sixkiller's face lit up. He was on top of the hill, just his face, but it was so plain in the light that I felt like I could touch him. The striking match made his face run red and greasy. The match moved down and a bigger flame spurted in Pem's hands. His face was gone.

I yelled *"Wooooooooeeeeeee!"* like one of Grandpa's Rebel Yells, without thinking what I was yelling, and then called Papa. I heard Papa's whistle.

Up the hill the fire grew, blue at first, then yellow, and I saw Pem standing and holding the fire. Then there were two fires. They drew apart. He had torches. Before I knew it, there were four torches. One of them shot down through the air like a rope of fire and landed in the shed roof over my head. The dry leaves crackled.

Now the torches started downhill, three of them, guttering. Then I could understand. Pem and somebody else were running straight for the barn with corncob torches that had been dipped in kerosene. I shucked the quilt and stooped, ready to throw. I made myself wait until they were near. The light grew, but I didn't stop to look up at the burning roof of old branches that we had cut the summer before.

When the torches were so close that I heard those two grunting at every step, I let fly with a rock.

Nobody had to tell me. I had missed Pem. The rock sizzed past him so close that he yelled, "Watch, Jiggs! He's rocking. Get him!"

I was nervous, but I had the next rock in my hand so fast that Pem had moved only a foot or so when I threw again. It was as hard a throw as I ever made, and I caught Pem in his bread basket. The rock was almost the size of a fist, but flat. He sat down like he'd been sledged, and the torches hit the ground in his hands.

Bits of fire showered me from the burning roof over my head and I had to tear myself from looking at it to see Jiggs coming. He was near the bottom of the hill, holding his other torch high, when he jumped for me. He yelled, "Look out, white boy!"

Jiggs was no more than ten feet from me when I threw, and I thought at first that I had killed him. His chest thumped like it was broken and he pitched down against the side of the barn with the burning cob still in his hand, and gagged and gapped his mouth without making a sound. His eyes were open but he wasn't seeing me. He was trying for breath.

One end of the roof came down over me. All I could see was fire, falling in rods and forks and long coals that splintered and spread sparks. I fell over Jiggs and tried to pull him out. My britches and coat were burning, but I was too addled to go for a water bucket. I snatched the quilt to wrap around both of us, but it was running sheets of fire. I dropped it and left Jiggs so that I could whip at the fire on my overalls legs. I rolled and beat and yelled, it hurt so bad, and then I got hold of Jiggs by the legs and we fell over in the leaves just as the whole roof came down from the shed behind me, with the poles popping fire.

I thought somebody was calling me, but it was far off and grew fainter. I wanted to get up again and go with Jiggs on my shoulder, but I sank down and it seemed to get darker. Something hurt me so that I couldn't stand it another second. I passed out.

The first thing I saw was butter on the bed. One of Mama's half-pounds was on a plate and a hand came and took some and went away, with butter curling under the fingernails as it grabbed. Something tickled me. It was Mama rubbing butter on my leg. It was funny to me, but I tried not to let her know I was awake. When I noticed again, she was gone. My leg was heavy and my arm was in a sling, strapped to my neck and belly. My face was hot, and when I felt it, crusty under the butter grease. My tongue was thick in my mouth.

Papa came and fed me corn mush and it was good, but I could hardly swallow.

Papa looked me over like I was new to him. "You're a good man," he said. "Your own man now, pretty near."

When he had left, I saw one of Papa's old shotguns leaning on the foot of my bed. It was the wrong room for it, and I knew that he meant for that to be my gun.

Soon they all came in and I could manage to eat a little and they told me over and over the story of how I had crippled Pem and Jiggs Sixkiller. They told it like I hadn't been there at all and could remember nothing.

"You raised a welt on Pem like a mushmelon," Jimroe said. "There's one Indian won't forget you as long as he lives."

"We'll have to keep rocks away from you," Papa said. "You're worse than Little David and the Philadelphians."

I got a crack in the corner of my sore mouth trying to grin at him.

Doc Kiger came and changed something on my leg and smeared on a smelly medicine. I heard him in the hall talking to Mama and Papa. He said that I was burned to the bone, and it scared me so that I hurt worse than ever that night, and cried a lot. Mama came and put cold towels on my head and face. She cried, too.

"Out of all the rest," she said, "to think it had to be you. The only shy cub in the litter."

I felt better in the morning. Tree hobbled in on his crutches and grinned from the door. The skin of his face was as loose as a hound's. "Now ain't we a pretty set of things?" he said. "And us supposed to be particular hell in the woods at taking care of ourselves."

He said he was ashamed to hear that I was so bad to throw rocks at folks, and that the sheriff at Randolph was complaining about me filling his jail. He said they had taken Pem to Randolph, and that the Judge had sent Jiggs somewhere, and for me not to think of a thing but getting well.

Papa came and put an arm around Tree and joked with both of us. He looked at me like he wanted to say something but didn't know just what, and finally pulled a big plug of tobacco from his pocket and cut me off a chew.

"Put it under your pillow and chew when you can," he said. "Just a little at the time till you've got used to it. And for God's sakes, don't swallow your cud and let Mama find us out."

I popped it into my mouth and had to pretend that it was my first real chew, and gagged and carried on a little to fool him. Tree didn't bat an eye, like all the dozens of chews he had slipped me had gone clean out of his mind.

"There's just one thing," Papa said. "How in hell come you didn't come to me with what you knew about Pem and Jess? It kind of hurts me to think you wouldn't. We might have saved all this."

I didn't look at him or Tree. "I wanted to, Papa. You know I would want to. But I couldn't. At first, there wasn't much to tell—and then, one thing and another. I couldn't . . ."

Tree broke in. "Hell, Hence. It wasn't no fault of his. He was all ready to tell you, when he found out for sure, but I made him hold off. You know, there's times you've been known to fly off the handle. We were just trying to help out, without kicking up a big fuss."

Papa thumped my head. "By God, I'll say you helped, whatever it was. The thing that ails you, boy, is being fifteen years old, no more and no less—and there ain't but one way out of that. You'll do it in a few weeks."

He and Tree talked a little more, and Tree went away.

Papa winked at me. "Well, we're still keeping watch around here, just in case, even if the wagons are all gone over the river. And we've got a place for one more good shot. A man with a gun, I mean."

A day or so later, when I was better, Tree sat on my bed and we tried to play two-handed setback, but it wasn't much fun. He said that if I didn't hurry, he'd beat me up. He said that the first of the wagons had already come back across the river, and that folks were growling about the little dabs of money they had been paid for tobacco in the Danville warehouse. Even the best tobacco, he said, had brought only ten cents a pound, and after all that long ride the farmers were sore, and some of them had burned their tobacco in the Danville streets, and dared the law officers to try and stop them. More of the leaf had been ruined at the river crossing because men plunged wagons carelessly into the river.

Papa and Mama came in with Grandpa and Aunt Lumbie, who had come to be with us for Christmas, and Aunt Lumbie made over me while Papa told the story of our barn burning again. Grandpa didn't pay much attention. "Hell's fire," he said. "When I was your age, boy, I had done caught three or four women."

The doctor came again that day, and when he had gone Papa was in with a big red grin and said I was all right, or would be before long. "You'll be up before you know it. We never thought you'd turn out like this, the toughest knot of all, when you've always been so stand-offish, and wanting to read books and all. We'll make it, boy, working together. Lord knows how, with all that worthless tobacco. But don't you worry. This place will be yours one day, and it'll make you a living. The Lord never let us down yet, despite all the times I've tempted him."

I slept better that night, and when I woke up in the morning my leg itched like fury, beginning to get well.

21

How It Rained Money

I was the first one to see Biscoe Allen coming toward our house. I spotted him from my window when he was still far off, but it was a while before I could believe it. He was driving fast in a new Ford touring car, a 1917, and had somebody with him. When he wheeled in our lane on a skid I saw that it was his wife and Wash Strawn, both sitting stiff like they didn't expect to enjoy themselves. They dropped out of sight for a second or two, until they came up our hill.

Grandpa was down in the yard by the porch, sunning himself in a rocker. Trout was by the lane, coming home from school, and he had some strange black-and-white dog following him. Grandpa yelled, "Steamer, Buddy. Goddle-mighty, watch the Steamer!"

Trout wasn't in the way, but he dodged across to be nearer the house and the dog cut over the lane after him. Biscoe's front wheel knocked the dog sky-winding, and it yelped like death, then cut off in the midst of the howl. It was flung in the lane at Trout's feet, limp as a rug.

"Hurraw, there!" Grandpa said.

Biscoe slammed to a stop and threw his leg over the door to the running board.

"Boy, boy."

Trout just looked at him.

"I'd not have had this happen for the world, son."

"Mister, that dog . . ."

"I know it, boy. I know what he must've meant to you. If I could buy him back to life I sure God would."

"Damn a dog-killing Steamer to hell, anyway," Grandpa said.

"It jumped under us, Biscoe," Mrs. Allen said. "I don't know where he come from."

Biscoe grinned at her like a mule eating a mouthful of briars and said slow and polite, "I just killed the boy's dog, lovey. A time like this, how don't matter."

He turned to Trout.

"Is there any way you can say what he was worth to you, son? Any way atall?"

Trout looked at the dead dog.

"I wouldn't hardly know, Mr. Allen. Not for this dog . . ."

"Now, now. I know just how you feel."

Biscoe pulled money from his pocket and handed Trout a bill. It was five dollars.

"Hell's fire," Wash Strawn said.

Biscoe barked at him, "Dry up. Ain't you done harm enough, without making light of a boy's dog when it dies?"

"I appreciate it," Trout said.

"It's nothing, son. I know it's nothing," Biscoe said. "I just want you to have that money at a time like this. It makes me feel a little bit better about things."

Papa went to the porch. "I never thought to see you out here again," he said.

Biscoe held up a hand. "I know what you're thinking, Hence. I don't blame you—but lots of things have happened that were no fault of mine. And we come to talk. I mean money talk."

Biscoe handed his wife out of the car like he thought she might break, but was watching Papa all the time.

"They say you've still got your crop, Hence."

"Yeah. A precious lot of good it does me."

Biscoe rubbed his hands and laughed so loud that he surprised Papa.

"Well, I don't know how it happened that you wouldn't cross the river with the rest of them—but it looks like it turned up luck for both of us."

"How's that?"

"Why, the companies are hollering for more leaf all of a sudden. They say so much of the prime tobacco was burnt and lost in the South, and thrown away on that Danville foolishness, that they've got nothing but sorry tobacco."

"You mean you want my crop?"

"Hence, me and the Madam and Mister Strawn would like to set down with you, if it was so you had the time."

They went in the house with Biscoe doing all the talking, almost drowning out Mama when she came to speak to Mrs. Allen. They scraped chairs on the parlor floor. Biscoe said that Wash Strawn had a word to say, and Wash growled at Papa, "I never thought you'd be fool enough to think I'd set the halfbreeds against you. You know damn well that the burnt barns were no thought of mine. I never did a thing more than tell folks we would have bad markets, cheap tobacco."

"It's the Gospel," Biscoe said. "Now, if it happens that we

can get together on a price—why, maybe both of us can save something out of the season after all."

Grandpa hadn't even turned in his chair to watch them go in the house, but kept looking at Trout, who was reading everything he could find on his five-dollar bill.

"Big boys don't cry about dogs or nothing else," Grandpa said. "I hope you ain't going to blubber now, Buddy."

"I just wonder where that fool dog come from."

"You mean he ain't yours?"

"Never saw him in my life till we come up the hill."

Trout folded the bill into his pocket and winked at Grandpa. Grandpa gave a Rebel Yell.

"Ah, you've got the old Starling ice in your kidneys. Another real Starling, by God. We'll never starve out—got us another trader coming on." But he soon lost interest in Trout and nodded like he was going to sleep.

When Trout walked across the yard he even looked like Jimroe.

The talk in the parlor was careful.

"I know we ain't always winked eye to eye, Hence," Biscoe said. "But now I'll trade you for your crop like neighbors."

"You want to buy it—all?"

"I'll say."

"Biscoe, I've owed you money for a long while . . ."

"It's just business. That don't enter into it. Fact is, I'd have been out here sooner, but I thought you might run me off—the misunderstandings and all."

"Well, I don't know what you mean to do. I know I'm stuck with the crop as it stands—but I'm damned if I'll give it away."

"Nobody's asking you to."

"I want you to know that I'd let every leaf of it rot before I'd let anybody steal it—you or anybody else." Papa's voice was rising.

"Hence," Mama said.

"Now, hear me out," Biscoe said.

Papa was quiet while Biscoe told how sorry he was that things had turned out sour for the county, and that hard feelings had come up between folks, and that he and Mrs. Allen had talked it over and thought they would come and make it right with Papa, as best they could.

"And then, of course, I heard you still had all your good leaf, and wondered if you might not be willing to sell, seeing a ready market for it. So I thought we'd better make our peace and have it over with."

"What kind of a dicker have you got in mind?"

"I never came to dicker."

"You didn't?"

"No, sir. I'm going to lay down all my cards. You've got one of the only two or three prime crops left in Corona and it's worth top money, little as I thought it could be. Almost all the rest is gone—all that's worth a damn."

"Well, sir."

"Oh, I don't mean it's all gone. Slim Poindexter and Billy Lufler held back a barn or two. Now, I've talked with the Runnels buyers . . ."

"Uh, oh."

"Hold on, Hence. I'll pay thirty-eight cents a pound."

"You mean it?"

"Right across the board—lugs, first primings and all."

"Well, I've no idea what it would all come to—and then, there's the debt we owe you, and all."

"We won't argue about a thing. I expect you'll wipe out the debt on the first two barns."

"I never thought we'd do it."

"I'll tell you what I'll do with you. I've brought along the old notes you signed, just in case. If you're willing, I'll cancel them out in exchange for your first two barns, no matter how light they weigh. You ought to make mighty nigh two thousand dollars."

"Hell. It's like a fresh start. Better."

"All right," Biscoe said. I could hear paper tearing, being snapped in two, over and over, and Biscoe said he was glad to hand Papa the scraps of the old fertilizer and seed debts from all the way back.

"I'm relieved to see this day come," Mrs. Allen said. "I can breathe easy, not feeling like Biscoe and Wash are going to pull the county down on our heads."

Mama said it had seemed like a long year. "But now it's looking shorter. Looks like old times around here."

They joked for a few minutes until things had warmed up, then Biscoe said, "I don't want you to think that I was trying to drive you to make a mortgage for your little debt to me—or anything like that."

Papa laughed a little. "Well, if I ever did think of it, we can forget it now. It's all over. I'm ready to live and let live, with a tobacco price like that. I get right sentimental over money."

When the Allens were leaving, the family followed them to the Ford like we were the best of friends with them. Mama and Papa hung around the car until Biscoe cranked up and tore away down the lane. Biscoe and Mrs. Allen waved. Wash Strawn lumped down in the back seat.

Mama cried and held on to Papa and the kids ran around yelling about all the things that they could have for Christmas now. Papa soon walked out the back way by himself, down to the barn, and stood there. I knew he was thinking it over, trying to get used to the idea of having money for his crop. Mama walked down to him and he took her by the arm and they went to the nearest shed and opened the door, looking at the tobacco piled in there. They looked for a while, then Papa closed the door carefully and they walked up the hill toward the house holding hands.

Late that evening, after I had gone to sleep, Jimroe and Miss Cassie came in from somewhere, and there was a whooping over her downstairs and Papa told them about the sale. Miss Cassie sounded like she had never had such good news.

Papa broke a rule and poured everybody a little drink in the kitchen, and instead of blessing him out, Mama took a little one with them. They laughed over her coughing and spluttering.

Miss Cassie said, "I hope you haven't forgotten who it was that saved the fine crop for you. Fax. I'm so proud of him."

Not long after, I heard Papa tipping up the steps, but when the creaking boards came near my door I pretended to be asleep.

22

Our Runaways

Grandpa was taken sick the next day. They put him to bed
in the room where I was lying. Papa brought him up in his
arms like he was a doll, weighing next to nothing, and when
they had him under the covers he hardly made a wrinkle, he
was so slight.

He lay with his hands outside the quilts, across his chest,
fidgeting his fingers. Mostly he just looked at the ceiling
with his cloudy blue eyes, and now and then swallowed with
a soft noise. His nose was so sharp and thin that light shone
through the edges and it looked like a blade of glass.

Once or twice Grandpa rolled his eyes at me and I

thought he knew who I was, but he said nothing. He didn't speak at all until late in the afternoon when Miss Cassie came in. She talked to me because I was going to have to miss the big school Christmas party, but she took time with Grandpa and touched his cheek.

"We all hoped that you could come and dance for us," she said. "Next time, sure."

Grandpa wet his lips. "You're that yeller-headed Jimroe gal."

Miss Cassie laughed. "I hadn't thought of it that way."

"Mighty nigh all I think about is gals," Grandpa said. "Mostly they run to yeller-headed ones. I used 'em up by the dozen when I was a boy."

"I'll bet you did and that they didn't mind."

"I never had no complaints."

Aunt Lumbie and Mama laughed a little but they were worried that Grandpa had got worse.

Miss Cassie left her lemon smell in the room and I breathed deep until it was all gone.

When it was quiet again and began to get dark, Mama set a lamp on a hall table outside our door so that we could see but still have a little shade for Grandpa. I lay there and thought of Grandpa dead, and felt funny because I couldn't make myself sorry enough to cry. I thought that I wouldn't be able to cry at the funeral, much as I loved him, and that people would look at me and wonder why I was such a cold stick.

In the next bed Grandpa looked the same as ever, still as a log, batting his eyes once in a great while, like he was only waiting for somebody to tell him that he could get up and go again.

They fed us, and Grandpa ate like a bird. The only thing he said was about whiskey.

"I'll have my tod now," he said. When they went downstairs to fetch the liquor he said, "Damn a place where they forget a body's tod."

When the whiskey came he drank more than an inch from the bottom of the glass and lay back saying "Ahhhhh." He soon raised his head and asked for more. "And this time, dammitall, lay it down in a little warm water. It grabs quicker that way."

About dark there was a racket of people leaving from downstairs to go to the school Christmas party, and Judge Bucktarrel came by with Aunt Ly Sue and took the little kids along. Tree was down there with them, hopping around on crutches, and they got him so fired up that he went to the school with them, and said he had no idea of going home until after the party was over, he didn't care how long he had been away from his folks.

Mama and Aunt Lumbie were left alone downstairs. I heard them talking about Grandpa. Aunt Lumbie and Mama were knitting, snicking their old ivory needles like they were keeping time to some music. Grandma sounded cool about things.

"I guess we ought to bury him at White Oak Limb with his people."

"That would be nice," Mama said.

"I think his children would want it. Beside his first wife, poor thing. I guess he's forgot her name by now."

"It makes me sad—but he's had a good, long life and lots of enjoyment in it."

"Well, I reckon I'll go on the other side of him in the plot when my time comes," Grandma said. "He'll go to Glory with a woman on each arm. He'd like that. The more the merrier."

"I just hate it that it had to come this time of year, with no other flowers but Christmas cactus. I'll have to scratch some galax and laurel leaves from a snow bank somewhere, for sprays."

"Oh, I just hope it won't be snowing, or icy, when the day comes."

Grandpa raised his head. "What say?" he said to me.

I shook my head at him and he grinned and laid back. I wondered if he could have heard them.

Once Mama started talking about Miss Cassie and Jimroe, but quit. "I hate to think it, but I wonder what it is she sees in him—making such big eyes at Jimroe."

"I know what Grant Starling says," Aunt Lumbie said. "He says Jimroe's the only Starling alive with enough get up and get for anybody to make anything out of."

Mama went "Shhhsh!" and I knew she had thought of me.

It was dead-still that night and the noise from the school-house party came clear across the valley, so strong that I could almost make out the words when people yelled. When the music started they sounded like they were about to tear down the building. The fiddles were good and fast. They played all the old tunes, "Boil Them Cabbages Down" and "Bully of the Town" and "Sourwood Mountain" and Grandpa's old favorite, "Nellie Had a Pair of Shoes."

At last, when it was time to break up, the band played one without a name that went:

> "Eat the meat, gnaw the bone,
> Grab your honey and go on home . . ."

There was another ruckus downstairs when they came back from the school. At first they whispered because Mama shushed them, but they got louder as they went and were full of laughing. Jimroe bragged about how Ivy and Trout had won the spelling bee and said he bet I would be jealous-hearted.

Judge Bucktarrel told a tale about how Red Dowd had taken Tootsy Kinnamon outside courting during the party, and she'd been wearing a homemade bustle pad that was only a sack stuffed with bran, like they fed to stock, and that somehow she'd poked a hole in the sack while they were out.

"They just broke up everything when they came back in

there with a whole taggle of pigs on their trail, gobbling after that trickle of bran and getting all into our dance."

They talked for a while before Mama and Miss Cassie came up to peep at us, and Miss Cassie touched me with a fluttery little kiss.

The next thing I knew it was nearly daylight. Outside the window everything was slicked over in ice, the roof and sheds and trees cased in ice to the least tip and twig, as far as I could see in the dim light. I heard a rumble in the kitchen. It was Papa grinding coffee, the only thing he was ever known to do in that room to help out, and he was at it early only because they would be going hunting, like they did at every cold snap. It was a chance to get red meat for the table for several days.

It was as cold as the blue flugins in the frosty air and I pigged back into my warm place in bed. Boots thumped on the floors outside and dogs came whining up on the porches and I could hear the breeches of guns being broken open and snapped shut. The men went on the back porch and light washed in my window. It was so cold that the least sound came up to us.

Papa stretched and yawned with a shiver in his voice. *"Rowwwrr!* It feels like there's nothing between us and the North Pole but one bobbed-wire fence, and two strands of that down this morning."

"Cold as a mother-in-law's breath," Frank said.

They stepped off the porch and crackled away on the ice to get in the sedge fields before the light got too strong, so that they could really lay the rabbits about them. In less than half an hour the shotguns began firing and I knew there would be meat as long as the cold snap lasted. I sat up and watched them come. They had a couple of dozen rabbits and a squirrel or two. They cleaned them on the yard table, and when the skinning and cleaning were done, Papa ran a wire through the heads of the animals and hung them on the back porch, where they froze stiff as boards, raw and red, and swinging furry feet in the wind.

When Mama went out to admire them, Papa took off his hunting cap and bowed to the row of rabbits and squirrels, pretending that they were Poindexters. "Morning, folks. Ain't it a mite early for you Red Muzzles to be up and about?"

Mama laughed and said it was a shame that people didn't even consider Starlings worth shooting. Papa scooped her up and carried her in the kitchen like she was a bride in a new house.

For the next few days Mama would be able to reach out and bring in three or four rabbits any time she wanted to make a game stew, or cook what she called Jugged Hare. They were still having fun at breakfast in the kitchen when I dropped back to sleep.

When I woke up Mama was standing at the foot of my bed with a bowl of corn mush. She was wild-eyed.

"Where's Grandpa?"

He was gone.

There was a fuss downstairs just then, and Grandpa was yelling, "Turn me aloose! Great God, Miss Agnes, can't a man step out to answer Nature, without you having hissy fits?"

"Pap! What are you doing out of bed?"

"Ah. I just felt like resting a little, and now I'm done with it. By God, I know when I'm ready to die and when I ain't. I'm going to help Hence down at his new tobacco-plant bed today, sure as hell."

They calmed him down and led him in the kitchen, but he kept grumbling and wouldn't be brought back to bed. The girls and women said that it was a miracle, but Grandpa said he'd been getting out of bed every morning for ninety years, just about, and felt like he might keep it up for another ninety.

When that excitement died down, Papa began getting louder. Frank and the other big boys drank the last of their coffee slowly and provoked Papa. He was as impatient as if nobody had struck a lick of work on the farm for a month. He complained until you'd have thought he'd swallowed a small kitchen knife. It made him almost sick to think of wasting a minute's work.

"We'll clear new ground this morning," he said. I could tell what was on the faces of my brothers as well as if I'd been down there myself. They were looking as if they had tasted something bitter, because Papa said, "All right, if some of you don't need a mouthful to eat all during next year, they can lie up beside the fire all day or go back to bed. The rest of you come on with me."

He didn't mean for them to make the choice, because he would put up with nothing less than a full day from any-body—still thinking ahead for us a year at the time, beyond Biscoe Allen and the tobacco companies and the worms and hail and drought and everything else.

They went to work in the plant bed, and I lay up there wanting to be with them, as hard as the work was.

They worked even faster than I thought they could that morning, and just before dinnertime the sweet smell of green wood burning came up the hill and I knew they were half done with the clearing, anyway. When they came to the house for dinner Cousin Tree was in the yard with Lize and some log chains. He was limping and grinning. Papa hooted.

"I hope I'm in time to save a little of the crop for Linden and the poor children," Tree said.

"I might know you'd show up when the worst was over," Papa said, but he was glad to see Tree out and walking, even as a cripple. They thumped each other on the back and Tree said he was game for work, but that it might take more Old Panther Sweat than usual to keep him going. I knew that he would have Lize working in the tobacco bed that afternoon, snatching the biggest logs out of the way. He and Lize could finish that job while the rest of them were thinking about getting started.

After dinner they had more trouble with Grandpa. He wanted to go down with them to see the new ground burned off, and said they'd never get it right for the new plants if he didn't show them how.

"That Hence never could get the ground just right," he said. "His plants come up so dense. He ain't so bad on water-million, but on tobacco he ain't worth a damn for nothing."

Papa laughed, but Grandpa was in a mood to argue and they had to go off to work and leave him, still yapping. The women tried to keep Grandpa from following Papa, and picked at him for a long time before he promised to do no more than walk on the porch. They bundled him in a coat and he went outside, tapping along with his hawthorn stick and growling pretty rank and rambling about the Confederate Army.

Grandma gave up after a while and told him she would take him home before he threw a fit. He yelled at her, "It's by God about time, Lumbie. Devil take it, if I was to happen to want to die, I'd not want to do it off somewhere like this with a parcel of strangers. I want to be home."

Mama sent Trout to the barn to hitch Ladylove to Grandpa's old buggy for them. He ran back in a few minutes. "There's nothing to hitch," he said. "The mare's gone —the buggy's gone."

They had excitement over that and somebody hurried to the barn to see if it was true, and then to the plant bed to tell Papa. Grandma was talking about thieves and barn burners and the like, when Grandpa cut her off.

"It's all right, woman. It ain't our rig no more. You know I willed that thing to that Jimroe boy. Hadn't he might as well have it now, when it can do him some good? I just up and gave it to him."

"Grant Starling."

"Yes, hell. I told him to take that damn rig and shake a leg out of here—and take that yeller-headed gal with him. I couldn't abide to see him standing around on one foot with that toothsome wench waiting."

In the squealing downstairs Mama said, "Why, I thought somebody was missing, with all those biscuits left over. I haven't seen Jimroe for a long time—and that Cassie was just in and out."

Papa was tickled to death when they told him what had happened.

"So that's why he's been looking like a sheep-killing dog."

"I told him by George I'd give that rig to that Trout boy if he didn't get away from here," Grandpa said.

"Where'd they go?"

"How would I know? These fools wouldn't let me step off the porch. They went to the nearest place, I suppose. Where would you go, with such a gal? If he'd had any sand in his craw he'd have been gone with her long before now."

They milled around, talking about Jimroe and Cassie running away and fooling them and Grandpa said, "It ain't been so long since they got away. I expect they'll be clearing Wildkitten pretty soon."

People went on the porch and stood in the cold, stamping their feet until they thought they had been too late and that the buggy had already crossed the mountain. But at the last minute Frank yelled, "Yeah! There they go. Just topping the ridge."

Mama said she thought she saw Cassie waving, a speck of white handkerchief, but nobody could be sure. Mama cried. "Gone to Randolph! You remember, Hence? Oh, my. Do you suppose they'll ever comb gray hair together?"

"Well, sir," Papa said. "That Jimroe. He'll have a handful."

"Done got one," Grandpa said. "I could see 'em hugging all the way up on Wildkitten. They didn't need no practice."

The little ones whooped and Trout said he was glad of it, since there would be no more school for a while.

"Oh, no," Mama said. "She's sure to come right back, first thing after Christmas, and you'll catch it worse than ever."

I knew that was true, and that they'd be back inside a week, but that things would never be the same.

Grandpa said he wished that it was him driving Ladylove.

"By God, I'd give that mare her head and to hell with the reins, and tend to my business."

He barked at Papa, "Hence, I'd be obliged if you'd quit fiddling around, and have me a horse hitched to something and let me get along home."

Papa sent Trout back to the barn.

Grandpa did a jig on the porch and squalled as loud as I ever heard him:

> "Oh, Nellie had a pair of shoes
> She could wear 'em if she choose.
> Hi, Barefoot Nellie!
> Ho, Barefoot Nellie!"

I watched the ridge of Wildkitten where they had disappeared and thought a funny thing. I thought, Nobody knows how I'm going to miss that damn Jimroe.

Then I heard them coming upstairs to tell me all about it.

 *About the Author*

BURKE DAVIS is a North Carolinian who now lives in Williamsburg, Virginia. He describes himself as a reformed but unrepentant journalist, Civil War historian and sire. He was educated at Duke University, Guilford College and the University of North Carolina.

He was born in Durham, North Carolina, in 1913; he is six feet four and speaks with a not unexpected accent. He says that he has been working on *The Summer Land* since 1937, aided by a large band of folklorists and renegade sociologists of the Carolina-Virginia border.

Mr. Davis is married to the former Evangeline McLennan, who is also a writer. They have two children, Angela and Burke.

The Summer Land is the author's fourteenth book, and fourth novel.